Wheels' End

Book IV in the
Wheels and Zombies series

by M. Van

Wheels' End

Book IV in the
Wheels and Zombies series

by M. Van

42Links Publishing
Visit: www.42Links.net

Cover design by Shezaad Sudar

Edited by Book helpline
Visit: bookhelpline.com

All rights reserved.
ISBN: 978-90-824472-8-6

1

Mags

Snow crunched under my boots as I forced my near-frozen feet forward. My hands were cold, and my finger felt numb as it hovered over the trigger. For a moment, the sun peeked through the deck of clouds, and its beams glinted off the snow before disappearing behind an overcast sky. With ease, I moved the barrel of the M4 carbine over the makeshift houses, alternating my attention between peering through the scope and checking my surroundings.

Angie trailed behind me. Her feet moved in sync with mine, and the sound of the snow crunching under our boots seemed to be the only thing to break the silence around us. She knelt at my side as I stopped behind a crate to survey the narrow street.

"Having fun?" she asked. I shifted my gaze from the street to her and was met by her balaclava-covered face. The glint in her eyes betrayed the mischievous grin that I was sure to be hiding behind the layer of fabric.

"I'm freezing my ass off—again," I replied,

although that wasn't exactly true.

Both of us were decked out in several layers of clothing made from all kinds of materials. Polypropylene underwear, polyester-fiber pile shirt along with bib overalls, lined field coats and matching trousers. The ensemble was topped off with a water- and windproof layer of camouflage. I felt like a marshmallow, and if we had worn the layer of snow camouflage, I would have looked like a marshmallow.

The layers of clothing gave decent enough protection against the cold, but being a girl from a country where winter might give you about two inches of snow if it weren't raining all the time, the Alaskan weather meant a whole new challenge for me.

"C'mon," Angie said, sounding exited, "you have to admit this is kind of fun."

I glared at her before shaking my head.

She shrugged as she adjusted her helmet without losing the sparkle in her eyes. It was good to see those eyes without the darkness that had lingered there before. Who would have expected that something good could have come from a zombie apocalypse, giving Angie and me a second chance at life?

Angie chuckled as I refocused on the narrow

street. Then she tapped my shoulder and said, "Let's get this over with so we can get you warmed up."

I got up from behind the crate and continued to move down the narrow street with Angie on my heels. The fake houses lining the street looked like metal boxes stacked on top of each other. Square holes representing windows revealed nothing but blackness. Several cars that had seen better days crowded the street along with Dumpsters and other junk. It made for easy cover.

The crack of a gunshot in the near distance made me flinch, but I didn't lose my focus as I led us further down the street. The sound of metal on metal, as if something was moving on a pulley, drew my attention to the left, and an image of a disfigured man on a sheet of cardboard appeared behind a square hole of one of the fake houses. I caught the figure in my sight and fired two shots. Seconds later a similar sound came from my right, and I shifted my gaze to find a different cardboard image as it appeared from behind a car—again I fired.

I increased my pace until I reached that same car and crouched next to it. My eyes flickered to the image on the cardboard, and I silently cursed myself. The image of an old lady appeared to be nothing more than that—an old lady. Angie's weapon fired just before she reached me and knelt by my side. Glancing at the image of the old lady, she excessively cleared her throat.

"Shut up," I said before she could add anything, and I fired my weapon at a cardboard picture that couldn't be mistaken as anything but a zombie.

We moved in tandem through the narrow street, picking off cardboard figures as we went along. Weeks of running through these courses had taught us to synchronize our movements, and anticipating each other's actions had become second nature.

As we reached the end of the street, my weapon clicked empty, and I took cover behind the shell of a burned-out car. I started to reload while Angie fired her weapon from the other side of the street where she sat behind a couple of wooden pallets—pretending to hide from invisible enemies. Our gazes met as a disembodied voice crackled over the speakers mounted on poles along the course.

"Cease fire. Course finished. Repeat, cease fire," the voice over the speakers said. The voice added a safety confirmation that the firing range was cleared to enter. I blew out a breath as I felt a trickle of sweat roll down the back of my neck. Though I knew this to be a training session and the targets to be fake, running this course didn't stop my heart rate from nudging up to some uncontrollable level. It felt as if an animal raged inside my chest.

Angie got to her feet, pulling the fabric masking her face down. She grinned from ear to ear as she walked over and stuck out a hand to help me up. I understood that grin, even though society had come to a halt while zombies claimed the land. Well, they weren't zombies exactly. To be that they would have to have risen from the dead. In this case, a man-made virus had rendered the brains of the infected effectively useless while they had an unquenchable craving for human flesh. To me, this behavior came pretty close to what I had seen in all those movies over the years. Besides, it didn't take long for them to start looking like zombies, and so that's what I called them—zombies. The irony was that the same virus that had killed millions had saved Angie's life along with my own.

I didn't understand all the science behind it, but not that long ago, we'd both faced a slow death as cancer ate us up from the inside out. The zombie virus exposed to the cancer in our systems had caused a mutation that rendered us immune to becoming one of those walking dead ourselves.

So instead of being dead, Angie and I were running around this makeshift shooting range at the Joint Base Elmendorf-Richardson or "J-Bear," as the men and women stationed here called it—located in Anchorage, Alaska. As it was, we didn't have too much to complain about, except for the cold weather and the fact that I wished Ash and Mars were here.

"This place is too cold," I said as I walked at Angie's side. We crossed a snow-covered open field, heading to one of the bigger buildings lining what was supposed to be a parking lot. A couple of snow mounts with the distinctive features of cars hidden underneath told me as much.

We had relinquished our weapons with the TI, or training instructor. I didn't even know the man's real name. After he yelled at us for a while or, more exactly, yelled at me for shooting the old lady's cardboard image, he had dismissed us. I had to remind myself of the fact that he didn't have it in for me but was doing everything in his power to teach me the things I needed to know to survive out in the field. Still, I'd had better conversations.

"Just be glad you don't have to go through basic training like the rest of the recruits," Angie said, "or else we would have been out here a lot longer."

I glanced over my shoulder and saw the TI assemble his platoon for what I could only assume to be another round of agonizingly exhausting exercises. Our training sessions were private, but we caught glimpses of what the rest of the troops had to go through. I shoved my hands deeper into my pockets and sighed in relief.

"That I am," I replied and added, "I don't understand why Marshall wants us to tag along on some of those excursions anyhow. It's not as if I was ever cut out to be a soldier, and you already know most of this shit."

Colonel Lauren Marshall of the United States Air Force and commander of this joint base had been more than welcoming on our arrival. The woman, who I guessed to be in her mid-forties, had made quite a first impression. With her stern expression and her straight posture, she was in no way inferior to the military men in charge that I had met these past few months. Ever since we had arrived, she'd taken an added interest in Angie and me. After our intended three weeks' stay was extended, she'd insisted that we participate in some of the training and contributed to the community of this base. I had no problem with the latter, and handing out household goods at one of the logistics readiness squadrons wasn't a problem, but running around in the Alaskan snow was something I wasn't yet used to. Perhaps if things had been different, I would have been able to appreciate the beauty this place had to offer, but unfortunately there hadn't been much time for sightseeing. The irony of that hadn't exactly escaped me.

"I was trained as an FBI agent and not a soldier," Angie said.

"There's a difference?" I asked, keeping my tone serious. Her head shifted in my direction with a scowl on her face.

I grinned and said, "Hey don't blame me, I'm a tourist, remember."

"You're a tourist, but I don't remember ever hearing the Dutch were idiots."

"Yeah, well, this one got herself stuck in a big foreign country with zombies running wild," I replied.

"But you're still alive, right," she said, "and you kept Ash alive."

My gaze fell to the ground where my feet plowed through the snow.

"We kept each other alive," I said under my breath.

I missed the loud-mouthed kid with her thick Brooklyn accent rolling around in her wheelchair. Ever since we had met at that hospital over a year ago, we had been inseparable, and now, except for video calls, I hadn't seen Ash in over three months. General Whitfield had promised us that it would take about three weeks for the lab to synthesize the serum they needed to inoculate the population and make them impervious to the zombie virus. Unfortunately, things hadn't gone according to plan, and because Angie and I were the only ones who carried the nonsynthesized version of the Divus serum in our bloodstreams, we had been kindly asked to stay put. Ash also carried the antizombie juice inside her body, but because she was stuck in a wheelchair and fourteen years old at the time, it had been decided that she would stay with Mars's family in California in a town called Carmel-by-the-Sea.

A sigh escaped me at the thought of Ash followed by thoughts of Mars, which hadn't gone by unnoticed by Angie.

"Have you heard from them?" she asked.

I looked up to face her but noticed we had reached the steps that would lead us inside the building where the mess hall was located. Angie led the way, hopping up the few steps and opened the door for us both. The mess hall for this part of the base was located in a building that looked like a hangar—all metal with an oval roof. The interior was as nice, with a wooden finish and huge windows that gave an excellent view of the mountains. The foyer held an enormous amount of coatracks, which were mostly empty now. We had arrived early, and it would be a while before the famished recruits piled in looking for their chow. A hallway veered right where a bunch of offices were located, and straight ahead a set of doors led to the mess itself.

Angie had already relinquished her coat and stared at me, waiting for my reply.

"Not since the last time we all talked, about two weeks ago," I said. "You were there—remember."

"Yeah, but I thought, Mars might have ..." She started to say and then wiggled her eyebrows as she paused. "You know," she added with a sly smile.

"And what?" I said, unable to keep a grin off my face. "Indulge in some R-rated steamy, hot phone sex?" I shrugged out of my coat as I entertained the thought and felt the heat rise in my cheeks. "I'm sure that would have gone over quite well in the com-room."

Angie chuckled, and from the expression on her face, I could tell she was imagining the reactions of the people working behind their computer stations inside the communications room where we needed to go to make our secure video calls. Because the knowledge we had obtained concerning the Mortem virus that had created the zombies and, of course, its potential cure, we weren't allowed to use unsanctioned lines of communication. In fact, we weren't allowed to talk to anyone outside the appointed circle.

Fortunately, Ash and Mars were included inside that circle. Even with Angie, who I'd come to see as part of my extended family, by my side, I would have gone mad if I hadn't been allowed to talk to those two for over three months.

Ash had become closer to me than my siblings ever had, and although I never had any children and probably never would, it almost felt as if I had found that kind of love with her. Mars, however, had turned into a story of his own.

I had met Angie's partner with the FBI while escaping JFK airport in New York. Of course at the time, I hadn't known he'd been working undercover, trying to catch the bad guy who had set the zombie virus loose on the population.

I had tried to keep my distance. When you're dying of cancer, diving into a relationship was the furthest thing from my mind. Besides, zombies were chasing us. Still, it was hard to ignore his beautiful dark skin with that brilliant smile and those pale jade eyes that made me wonder if he could read my soul. Fortunately for me, Mars turned out to be a persistent man who wouldn't allow himself to be pushed away and whose presence would make my heart jump in all kinds of ways. He had opened me up to a range of feelings that no one could truly believe in unless they had experienced it at least once.

Angie was staring at me again.

"What?" I asked.

"You were so far gone that I doubt even the Enterprise would have been able to locate you," she said with a grin.

"Shut up," I replied and opened the door to the mess hall.

2

Ash

"Come on, Ash. Again, again," Rowdy called out and followed it by a squeal. I sighed and internally cursed for letting myself being used like that. Ever since I had arrived, this forty-inch-tall midget had started to use me as his own private taxi. If it weren't for those big brown eyes and that million-dollar smile, I might have chucked him from my lap.

But that was just it; this four-year-old kid had the ability to wrap me around his chubby little fingers, with his frizzy hair and dimpled cheeks. Except for the eyes and a slightly darker skin tone, he looked exactly like his dad. He even had Mars's charm, the little bastard. "Just one more time, Ash —please."

He drew out the last word, and I was sold— again.

"All right, all right," I replied, "just give me a sec to line up." I pushed my wheels until I reached the middle of the sidewalk and started to balance on my rear tires. The sun had already started its descent at the end of the ocean, and the cooler temperatures had left the beaches mostly empty. It wasn't exactly cold and nothing like the winters I had experienced in Brooklyn, but it wasn't beach weather either. I inhaled deeply, smelling the salt on the air as the waves crashed on the beach. From Rowdy's smile, I could tell he was getting excited. "Hang on, okay."

"Okay," he said. It wasn't necessary for him to hang on, because I had extended the belt that kept me seated in the chair and had looped it around him too. He was basically strapped to me and with his little skateboard helmet, I figured he'd be safe enough. Besides, I knew what I was doing. That didn't mean I didn't like to mess with him.

"Are you really hangin' on?" I said in an exaggerated voice.

"Yep," he said, undeterred.

"Okay then, keep your tiny hands inside the vehicle at all times," I replied and started to spin. I started slowly first, but gradually picked up speed. The excited *wheeeeee* that followed had me thinking I was doing good. As dizziness set in, I slowed us down. Rowdy's giggling as he held on to my shirt was infectious, and a grin tugged at the corners of my mouth. I hated to admit it, but this kid was kind of fun to hang around with, especially since I had nothing better to do.

Ever since Mags and Angie had left me behind

in Colorado, life had become a lot less exiting. Not that this lack of excitement was a bad thing, but I missed them both. They had become my family, and I hadn't experienced that in a long time. Of course, Mars came to visit Rowdy, and Mr. and Mrs. Marsden were really nice people, and I was grateful to them for letting me stay. The fact that they lived in the cutest blue house by the beach was a plus, but I didn't know them as well as I did Mags or Angie. It's kind of nice to know what to expect from a person in certain situations, and I had that—especially with Mags. I missed our banter.

General Whitfield had promised us that the trip would only take a couple of weeks—three at the most—but Mags, and Angie had been stuck in Alaska for months now, and I didn't think any of us were happy with it.

"C'mon, little man," I said as I made the last turn, "it's time to go home or else your grandma will leave me to do the dishes all on my own."

"Awww," Rowdy replied, but I ignored him. We were only a couple of houses down from where the Marsdens lived, but the elderly couple was very protective of their grandson. I couldn't blame them for that—they had almost lost him in the same car crash as that had killed their daughter-in-law.

I'd seen pictures of Lisa on a side table in the

living room and in Rowdy's room. The Marsdens did their best to keep the memory of Rowdy's mom alive and talked about her a lot—well.

Mars hadn't spoken about her with me, but I figured that might have something to do with him being with Mags and all. I did know that Lisa had died in a car crash when Rowdy had been a year old. The little man had been with her inside the wreck, but had thankfully come out unscathed. As a family they'd gone through a rough time, but at least they've had each other.

I rolled down the sidewalk while Rowdy stuck his hands out and pretended to be a plane. He was making engine noises as I spotted a man at the front door of the blue house. Mrs. Marsden stood in the doorway, talking to the man, who was wearing black pants, a yellow jacket, and a red baseball cap. He seemed to be delivering something. I rolled up the pathway that led up to the house. Mrs. Marsden waved as I stopped at the steps of the small porch.

"Thank you," she said in a warm voice as she accepted the package.

After I undid the clip to release him, Rowdy wriggled down my lap and climbed the porch to meet his grandmother. I turned to roll around the back where it was easier for me to get inside. Mr. Marsden had offered to make me a ramp, but I had declined his generous offer. This was supposed to be a temporary arrangement, and I didn't want to be any trouble.

"Here you go," Mrs. Marsden said as she signed the tablet that the man held out to her. I was about to push off when my chair started to move on its own. Of course, it hadn't moved on its own, but the friendly delivery guy probably thought I needed help.

"Hey," I said, sounding not so friendly and instantly the pushing stopped. I turned to face my wannabe do-gooder. Tablet in hand, the man had raised his hand apologetically, but the expression on his face told me it wasn't sincere.

"My apologies, Miss," he said in a tone that added smugness to his condescending look.

"How'd you like it if I pushed your around?" I said with a sneer. Lots of people had a tendency to be helpful when it wasn't called for, but annoying as it was, I usually managed to maintain some form of politeness. With this guy, that didn't seem possible. With that nasty smirk on his face, it felt as if he were looking down on me for no reason and it wasn't just the fact that I was sitting.

"Ash," Mrs. Marsden said. She sounded a bit annoyed. I glanced past the deliveryman, who stood with his back to Mrs. Marsden, so she couldn't see his expression. A frown added to the creases on her wrinkled face.

"It's quite all right, ma'am," the deliveryman said. His voice was friendly as he spoke with Mrs. Marsden, but he sneered at me as if he'd found me sticking under his shoe.

"Ass," I called after him as he walked down the path.

"Ash," Mrs. Marsden said, and this time she sounded really appalled. "You get inside right this minute, young lady, and I think tonight's dishes belong wholly to you."

"Great," I muttered under my breath as I watched the deliveryman get into an unmarked white van. Which I might have noted as being odd if it weren't for Mrs. Marsden calling out my name again. I turned to face the porch and saw Rowdy sitting on the top step as he watched me with wide eyes.

"Yes, ma'am," I said as I started to make my way around back.

"I said I was sorry," I said as grabbed a plate from the dry rack and started to run a towel over it.

"I would just appreciate it if you'd check your attitude, especially in Rowdy's presence," Mrs. Marsden said. "I thought we had passed that stage."

I placed the dried plate on my lap, and as I rolled to the proper cabinet, I caught Mrs. Marsden eyeing her husband as if in search of his support.

"Well?" she said, confirming my suspicion. Mr. Marsden raised his eyes from the paper he sat reading at the kitchen table.

Avoiding his gaze, I turned to fetch another plate and exhaled. I wasn't sure how to feel about this parenting stuff. These people weren't my parents, and besides, I had turned fifteen last September, and it wouldn't be as if they could bring about big changes. Mags never seemed to have any problem with my behavior.

Still, I understood that they were helping to raise a small kid and that they needed me to use a little finesse once in a while. I was really trying not to ruin his upbringing.

"I didn't even use a bad word," I said, feeling the need to defend myself.

"I think that three-letter word you called after that poor man definitely counted as a bad word," Mrs. Marsden said. I shook my head in defeat and conceded to the fact that I had gotten myself stuck in the Twilight Zone.

"Have you considered asking Ash about her reason for lashing out at the man?" Mr. Marsden said. His calm deep voice always made me smile. He sounded like that actor who played God in that Jim Carrey movie. Mrs. Marsden sighed, and I took that as my cue to turn and face them both.

"Because he looked at me like I was dirt," I said. I flicked a nervous glance between the two of them, but I couldn't hold their gazes and glanced down at the tiled floor.

"He did not," Mrs. Marsden said. My head shot up, and I guessed my glare spoke volumes, because Mrs. Marsden's eyes widened.

"I think Ash might see that differently." Mr. Marsden stood from the kitchen table and nodded in the direction of the living room. "Why don't you relax a little?" he said to his wife. "And I'll help Ash finish up." He came up behind me and grabbed the dish towel from my shoulder.

He waited for Mrs. Marsden to leave the kitchen before he spoke.

"It's not always easy," he said, "being different."

I didn't know what to say to that because I wasn't different—was I? I shrugged instead.

He paused drying the plate and stared out the window for a moment. "My old man, he was a proud man who had worked hard all his life—"

"Wait," I said. "I remind you of your dad."

Mr. Marsden raised an eyebrow as he looked down at me and slowly quirked a smile. "You wanna hear the story or not?"

I grinned and nodded. I always liked it when Mr. Marsden started telling me his stories. It kind of reminded me of Chuck, an elderly gentleman I had met at the hospital where I had been staying before all hell broke out. The two men looked nothing alike of course. Mr. Marsden was a big man, tall, with broad shoulders. He must have been a catch in his day with his dark skin and muscular arms. Now, the gray hair and the belly that had started to hang over his belt began to abate his dashing appearance a little, but there were still enough ladies who turned around as he passed. I had seen it at the grocery store. Chuck, however, had been ill at the time I had met him, with skin as gray as the ash of the cigarettes that he smoked and his face a wrinkled mess. He had taken a liking to me, though, and treated me like a normal person and not as a disabled kid in a wheelchair.

"Like I said, my daddy was a proud man, and even after he had lost his leg," Mr. Marsden said before stopping himself. "I told you about my daddy's leg, right?" He glanced down, and I nodded emphatically yes. In fact, he had told me several times how his dad's leg got caught underneath the wheel of a tractor and had to be amputated. As Mr. Marsden continued, he fortunately skipped that part of the story.

"Even after he lost his leg, he was a proud man. It hadn't changed him, because that was the kind of man my daddy was," he continued, "but that didn't mean that others didn't see him in a different light —or treated him differently."

Mr. Marsden handed me another plate, and I rolled to the cupboard. To help me out, most of the essentials like glasses and plates along with the Twinkies and other snacks had been moved to lower shelves and cupboards to make them easier for me to access.

"How did he deal with it?" I asked as I closed the little door. Mr. Marsden glanced at me with a half-smile and a look that seemed as if he had been in a faraway place.

"Pretty much like you did," he said as that half-smile turned into a grin. "With a shrug and by staying the person he had always been."

We finished the last of the cups and utensils. After I had cleared them all away, Mr. Marsden threw the towel in the sink and leaned against the counter.

"I almost forgot," he said, giving me a curious glance, "what did the guy bring?"

I shifted my gaze and gestured at a small brown box that rested on a shelf mounted on the wall next to the pantry.

"Hmmm," he said as he walked over to the box and picked it up to inspect it. He gazed at it a little while until I saw his eyes widen. "Must be the spark plugs I ordered. Jack from the auto shop must have been kind enough to send them over. I'll have to thank him for that." He placed the box back where he had found it and then headed in the direction of the living room.

"I'll take them to the garage tomorrow morning," he added before he left the room.

3

Mags

My feet had started to warm up a bit as I pushed the food around on my plate. As the lack of coats on the racks had predicted, the spacious room with rows and rows of tables sat almost deprived of people. Though the sun had started to set, it was still early. It was mid-December, and that meant that by the time it was five o'clock it would be dark outside. That was also the time when most personnel would find the mess for dinner, which meant Angie and I had about thirty minutes of quiet left.

I lifted my eyes and watched Angie saunter between the rows of tables as she approached the table I had picked in the furthest corner from the food line. She had stopped commenting about my choice of seating arrangement after the first two weeks.

Angie placed her tray on the table and plopped down in the chair across from me. Our eyes met, but I soon dropped them to my plate, shoved some peas onto my fork, and forced myself to eat them. It had nothing to do with the food, but soon my fork started digging aimlessly into the mashed potatoes again instead of shoving them into my mouth.

I missed being around Ash and Mars, but that wasn't what kept me from eating. Not even this strange, cold place with its days too short and so far away from everything I knew and loved was the reason. My mind kept wondering about what the hell we were still doing here. The only reason that we were supposed to come here was to get Dr. Kelly Matley's research into the hands of this Dr. Theodore Chen, and we had done that.

Everything Dr. Matley had found out about the virus causing the zombie mutation and the reason that neither Angie, Ash, nor I had become infected was in the files we had delivered. I had expected to be here for a couple of weeks, because without Dr. Matley around to explain her research, Dr. Chen would have to do some digging of his own, but it had been over three months now. Dr. Matley's death had set the research back, I knew that, but this was starting to get ridiculous.

"Okay, spill," Angie said out of the blue. I looked up to face her. "You've been poking at your food for the last ten minutes, and it's not that bad."

"And you managed to notice that in the two minutes that you've been sitting there?" I said and looked up to face her.

Angie's dark eyes bored into me with that commanding quality they held. I still needed to ask her how she did that—get people to comply with just a stare. I managed a half-smile, but then sat back in my chair and pushed the tray holding my plate away. I held Angie's gaze for a moment but knew I would lose that battle, so I shifted my gaze to the door as a couple of airmen entered the mess and walked past our table.

"Why are they keeping us here for so long?" I said. I kept my voice low, but probably more out of resignation than out of concern someone might hear. "I mean, Chen has been checking our blood every two days since we've gotten here."

"Well, you got yourself bitten again, and that thing with your eyes wasn't pretty," she replied. I gazed at my right hand that as of late was missing a pinky and a ring finger. A fleeting image of running down hallways inside Cheyenne Mountain complex flashed across my eyes. The memory of trying to lure the zombies away from Angie, Ash, and especially Mars sent a shiver down my spine. Although zombies usually didn't show interest in me because of the Divus serum that had formed in my system, a bloody rag drenched with Mars's blood had been too much of a temptation to one of the zombies, and it had sunken his teeth in it. The rag being wrapped around my hand at the time, the bite had caused me to lose the fingers. I shook my head to shove the memory from my mind.

"I know," I said in a whisper, "but that was months ago. Why is Chen still checking my blood, and yours for that matter?" Angie placed her utensils on her tray as I added, "And don't tell me you haven't wondered about that."

Angie moved her mouth as if she were poking at something between her teeth before she said, "I truly believe that they are checking to make absolutely sure that once injected with the serum the turning into a zombie process isn't just delayed." She paused as her eyes scanned around us. The crowd had started to grow, and men and women in mostly green fatigues were piling inside.

"But?" I said. Though the tables around ours in the far corner of the room sat abandoned, Angie leaned in closer.

"The fact that the three of us are practically contagious ourselves kind of concerns me," she said. "We're basically incubators for this virus that is killing the world, and I have no idea how they are planning to deal with that. It's not a coincidence that it's just the two of us when we get to do any kind of training."

I hadn't thought of that. Except when I'd been

with Mars, at which point the incubator part had been more of a worry to me than it had been for him. Angie had a valid point. It seemed unlikely for the government to distribute a cure that could potentially worsen the situation. Maybe Chen had been working on a method to get around that and that was the reason he had needed us to stay so long.

"So you don't think it has anything to do with …" I started to say, but hesitated as it came to mentioning his name, "Warren." The memory of that man tended to make me physically ill, and I felt my stomach churn as his name fell from my mouth. The things he had put Ash and me through, the tests he'd performed on us, which had been basically torture, still woke me up bathing in my own sweat at nights.

Angie frowned as she said, "You mean the super soldier thing." I nodded in reply. Angie held a thoughtful expression for a moment, but then shook her head. "I don't think anyone has forgotten about it, but I don't think that it's on the top of the list right now," she said after a moment. "Getting rid of the zombies is."

"Yeah, but don't you think that super soldiers might give them an edge on that, making it a reason to bump it up on their list?"

"I hope not," Angie said as she leaned back in her chair.

"Well, I'm thinking of asking Dr. Chen tomorrow," I said.

Before she could answer, the voice of a young man pulled us out of our conversation.

Private First Class Jon Hickey stood awkwardly at our table, his brown eyes darting nervously between Angie and me. The young man clenched his jaw, which sharpened his features. A combination of freckles and acne riddled his face, but I figured someday he'd grow out of that to become a decent-looking man.

Angie blew out a breath as a sudden irritation flooded her eyes, and she glared at the already tense-looking private. "What?" she asked in a harsh tone.

The private's hands twitched at his side, but he held his composure as his eyes met Angie's. For a brief moment he managed to hold her gaze before he trailed his eyes to mine, but I would have applauded him for the effort.

"Ms. Vissers, Ms. Meadow," he said with a nod.

"Hey, Jon," I replied, trying to sound a bit more welcoming than Angie. It took some effort. The topic of our discussion wasn't the most enjoyable one.

Jon gave me a faint smile and nodded again. "I am instructed to inform you of a scheduled video call," he said. "You're expected at coms tomorrow at nineteen-hundred hours sharp."

His words lifted a smile on my face, and I felt some of that earlier built tension fade. A video call, that could only mean one out of two things—Ash or Mars. Both would even be better, but I didn't want to get my hopes up. I still maintained a love–hate relationship with hope in an effort to keep myself from getting hurt. But as I had learned this past year, a little hope wouldn't kill you.

"Thanks, Jon," I said, adding a cheery note to my voice. Angie shot me a look and raised an eyebrow. I ignored her. "Have you eaten? You could join us."

Jon's gaze shifted over the table and then to the food line before it settled back on me. Although the young man had been nothing but polite ever since we had met him that first day we'd arrived, he never seemed comfortable around us. He had shown us around the base and explained the basics for us to get around this massive place, but he'd always kept his distance. If we needed anything, we only needed to ask and he'd make sure we got it, but conversations never went any further than the basic yes, ma'am, and no, ma'am. Jon shifted on his feet as he cleared his throat.

"Thank you, ma'am, but I've ..." he said, hesitating as his eyes traveled over the large space filled with soldiers eating.

Bodies seemed to have filled the mess in a matter of minutes. The noises of conversation, chairs scraping the floor and utensils raking plates permeated the room.

Jon's eyes seemed to find what he was looking for, and he visually relaxed. "I'm meeting members of my squad for dinner. If you'd excuse me."

With that, he nodded and turned on his heels.

"You might come to believe the boy thinks we're infected with some kind of contagious disease," Angie said, her gaze following the young soldier as he made his way down the aisle. She turned back and indicated the two empty tables next to ours, which seemed to be the only empty tables inside the room. Our so-called conditions hadn't been kept a secret. Colonel Marshall felt that it was her responsibility to inform the men and women under her command and had arranged for detailed briefings, which included information about us being a potential solution to the zombie problem. This had led to a respectful but distant reception from the people working on this base. I suspected that if they could, they would avoid us like the plague. But we had gotten used to it after a couple of months.

I grinned. "Now who would be spreading a rumor like that?"

| 4

Ash

I awoke with a start as I hit the floor. My eyes shot open, escaping the images of clawing hands trying to grab me. I drew in a breath to calm my racing heart as my eyes searched the small room. It took me a second to remember where I was, before the Marsden family guest room came into focus.

A desk minus a chair stood propped underneath the window, a dresser stood against one wall, and the single bed out of which I had just fallen was set against the opposite wall. Mr. Marsden had cleared out the two chairs and the enormous plant that used to stand in the corner to give me some more mobility with my wheelchair.

I propped myself up on my elbows and noticed my left leg still lying on the bed, entangled in the sheets. Pulling it free, I sat up and tugged at the cord of the earplugs blasting music into my ears. Rage against the Machine probably wasn't the best choice to wake up to.

Cursing myself for falling asleep with the damn things in—again, I checked my phone. Technically, it was still Mags's phone, but I had no intention of giving it back. The thought triggered a grin on my face, because I didn't think she would ever ask for it anyway. Fortunately, I had plugged it in last night, and the battery read 100 percent. The time on the device read six a.m., but pretty sure that sleep had left me, I wriggled into the faded jeans that had broken my fall.

I fished a clean T-shirt and a black hoody from the dresser, slipped my phone in my pants pocket, and grabbed a steel cylinder from my nightstand. I had found the tactical baton in Mars's old room, and since Mr. and Mrs. Marsden didn't allow me to roll around with a loaded gun, this was at least something. Of course, I hadn't told the old couple I had found the thing, but I shoved it in the front pocket of my hoody anyway and then rolled my way to the bathroom. I tried to keep the noise level down at this early hour, but I couldn't always help bumping into things. Though if it weren't me waking them up, I'd bet Rowdy would have Grandma and Grandpa Marsden up within the hour.

After freshening up and cleaning my teeth, I found myself in the kitchen, eyeing the content of the fridge. An orange caught my eye, but I decided against it. Those things were expensive these days, and I knew Mrs. Marsden was always on the lookout for healthy, vitamin-rich foods for Rowdy. I think she might have been afraid that, once that kind of food became too expensive to buy or ran out, the kid might stop growing or something. But even at this young age, it seemed pretty obvious that the kid would grow up to be as tall as his dad. I closed the fridge, grabbed an energy bar from a drawer, and headed out through the back door.

This neighborhood was practically dead in the mornings except for one or two joggers and Mr. Jackson from across the street, who deemed it necessary to intercept the kid delivering the newspaper every morning. Considering the neighborhood mostly consisted of retirees, the quiet wasn't that strange. These people had made their contributions to society and, from what I could tell from the expensive cars and houses, had done it well. Now, sleeping in seemed to be their contribution.

I headed down the street and took the first left. The dead-end street gave room to park at least a dozen cars, but sat empty at this time of day. This wasn't exactly tourist season, although the beach always seemed to draw some people, and I totally got that. I loved to watch the waves hammering the sand, but preferred it without strangers giving me looks.

With ease, I hopped off the curb and crossed the parking lot to the stairs that would lead down to the beach. The curbs around here weren't that high, so I maintained a little speed, and just at the right moment, I lifted the front casters off the ground and used the momentum to hop on the curb. I stopped at the railing and gazed across the seemingly never-ending expanse of water.

The colors of the sky started to shift as the sun began to rise behind me, and I grabbed my energy bar. I took a bite and settled in as I savored the sounds and smells around me.

A bit further down the beach, a guy was walking his dog. The animal was big, and as I watched his owner clean up after it, that seemed like a good enough reason to never get a dog—at least not one that was that big. As I watched a few joggers run by, I couldn't help but recognize the similarities between this beach and the last one Mags and I had visited.

We'd made a pit stop east of New Orleans and had decided to take a swim. A grin formed on my face as I remembered how Mags had taught me how to swim—well, sort of. Unfortunately, our fun had been cut short.

"Enjoying the view?" a voice said behind me. I

jumped and then felt a little embarrassed about the yelp that had followed before I noticed Mars standing behind me.

"Jesus, Mars," I said, still a little in shock. "You scared the shit out of me."

"That might have been the point," he said and flashed a grin. As he came to stand beside me and leaned down on the railing, I punched his arm.

"Ass," I said.

"Hey," he said, rubbing his arm, "you better not say that with my mother around."

"Tell me about it," I muttered.

With a lazy smile on his face, he turned his gaze to the ocean. Within seconds, the smile faded and a frown creased his forehead. He wore jeans and a T-shirt—not his usual work attire, so I guessed he must have gotten some time off.

"When did you get in?" I asked. I wondered where he had come from and how the hell he had known where to find me.

"Late last night," he said. "I didn't want to bother you."

"Ah," I said, hoping that my waking up hadn't woken him.

"You didn't wake me," he said as if he could read my mind. "Not exactly."

I raised an eyebrow at his vague remark. "Not

exactly?" I echoed.

He glanced back at me and concern edged on his face. It was clear something had Mars worried.

"What's wrong?" I asked, my voice sounding an octave higher. A sudden rush of fear overtook my body, and I rolled away from the railing to get a better look at him. "Did something happen to Mags or Angie?"

"Oh no, nothing like that," he said. "They're both fine. In fact, I've arranged a video call for tonight."

I felt the relief wash over me, and I exhaled.

"But I would like to talk to you about something." He glanced around as if to check for anyone eavesdropping. Then he slid down to the ground and sat with his back against the railing. I couldn't help giving him a curious glance. He avoided me for a moment, gazing up at the sky as if the reason for living could be found among the fluffy clouds.

"Mars," I said, drawing out his name. That caught his attention, and his gaze landed on me. Those jade eyes predicted a coming storm before his mouth could drop the bad news.

"You didn't wake me," he said, "but I got a call as soon as you left the house, and I followed."

I needed a second to let that sink in and cocked

my head sideways. Holding off on the profanities, I said, "You've got eyes on me."

"Yeah," he replied.

"Just me?" I asked.

"Just you."

I hesitated to ask the obvious, not so sure if I wanted to know, because nothing good would come of it, but then Mars beat me to it.

"We have reason to believe that Dr. David Warren has arrived at Monterey Regional Airport a couple of days ago."

Shocked, I glared at him as the realization increased my breathing and I felt my heart racing inside my chest.

"We think he might be here to find you," he added. Fear took hold of me, and I grabbed the push rings as I felt a tremble take hold of my body. The look on Mars's face hit me then. I didn't want his pity, and I didn't want him to see me like this. I didn't want anyone to see me like this, because no one would be able to understand—except for Mags. A shudder ran through me as the memories rushed back, and I wished Mags were here to help me subside them.

I rolled backward as Mars shifted from a sitting position into a crouch.

"Ash," he said, his eyes wide. He reached out a

hand, but I shook my head and set off bouncing off the curb before rolling down the parking lot.

Sterile rooms with glass for walls, examination tables, machines wheezing and beeping around me, and him, Dr. David Warren, with that sly smirk on his face, the same bastard who had often visited me in my dreams, together with the zombies.

Behind me, I heard Mars call out my name again, but I couldn't face him—not right now. I felt tears sting my eyes as they threatened to spill. The time at that lab, locked up in the dark, surrounded by zombies and the tests—especially the tests, although nightmares had awoken me before, I had never reacted this strongly to the memories, and I wondered if this zombie-and-Warren-free environment had something to do with it. Maybe I just had too much time to think about things, but it felt as if something had broken inside me, and every time I thought of those events, it felt as if someone was trying to choke the air from my lungs. And I didn't want it to affect me like that. I hated that fear claimed its victory over me in those moments and that it was harder to reverse that claim without Mags, but that wouldn't stop me from trying.

Breathing hard, I rounded the corner. Sticking to the road instead of the sidewalk, I gained momentum. The early morning chill and the ocean breeze seemed to have a calming effect on me. I glanced over my shoulder to see if Mars had caught up yet, but I didn't spot him and considered going around the block instead of the Marsden home; maybe after that, I'd be able to face Mars. As the thought crossed my mind, an approaching car steered into my lane—effectively blocking the road.

In an attempt to slow down, I forced a turn, and by the time I stopped, my fear had been shoved to the back of my mind as anger surfaced.

"Are you blind?" The words fell from my mouth in a harsh tone as a man in suit and tie opened the passenger-side door and stepped out.

"I'm sorry, Ms. Reed, but you'll have to wait here," the man said.

I glared at him in surprise at hearing my last name. "Who the hell are you?" I asked.

"My name is Miller," he replied, "but if you wait here for a minute, then it will all be explained." A door on the other side of the big black SUV slammed shut, but I didn't immediately see someone. Miller took a step toward me, and on pure instinct, I spun my wheels and rolled backward away from him.

"Ms. Reed," he said, questioningly.

"Mr. Miller," I said, creating some distance

between us. Two options crossed my mind about who these guys might be, and it came down to either Warren's men or the eyes on me that Mars had mentioned. If I had to guess, I'd say friends of Mars, because in the past, Warren's men would have been waving guns by now, but I figured a little caution would hurt no one. Because of this, combined with the fact I still didn't feel ready to go back to the Marsden place, I decided to take my leave. "It was nice meeting you."

The words had barely left my mouth before I had spun my chair round and started spinning the wheels. Unfortunately, I bumped into a very burly looking man who grabbed the back of my chair and spun me around again.

"Get your hands off me," I yelled and jabbed an elbow into his side. The man gave an oomph, but he didn't release my chair. I punched him again, but still to no avail, and I reached for the baton in my pocket. With a forceful swing, the inner shaft extended, and followed by a fluid motion, I let it connect with the hand holding my chair. The burly man instantly released the armrest and groaned in pain and followed this by a string of violent cursing that sounded like music to my ears.

"Ash," Mars's exasperated voice reached me over the cries of pain coming from the big man. I turned to see him standing behind me with his hands at his sides. His eyes shifted for a moment from me to the burly guy holding his battered hand. Then he shook his head and gestured to me.

"Miller, Baker, meet Ash."

I whirled around in my chair and waved at the men. Miller gave me a strange look as his eyes shifted between Baker and me. The latter, though, had a scowl on his face from here to Tokyo.

"Hey, guys," I said.

"Sir, I think she broke my hand," Baker said through clenched teeth.

"I'd warned you in the briefing, didn't I?" Mars said. "You shouldn't have touched her chair."

My eyes shifted to Mars, and I couldn't suppress the grin on my face. It seemed weird, but this encounter kind of had my juices flowing and had made me feel a bit better.

"Coffee, anyone?" I said.

Over a cup of coffee, which had originally been one of Mags's vices and appeared to have become one of my own, Mars apologized for not mentioning Miller and Baker back at the beach. He also disclosed some details about what was going on. It seemed he had been tracking Warren for the past few months and had learned that the man had stolen some samples from a lab in Washington, DC. At least the current official assumption was that Warren had stolen the samples, but Mars hadn't been that sure. Unwilling to work with assumptions, Mars hadn't dismissed the idea that Warren might have acted under orders that could lead all the way to the White House.

Orders or not, Warren had gathered his stuff and had taken off, along with several vials of the next generation of Mortem virus that he had been working on.

Further digging had revealed that the vials contained a variation of the virus that created zombies with a sense of awareness. They had also found William's head in a freezer. William was a guy Mags and I had met in Brooklyn while we were hiding out, at the beginning of the outbreak. William had seemed like a nice enough guy who had helped us out, but he turned out to be Warren's aide. Mags had accidentally infected William with Mortem while he'd come after us inside Cheyenne, and, I guessed, Warren had decided to keep his zombie-head.

Our conversation halted as the other occupants of the house awoke and a certain four-year-old demanded Mars's attention. Mrs. Marsden had declared the day special and treated us to pancakes for breakfast. After we'd eaten, I retreated to my room to give the family some time on their own. With not much else to do, I dragged myself from the chair onto the bed and plugged in my earbuds.

Mags's playlist of over a thousand songs held the weirdest combinations that ranged from jazz to rock, hip-hop, dance, classic, and whatnot. Veering away from the raging music that had greeted me this morning, I searched for something easier on the ears and chose a song called Waves that fitted the scenery outside. I had never heard of this Mr. Probz guy, but I liked his soothing voice.

There was a knock on the door just as I settled my head on the pillow. I looked up and saw Mars standing at the door. With his hands tucked into the pockets of his jeans, he leaned against the doorframe in a way that only Mars could. He had this easygoing, relaxed attitude that made me wonder if it were even possible to freak him out. I also liked that it seemed to rub off. We had talked in depth about Warren this morning, and that was usually a subject I tended to avoid. Mars helped to make it easier.

Mars cocked his head as he said, "So, what are you doing?"

I sat up and prodded myself against the headboard of the bed before I raised the phone and pulled the plugs from my ears.

"Just," I said and shrugged, "hanging out." Mars pursed his lips and nodded as if he were thinking it over.

"I don't think so," he said. He pulled his hands from his pockets and clapped them together. "Get your stuff. The whole family is heading for the beach."

"But ..." I started to say and hesitated. Mars glared at me as if I were about to say the stupidest thing ever said. "I thought you would want to spend time with your family." With all that was going on, Mars had to be away from home a lot. He tried to squeeze in visits as often as he could, but this time, I hadn't seen him in over two weeks.

That look didn't leave his face, and the gleam in his eyes grew as he said, "That's the point, and we're missing two as it is, so that means your presence is mandatory. Get your ass in that chair and get a move on."

He brought a smile on my face with those words the way only a few people could, and he seemed to know it. "Bring a sweater," he shouted as he set off down the hall. "The wind might be a bit chilly."

Grabbing my phone, I left the earplugs behind and settled back into my chair. I took an extra sweater, shoved it into Mags's old backpack along with the phone, and hung it from the back of my chair.

Minutes later Mr. and Mrs. Marsden led the way as I rolled at Mars's side while Rowdy sat on his shoulders. Mars had been right: the wind was a bit chilly, but the clear sky gave room for the sun to warm us up.

As the others had found a spot for our blankets, I balanced my chair down the steps until I hit the sand. By that time, Mars was on his way back and stopped in front of me, inspecting the sand at his feet.

"That stuff is a killer for your bearings," he said and grinned. "Now if I were Mags, I'd probably throw you over a shoulder."

"And I'd be pissed," I said, shooting him a dirty look. He looked thoughtful as he inspected the chair. Then he bent down, clamped on the brakes, and moved around me, and before I knew, it was lifted into the air. I was sure my face flushed all kinds of red as he carried me across the sand, but I had to admit this was better than being thrown over a shoulder. Although I couldn't blame Mags for that. It probably wasn't the easiest thing to haul me around. From Mars's breathing I could tell carrying me, chair and all, was pretty exhausting for him too.

"Dude, you better not break it, or you're goin' to

be the one to fix it," I said teasingly. "The repair kit is mounted underneath the seat."

"I won't break it," Mars replied with a chuckle.

Moments later I was settled on a blanket, the chair at my side as I watched Rowdy. He laughed as he fled the water rolling onto the beach under the watchful eyes of his grandfather. Mrs. Marsden stood close by, snapping pictures with her camera. It all felt so normal, as if everything were right with the world. I felt glad to be part of it, although the feeling of foreboding that settled in my stomach warned me that it wouldn't last.

I glanced over my shoulder, seeing Miller and Baker scanning their surroundings. They had left their cozy SUV in front of the Marsden house and had followed us—supposedly to protect us. The sight of them fueled the twisting sensation in my gut, and I turned to Mars, who sat back as he leaned on his elbows while he held a prideful eye on the antics of his giggling son.

"You can't tell her," he said without taking his eyes of the kid.

A bit surprised, I opened my mouth, but my mind was still processing, figuring he meant not telling Mags about Warren, although unable to understand why, and so no words came out. Mars turned his gaze on me and, with piercing eyes, conveyed the seriousness of what he was saying. "She doesn't know it yet, and I don't want her to know. They're about to send her on a mission."

"Wait, what?" I said as my brain tried to catch up. Mags didn't go on missions; she was just supposed to be the guinea pig that helped with the development of a serum to prevent infection by Mortem virus. She wasn't a soldier or an FBI agent. "That wasn't the deal." The strain in my voice was evident, but I couldn't help it. A bad feeling had already settled in my stomach and this just added to that.

"I know," Mars said, "but they're close to a solution and need more people to test it on. Only a few soldiers have volunteered, and someone brilliant idiot has opined that people in the right circumstances might be more easily convinced."

"What does that have to do with Mags?" I asked.

"They would like her and Angie to join a team to seek out survivors in a zombie-infected area and help them get out with aid of the serum."

"This is bullshit," I said. Anger started to build inside me because this wasn't what General Whitfield had promised us. "This thing was supposed to take three weeks, and it's been months, and now you want to put Mags and Angie in danger again."

Mars sat up and turned so he could fully face me.

"Trust me," he said, raising his voice. "I'm not happy with it either, and I've tried everything to get them back." His eyes shot to his son and parents not far off, but they didn't seem to have heard his small outburst. His face looked sad as he turned back and lowered his gaze to the blanket. "I hate it, but there is nothing I can do about it."

"So why tell me?" I asked. "You said she doesn't even know yet."

He tilted his head up and said, "I don't want her to worry. She needs to keep her head on the game."

"And you don't mind it if I worry?"

He gave me a sheepish look and shook his head.

"You always worry about Mags," he said.

I shrugged. He was probably right. I didn't like being so far apart while our lives seemed to be in the hands of others.

"But I don't keep things from her," I said in a low voice.

"I know, and neither do I, at least not anymore," he said, reminding himself and me that he had lied to us before. Mars had told us we could come and stay at his parents' home in Colorado, but that had turned out to be a high-security military facility. His intentions had been good, though, but that didn't stop it from stinging. "But these are strange times, and God knows how someone might react. I need Mags to be compliant, or else someone might get the idea that she or Angie could become a security threat and lock them up—"

He broke himself off and stared of across the ocean. I didn't know every aspect of the situation and didn't even want to understand the political crap. What I did understand was that Mags, Angie, and I were security risks. Our blood could become the source of another outbreak if we weren't careful. The fact that I was staying with the Marsdens had been solely Mars's doing, with a little help from General Whitfield. It still amazed me that Mars trusted me with his son, and I was utterly grateful for it. If he hadn't, I'd probably be stuck in some isolation room in one of those refugee camps.

"I can't lose her," Mars continued. "So I'm asking you, please don't tell her tonight." Mars was referring to the video call he had set up for us. That was one of the reasons he was here today, to take me to Monterey. The military had a communication station set up at the airport over there.

If I were honest with myself, I didn't trust my answer. That's probably why I nodded instead of voicing my reply.

Mars blew out a breath in relief and then said, "I'll be inside the coms room with you, but you can't tell her I'm there."

Before I could question that, I was hit from the side and keeled over with a giggling Rowdy sprawled on top of me. The kid's laugh was infectious and made me forget my strain of thought. I rolled on to my back and lifted him into the air. That made him laugh even harder.

| 5

Mags

The day had dragged on and wouldn't seem to come to an end. The running and shooting guns had left my body drained of energy, but I'd been looking forward to talking to Ash or Mars the entire day. There had even been a little bounce in my step as Angie and I had approached the building where we would get to hold our video call.

After we'd arrived, the communications officer had told me that it would be Ash on the other end of the line, which was great. It was during these moments as I sat waiting behind this screen inside this tiny office that I realized how much I missed being around her. Although it didn't lessen the disappointment I felt over Mars not being there.

In hindsight, it seemed strange that a man with whom, over the year or so that I've known him, I had only spent a couple of days with had come to mean so much to me. He'd been a rock for me to lean on ever since the virus had claimed its first victims and zombies had started to roam JFK airport. He had saved me then and had come to rescue Ash and me from the hands of Dr. David when he held us captured at his research facility in Florida. It felt as if he'd been there for me all this time, but in truth, we'd spent only days together and mere hours in private.

I guessed many would consider this a fragile foundation for a relationship, and I would probably be the first to agree if it hadn't been for the fact that under normal circumstances cancer should have ended my life over ten months ago. I had been given a second chance, and if this disaster that had struck the world had taught me anything, then it was that you should embrace the gifts you were given, and Mars had just been that—a gift.

I blew out a breath as a young female soldier poked her head inside the room.

"I'm sorry for the wait, Ms. Vissers, but there should be a connection now," she said in a perky voice. I shoved the mouse, and the screen turned from black to blue. A bar on the bottom of the screen filled up, and then Ash's face appeared.

"Got it," I said and glanced back at the young soldier. She nodded, offering a polite smile and closing the door behind her.

Left alone in the room, I stared at Ash's image, as it seemed to be stuck in place. Her blond, near-white hair looked shorter than it had the last time and sat tucked behind her ears. The expression on her face took me aback a little. Those big blue eyes of hers looked sad, and something of concern radiated off her. I dismissed my observation, knowing it might have just been an awkward moment as the frame had stilled, and I wondered if I had spoken too soon by indicating to the young soldier that a connection was made, but then the image was set in motion.

"Hey, kiddo," I said as my lips curved into a smile, "what's up?" Ash smiled, and those big blue eyes of hers brightened, although I could still detect a hint of concern in them.

"Hey," she replied, "it's about time. I've been waitin' like two weeks and twenty-five minutes out here." I grinned at the familiar retort and the thick Brooklyn accent I had missed. "How long we got?"

"They didn't say," I said, "but I'm guessing fifteen minutes or so." Ash huffed as she adjusted her chair. She seemed nervous and kept glancing over the screen beyond the camera as if there were someone else inside the room.

"How is everyone?" I asked.

"Mr. and Mrs. Marsden are okay. They send their love and Rowdy is drivin' me crazy," she said as some of her spunk returned. "The kid is like a whirlwind—always wantin' to ride along with me in my chair. I swear he sees me as his personal transportation device."

The smile as she spoke of Mars's son was infectious. I hadn't met the little guy in person, but on the screen he seemed like a handful. This, of course, veered my mind into a different direction.

"Have you heard from Mars?" I asked.

"He's been around," she replied, "but he's busy doin' FBI things and such."

I wanted to ask more, but Ash fiddled with the fabric of her sleeve, which was another indication that something was up.

"Are you okay?" I asked hesitantly.

Her eyes widened a bit as she gazed at the screen. "Yeah, why?"

"You seem …" I said and hesitated. Ash wasn't the type to be fussed over, and I didn't want to be the person that did that. I wanted her to have the space she needed, but then a fifteen-year-old kid might not see my intentions. "I don't know—distracted."

A half-grin slowly formed on her face as she peered into the camera as if I had caught her in the act of doing something she wasn't supposed to. But as soon as I felt some relief that she was okay, her eyes dropped to inspect the table in front of her.

I was about to ask again when someone knocked

on the door and, without waiting for a reply, opened it. Angie stood in the door with a grin plastered on her face.

"I think you two have had about enough alone time," she said. "I wanna see the kid before the connection goes down."

Angie maneuvered around the table with a goofy smile on her face.

"Kid!" she said, drawing out the word as she leaned over my shoulder to stick her face inside the frame.

"Hiya, Angie," Ash replied. At that, Angie shot me a look and raised an eyebrow.

"What's up? Have you been tearing up the beach with those wheels of yours?" Angie said as she continued, but I had caught her insinuation, and it confirmed my assumption that something was on Ash's mind. If there weren't, she would have never let that kid remark slide. It had become like this thing that mostly Angie did to tease Ash and also to remind her sometimes that she still was a kid.

Ash had been through so much as a young child. She had been a vessel from birth to help save her sister's life, only to lose her anyway when Alison had taken her own life to protect Ash from further medical procedures. And then Ash fell ill herself. No one should have to suffer through those things, and it had caused Ash to grow up fast.

So sometimes Angie and I felt as if we needed to remind her that she was actually still a kid. The opposite side of that coin was that Ash would never let that remark slide without some harsh retort, and if she did, then something was off.

I wasn't sure whether I should ask about it, and with Angie in the room, the conversation quickly shifted to the usual banter, which was something we all needed. I decided I would talk to her about it next time.

"You've been quiet," Angie said as she stomped up the three wooden steps that lead to the door of the apartment building that held our quarters. I glanced up at her and then turned to see the row of buildings we had just passed without me even noticing it. Streetlamps reflected on the freshly snow-covered streets. Other lights gleamed behind the tiny windows of the still-occupied apartments, although most were dark. Except for the sound of an occasional truck passing by, it was quiet—too quiet.

This base was the size of what I would consider a large town, although I didn't know whether anyone in this country shared that opinion. Nearly nine thousand deployable soldiers and airmen, with

God knows how many men and women working support services, were hosted on this base. Except now, nearly half of them had been sent all over the country to join the fight against the zombie infestation.

Most of the activities in and around the base had been centered on certain areas, but it seemed Colonel Marshall had deemed it necessary to stick Angie and me in housing as far away from the rest as possible. We had joked about it before, but being treated as a leper had started to wear me down.

Angie stomped her feet again to rid herself of the snow stuck to her boots.

"I don't know," I said as I climbed the steps, "I've just been feeling …" I paused, not sure how to vocalize what I meant.

"Like something's off," Angie offered.

"Maybe," I said and stomped my boots, but then shook my head, "I don't know."

Angie opened the door and stepped inside a hallway that would lead us to the small apartment assigned to us. Just before the door slammed shut and she left me to stand outside in the cold on my own, I heard her say, "There are some things left. You do know, right."

I exhaled and watched my breath billow out into the cold night air. A chill ran down my spine, and I turned to follow Angie inside.

"Something was definitely up with Ash," Angie said as I closed the door to our apartment and started peeling off the layers of clothing.

Our housing for the past few months had a small hallway that held all the stuff and gear we needed to even set a foot out the door. This meant the tiny space was clogged with coats boots, mittens, parkas, and all the other things we needed to keep ourselves warm. The tiny hallway opened up into a single room with a small kitchen on the left, a sitting area in the middle, and two beds tucked away at the far right. A small bathroom sat around a corner.

I didn't know whether all the apartments looked the same or if this one was just meant for the misfits, for the likes of us. On socks, I moved to the seating area and sank into one of the two armchairs without even bothering to change out of the moisture-wicking layer of underclothes I was wearing.

"I know," I replied, "and I tried to ask, but ..."

"What?" Angie asked.

"I had a feeling she wasn't alone in that room," I said.

Angie was rummaging around in the kitchen and stopped to look at me. "You mean like monitoring what she said."

"In a way," I replied. "As if she wasn't supposed to mention something or something."

"Hmm," Angie said and frowned before she continued her search for whatever it was what she was looking for.

I glanced at our bunks. Angie's side was pitch-perfect, ready to endure that bouncing-coin test I had seen on TV. Neither of us had much stuff, but the things she had gathered up lay neatly on her nightstand, and though her clothes were hidden inside a locker, I knew they'd be neatly folded and stacked.

My stuff, mainly clothes, lay scattered on and over a chair. An olive-green shirt had missed its target and landed on the floor next to that same chair. I sighed as Angie closed a cupboard door and walked into the sitting area with two glasses and a bottle.

She also still wore the sand-colored underclothes as she sat down in the other chair and placed her feet on the small table in front of us. I narrowed my eyes and focused on the bottle she swung challenging in front of me. I gawked at the bottle with the golden-brown fluid.

"Good old No. 7," Angie said with a grin.

"Where'd you find that?" I asked.

"Well," Angie said as she started to pour,

"remember what Marshall had said about our friend PFC Hickey."

With a shrug, I shook my head.

"That if we needed anything, we should just ask. Yesterday, I decided to test that."

I smiled as she handed me a glass, saluted, and took a sip from the whiskey. As far as whiskey was concerned, I preferred a single malt, but nonetheless, I savored the taste in my mouth and then felt the liquid's warmth trail down my throat.

"So, Ash," Angie said.

"Am I being paranoid?" I asked.

"Considering the fact that you both have been abducted by the psychopath who released a zombie virus into the world and then chased you across the country all the way into a high-security military facility," Angie said before pausing. Then, she creased her brows and scrunched up her nose. "Maybe just a little." She let out a chuckle, and I shook my head.

"You're not exactly helping here."

"Well, I don't have any experience in dealing with kids Ash's age," Angie said.

"You were that age once," I said. Angie shook her head.

"When I first met her at that hospital, I thought I'd be able to relate to her, you know, growing up with cancer," Angie said. She regarded me, and I nodded to confirm that I did know. The three of us had all gone down that road.

"But when I learned what had happened with her sister, that she'd killed herself to spare Ash a life as a guinea pig," Angie said and blew out a breath, "I can't imagine how guilty I would have felt if it had been my sister."

Angie stared off into space, and I pondered for a moment whether I should derail from the topic, but she had handed me an opening and I felt curious.

"Are you close to your sister?" I asked.

Angie's head twitched as if I had just brought her back into the real world from some faraway place. A combination of a smile and a grimace grew on her face, as she seemed to think about her reply.

"She's the overachiever type, and don't get me wrong: I love her," she said. "But she reached for the things that were expected of a woman in our family—college, career, then the golf-playing husband and a bunch of kids. For a long time I felt like I should at least emulate that." She took a sip from her glass and shrugged. "I couldn't do it."

I sank deeper into my chair. Maybe I should have changed the topic, because this was coming closer to home than I would have expected.

"I have a sister and a brother like that," I said.

"They run a big part of my father's company, selling the latest in computer technology. Well, sold, I think."

Angie nodded; she probably already knew that, having been with the FBI and all. She probably knew everything there was to know about my family and me.

"They're okay, right, your family?" I promptly asked. From what I'd been told, my family was okay, living back home in the Netherlands. The country had faced its share of the zombie plague, but it wasn't nearly as bad as it had been in the States. I had even been able to talk to my mom and dad, and they had ensured me everything was fine with them. Angie never spoke of her family, and it hadn't occurred to me to ask.

"My sister and her family are fine. My mom too," she said in a reassuring voice. "They live out west, far away from the nearest outbreak."

"Thank God," I said under my breath, relieved to hear that. We sat in silence for a while as we sipped our drinks. I had never been much of the sharing type, and fortunately Angie seemed to be the same.

Still, as if unsatisfied with the end of our earlier conversation, she said, "Maybe she's got an eye on a boy. Or a girl."

"Who, Ash?" I asked, taken a bit off guard. She wiggled her eyebrows at that. I chuckled as I replied, "God, I hope it's something like that. But I'm going to find out next time."

With that I shot a weary glance at my bunk. During the winter, the days in Alaska were short, but my body felt tired, as if the days went on forever. I yawned. Angie, however, poured another glass for the both of us.

| 6

Ash

Unable to find the pair of scissors I was searching for, I slammed the drawer shut. I must have gone over this entire kitchen and not one pair of scissors to be found. Cursing aloud, I picked up the bag of cookies with the packaging material from hell and hurled them at the sink. I rolled backward and knocked over a chair. As it clattered to the ground, I gripped the push rings and squeezed them hard in the hope of composing myself. I'd been agitated most of the morning and knew exactly why.

Usually being able to talk to Mags brightened my mood and it felt good to see her. She looked good, with her dark blond hair short. She had cut it even shorter again after the commander of the base had asked her to participate in training exercises. I preferred the familiarity of the shorter hair, because that was the way I had come to meet her. Besides the hair, Mags's complexion appeared a lot healthier than the last time we had seen each other in person, but then the loss of a couple of digits to her right hand might have had something to do with that. I hated how the conversation with Mags and Angie had gone. It had felt forced, and for all I knew, that might have been the last time I would talk to them. These days that could be a very real possibility, and although I thought I had learned enough to know that, I had lied to her. I had lied to both of them, and what was worse, Mags knew something was off. She just knew me too well.

"Fuck," I muttered under my breath and closed my eyes to calm my nerves. As I felt ready to pick up the fallen chair without the urge to break it in half, I opened my eyes. A pair of big, brown, fearful-looking eyes greeted me.

"Ash," Rowdy said in a tiny voice, "are you mad at me?" At the sight of the dazed-looking kid, I squeezed my eyes shut and internally cursed myself for a moment before opening them. With a reassuring smile, I straightened the chair and rolled closer to Rowdy.

"Hey, kiddo," I said as I placed my hands on his tiny shoulders. "Of course I'm not mad at you." Rowdy just stared at me with those big brown eyes, making me feel like an idiot. "I was just being a bit clumsy. And stupid. This has nothing to do with you, okay?"

His head gave a nod, but I could tell he was still upset. I wrapped my arms around him, pulled him onto my lap and into a hug. As I felt his small hand pat my back, I kissed the top of his head.

"You okay now, buddy?" I asked as I released him. He nodded and gave me shy smile. "Why don't you get back to your puzzle, and I'll find a way to open those cookies?" His face lit up. While Rowdy made his way to the living room, I heard a knock on the front door, and I groaned.

Mrs. Marsden had gone shopping with a couple of friends, and Mr. Marsden had locked himself in the garage where he worked on his hobby project. He had bought an old Camaro and had been fixing it for a couple of weeks now. When time allowed, which was usually after Mrs. Marsden had gone out, he'd work on his project. This left me in charge of Rowdy and the front door.

"Just a minute," I yelled as I rolled my chair from the kitchen into the hallway. As I steered past the hallway entry to the living room, I called out to Rowdy, "I'm gonna need a couple more minutes on those cookies, kid."

"'Kay," was the reply I got, and I opened the front door.

I was surprised to find a young soldier looking down at me. He stared at me, unblinking. as if he'd forgotten how to speak. Raising my eyebrows, I asked, "Can I help you?" He blinked, gave his head the tiniest of shakes before pointing a nervous thumb behind him.

"I ... uh ..." he said and hesitated. Then he gestured at the black sedan with Miller and Baker in the front seats. As ordered by Mars, they had sat in the same spot and watched the house after he had left this morning to head back to work. "I'm Bennett, Luke Bennett, uh, Private."

I glared at him, waiting for some more information, which seemed to unnerve the young private even more. "I'm sorry to bother you, but I just wanted to introduce myself." Another pause and this time he wiped a nervous hand across his forehead. "Agent Marsden has added me and my colleague to your detail." He pointed at another young man sitting behind the wheel of a green truck parked a few cars down from the black sedan.

I cocked my head sideways and took in the young man who shifted his feet, seemingly uncomfortable on the porch. He had short brown hair and blue eyes. A small scar cut his left eyebrow in two, which gave a bit more credibility to his baby-faced features.

"So they have twelve-year-olds working for the army these days?" I asked. For a second he looked shocked and shot a nervous glance over his shoulder at the black sedan. As his gaze returned, his eyes narrowed, studying me.

"If I'm twelve," he said, "does that mean I'm babysitting a nine-year-old. Besides, I'm not army." He held my gaze as he waited for a reaction. I had trouble keeping back the grin that desperately wanted to form on my face and was saved by Mr. Marsden's voice.

"Ash, have you seen that box that came the other day?" Mr. Marsden yelled. "They're parts I need for the car."

I quickly turned my chair and, with my back facing the soldier, released the grin.

"Just a sec," I said to Luke and rolled in the direction of the kitchen.

"It should be on the shelf where you left it," I called out at Mr. Marsden. I stopped at the door that led from the hallway into the kitchen, just in time to see Mr. Marsden find his box with a big smile on his face.

"Can't wait to get these in," he said. I didn't bother to remember what he had said was inside the box. My knowledge of vehicles ended pretty much before it started. "You guys okay?"

"Yeah, fine," I replied, "We're on the brink of finishing Rowdy's latest puzzle."

He walked to the backdoor and paused, turning back to me. A smile that reached his eyes sat on his face as he said, "I really appreciate you spending time with Rowdy, so that I can do a little ... you know." He pointed with his thumb at the garage behind him.

"I could say the same to you for letting me stay here Mr. Marsden," I replied and returned the smile.

"It's our pleasure," he said as he opened the door. "Now if only you'd stopped calling me Mr. Marsden and would just call me Joseph, things would be perfect."

"Perfect is just an illusion," I said before he closed the door behind him, muttering, "Yeah, yeah."

At the front door, Luke cleared his throat just as Rowdy called out to inquire after his cookies. I grinned as I watched the soldier inspect the doorframe as if it were the most interesting piece of craft he had ever seen.

"Why don't you come in and close the door?" I said as I made my way to the sink where I had last seen the bag of cookies.

"Hello," Luke called out, and I heard his footsteps approach.

"Second door on the left," I yelled. I pulled myself up on the counter, retrieved the bag from the sink, and plopped back in my chair just as Luke reached the door opening. I tossed him the bag, and he caught it with one hand. "See if you can open those."

I rolled to the cupboard to fetch a plate and cringed as I heard the packaging tear so easily in Luke's hands. Internally cursing the packaging companies, I placed the plate on my lap and rolled to where Luke was standing.

"I think they've had a rough time," he said while he gazed into the bag. I shrugged as I took the bag from him and poured some of the cookies-turned-crumbs onto the plate.

"It won't affect the taste," I said and made my way to the living room.

Rowdy was still playing with his puzzle, but his eyes widened as he saw me coming with the plate. He all but attacked the crumbled cookies and seemed to have no problem with the fact that they weren't the round variety anymore. He gave me an appreciative smile.

"Thank you," he said with a full mouth. I rubbed a hand over his frizzy hair before returning my attention to Luke who was standing at ease behind the couch with his hands on his back. He was grinning, but quickly stopped as he met my gaze.

"What's so funny?" I asked. He cleared his throat as he returned to his uncomfortable mode.

"I'm sorry, Ms. Reed," he said. Before he could continue, I cut him off.

"Call me Ash," I said. He stepped closer and held out his hand.

"Luke."

I shook his hand. As he released his grip, he nodded in the direction of the door. "Those agents out there, they, uh ..." he started to say and hesitated, "they said you'd be less than, uh, pleasant."

"I'm sure they phrased it differently," I said, "but they're not wrong." The words had left my mouth before I could think them through. *Why was I bothering Luke with my shitty mood?*

He cocked his head and pursed his lips as if he had to think about it before he said, "I'm thinking you're both wrong; I think I'll go with the kid's judgment."

He walked further into the room and kneeled next to Rowdy, who was leaning over the coffee table, holding part of a cookie in one hand and reaching for a puzzle piece with the other.

"What do you think, sport?" Luke said. Rowdy looked up to face him questioningly with his big eyes. "Do you like Ash over there?" Rowdy grinned widely and shot me a look before his eyes veered down, seemingly embarrassed.

"Ash and me are buddies," he said and then lifted his gaze to me as if to check that he wasn't wrong about that.

"That's right, bud," I said and raised my hand. Rowdy beamed and raised his own hand to complete the high five.

"Thought so," Luke said, patting Rowdy on the shoulder, "and I trust your judgment."

With that, Luke stood and started for the hallway. "Hey," I said as I rolled after him. I wasn't sure if was ready for him to leave. Luke had to be several years older than me, but except for Rowdy, he'd been the youngest person that I'd met in quite a while, and he seemed nice. He turned at the front door and raised an eyebrow. Of course, I had no idea what to ask him and lingered by moving my chair into the hallway and turning purposefully.

"I ... uh ..." I started to say and spotted the black sedan through the narrow window that lined the length of the door. "Do you have any idea what to look for out there?" Warren, obviously, but I couldn't think of anything else to ask.

"Well," he said as he opened the door and held onto it, "not specifically, although we have pictures of what Dr. Warren looks like, but it's more like things that are out of place."

That had me kind of curious, so I asked, "Like what?" Luke's gaze went over the hallway and then ventured outside.

"Like, I don't know, a car hanging around that doesn't belong in the neighborhood or someone leaving something behind at your doorstep."

Luke's words had me thinking. If Warren had gone rogue, that didn't have to mean that he was working alone. He always seemed to have someone to do his dirty work.

At that moment a strange-sounding car drove up to the house. Luke stepped outside onto the porch to give me a better view as the engine sputtered and groaned. Mrs. Marsden exited the passenger side of an old Dodge and waved at me as she waited for Mrs. Johansson to climb out from behind the wheel and Mrs. Freedman from the backseat. The three friends had left early that morning to head to the arts and crafts shop downtown. Apparently, the shop had a great sale on oil paints, and they had wanted to beat the crowd, although I couldn't imagine a crowd at an arts and crafts shop. Considering the heavy-loaded shopping bags they carried, it seemed they had gathered enough paint to knock out a canvas or two at their next arts club meeting.

"Sweetie," she called out to me, and as Luke gazed down at me with a goofy grin, I felt my cheeks go red. "Mrs. Johansson's car is making funny noises. Could you call Joseph for me?"

"He's in the garage," I replied.

"Aw, that's perfect," she said. "Don't bother. We'll find him." The three women waddled across the pebbled drive along the side of the house. As they disappeared from view, I looked up to see Luke's gaze and shook my head. The expression on his face told me he wouldn't let me off easy.

"See?" he said drawing out the word. "She thinks you're a sweetie."

"Watch it, soldier," I said, narrowing my gaze at him, "or I'll have to report you."

"I'm actually an airman," he said, "not a sol—"

As a loud scream pierced the afternoon sky, Luke's words seemed to get stuck in his throat. An endless wailing sent shivers down my spine, and I swallowed hard.

"What was that?" I asked. It seemed the words had left my mouth before the sound had registered, because it wasn't as if I hadn't heard it before. Luke placed a hand on the handgun holstered at his side and waved at the men already exiting their vehicles. Miller and Baker were quick to step onto the drive with their weapons raised. Luke's colleague, whose name I didn't know, followed. As they had disappeared from view, I rolled backward into the house, shooting a glance at the living room where I found Rowdy standing frozen. His teary eyes sat fixed on me. He flinched at the sound of gunfire, and the tears started to stream down his face.

"It's okay, buddy," I said, trying to sound normal. "Just cover your ears." I showed him by covering my own ears. "And stay where you are. I'll be right there."

As I rolled into the door opening, sounds that I had hoped never to hear again reached my ears, but that didn't make the deep-throated growls less real.

| 7

Mags

We hadn't gone off the deep end the night before. In fact, Angie and I had barely made a dent in the bottle of whiskey, but even so, after lunch my eyelids felt heavy and I could imagine myself crawling back into bed. Instead, we plowed our way through the snow to Dr. Theodore Chen's lab for our scheduled blood donation.

Originally, his research lab had been located inside the Alaska Cancer Treatment Center in Anchorage just outside the base, but for security reasons, it had been moved to a temporary facility on the base. We crossed the parking lot, passing a couple of buildings, and ventured upon a low, rectangle structure without windows. Guards stood posted at the metal door that would lead us inside.

The two men nodded in recognition, but still demanded to see our identification cards. It had been the same drill for us every two days, and though the guards rotated in shift, we often came across the same faces.

"Hey, Jackson," I said to one of the guards,

"how's the knee?" I had noticed one of the guards had gone AWOL for a while, and after inquiring about him, his colleague divulged that his moron buddy had twisted his knee after he'd tried to ski over a tree trunk.

"A bit stiff," Jackson replied as he reached to open the door for us, "but healed."

"C'mon, already," Angie muttered under her breath as she entered the building. I grinned, relieved to know I wasn't the only one having a difficult day.

After checking in with a desk clerk and shedding a layer of clothes, we were escorted to Dr. Chen's lab. My eyes were stuck to the linoleum as the soldier knocked on the door to announce our presence to Dr. Chen. Even after dozens of visits, my stomach still churned stepping into that lab. Any lab for that matter. Too many bad things had happened, and these damn rooms all seemed to look the same.

An examination bed stood in the middle of the room flanked by stainless steel tables. Lining the walls stood more of those tables along with shelves and glass cases filled with all kinds of tools and equipment. A shudder ran down my body, and I fought the urge to turn on my heels and flee the room. Angie, who had gotten used to my apparent discomfort, stuck close to my side as I sneaked a peek at the figure with his back turned to us before I returned my gaze to the ground. Dr. Chen had called out an *Enter* as he fussed with some papers at one of the tables, but hadn't bothered to turn around.

"That'll be all, Staff Sergeant," Dr. Chen said. I looked up from the sleek floor and noticed a second man standing up from behind a desk. He was tall, with dark hair, heavyset brows, and if I had to guess looked to be in his midthirties. Ignoring us, he closed the buttons on his green shirt, and I caught a glimpse of his chiseled chest. Angie prodded me with an elbow and dipped her head in the direction where my eyes had already landed. She pulled a face that clearly expressed that she liked what she was seeing before she whispered near my ear, "Who's that?"

"No idea," I whispered back as the staff sergeant sprang to attention and gave a curt nod at the doctor. Then he walked straight past us without giving any indication that we were there.

We were both still staring at the sergeant's back when Dr. Chen pulled our attention from the fine-looking soldier.

"Ms. Vissers, Ms. Meadow," he said. The doctor waved for us to join him. Only momentarily distracted by the staff sergeant's presence, that unsettling feeling returned with a vengeance and bedded down in the pit of my stomach. Dr. Chen was a short man, and even Angie had an inch or two on him. At six feet tall, I towered over him while Chen's eyes roamed around the height of my chest. I knew it wasn't the man's fault, but it seemed to me that my breasts were always the first things that caught his gaze. Despite the heavy clothing, it added to the discomfort I felt about being in his lab. Although he was approaching sixty, his hair was jet black, and there wasn't a crease to be found on his round face.

"Please sit," he said. Angie and I did as we were asked and sat down on the bed in the middle of the room. Chen had the things he needed all laid out on a tray and started the steps of drawing our blood.

"Who was that?" Angie asked as I rolled up my sleeve.

"Who was who?" Chen said, feigning innocence. Angie gave him a hard glare. The doctor seemed undeterred by Angie, and for a second I wondered if she had finally met someone who could defy her demanding gaze as he poked a needle into my arm.

"Doc," she said, emphasizing her previous question. The man smirked, but then relented.

"That was Staff Sergeant Eric Preston," he said. "He was here for his checkup."

He switched out a vial, and a second glass tube started to fill with my blood.

"Excuse me," I piped in at his unlikely answer. This laboratory was specifically setup for any research related to *mortem ostium inanimatum*, otherwise known as Mortem virus, the thing that had caused the zombie plague, and the Divus serum that was supposed to counteract the former. My stomach turned as my mind raced to my conversation with Angie the day before and the idea of experiments to create super soldiers.

"And he was being checked for what?" Angie asked. Her voice was hard and borderline threatening. I glanced up at her, and her eyes fumed in anger. Chen remained calm, ignoring the anger in Angie's voice, and started readying another syringe. He turned to Angie and gestured for her arm as he said in a soothing voice, "We have started the first trials of inoculating men."

"And they just volunteered," Angie asked as she offered her arm.

"Yes," Chen replies, "just as you did."

My mind started to race. My immunity to becoming a zombie had been a matter of sheer luck. As Dr. Matley had explained it in that conference room back in Cheyenne Mountain, this immunity only occurred in about twenty percent of female cancer patients, or neoplasma malignum carriers, as she liked to call us. It had something to do with the fluctuation in hormone levels, and at the time of ovulation as these levels peaked, a woman became impervious to the Mortem virus.

This occurrence had brought on the opportunity of creating Divus serum, something that had evolved naturally in my bloodstream by exposure to Mortem at the right time. And Angie had indeed volunteered to be injected by this man-made version of the serum, but for a man, this brought on a whole different set of complications. Men would need added treatment because of the lack of hormones.

Dr. Chen finished drawing blood from Angie and, after labeling the vials, placed them on the tray next to mine.

"And considering the insanity of that act," I said, ignoring the fake hurt look on Angie's face as I referenced to the fact of her volunteering, "the risk for these men would even be higher, considering the fact that you would have to expose them to active cancer cells."

"Are they aware that you've doomed them to a lifetime of being treated like a leper?" Angie added.

"If they survive, that is."

Dr. Chen held up his hand to silence us.

"Please," he said, "it is not up to me to fill you in, but a meeting has already been scheduled later this afternoon for you to speak with Colonel Marshall."

"Just tell me one thing," I asked and heard the plea in my voice. "Please tell me this isn't about Warren's super soldier theory."

About an hour later, we walked down a cozy, heated hallway inside one of the many buildings that we encountered on this base. Fortunately, Chen had driven us by car or else I would have never found it. Well, Angie might have, but I surely wouldn't have.

Still, despite the enormity of the base and the fact I had no sense of direction, I knew this place to be Alaskan Command. We had come here the day we had arrived to meet with Colonel Marshall, and now we were about to meet her for the third time.

It felt kind of strange that this woman who had dictated so much of our lives these past months and whose name I had heard mentioned at least twice a day was a total stranger to me.

As the outside of the building suggested, the inside had a warm feeling to it, besides the temperature. The structure looked like a ski lodge and could have come straight out of a brochure promising vacations in a winter wonderland. Inside the walls were sand-colored and alternated by wooden doors that had kept their natural color.

After a check of our IDs at the door, Chen led us past the reception desk with a wave of his hand. He guided us along a hallway, stopped at one of the doors, and knocked. I hadn't heard a reply, but Chen must have because he opened the door and stepped inside. I glanced at Angie with what must have looked insecure enough for her to give me an encouraging nod and then step in ahead of me.

Chen hadn't answered my question about the super soldiers and urged us to wait with any other questions for Colonel Marshall to explain. I hadn't liked that answer but had kept quiet as we drove over here. Now that same question gnawed at me. The things Dr. David had done in his pursuit of creating this new type of soldier had been horrific. Hundreds had suffered and even died from the pain he had inflicted. Ash and I had felt that pain first hand. I tried to keep those memories at bay, but I couldn't deny the fear and humiliation I had felt as soldiers had stripped me naked and strapped me onto a cold steel table. Dr. David had even come to gloat as they cut into my flesh.

I shuddered and shook my head as if to chase the memories into the darkest recesses of my mind where they belonged. Following Angie, we found Colonel Marshall sitting at the head a rectangular table. She stood as we entered and extended a hand in greeting.

She looked immaculate in her knee-length skirt, dark-blue jacket decorated with an eagle spreading its wings on her shoulders, and a whole range of metal and colorful insignias on her chest. She had short blond hair and a friendly smile.

Although she didn't look threatening, I didn't feel at ease, because to her right stood Staff Sergeant Eric Preston. The man kept his eyes on the wall at the other side of the table as if we hadn't even entered the room.

"Welcome," Marshall said as she shook our hands and gestured for us to take a seat. Fortunately, Angie had entered the room first and took the seat across from the staff sergeant.

"This is Staff Sergeant Eric Preston," Marshall said in a formal voice. "I believe you haven't officially met." The staff sergeant spared us a glance and nodded. "He is well aware of who you are and why you are here, so I suggest we skip formalities and go straight to the problem at hand." Marshall's eyes shifted to Dr. Chen, who had taken up a seat across from me, next to the staff sergeant.

"Of course," Chen said in that calming voice of his. "Ever since the outbreak of Mortem virus, we've been searching for a way to defeat the threat posed by the infected." He raised his hands off the table and gestured at Angie and me.

"You, along with Dr. Kelly Matley's research, have ensured that we were able to do so," he said. He didn't say that Matley had worked at Warren's side to create Mortem virus in the first place, but I didn't think it would be in my best interest to mention that. "Staff Sergeant Preston and two others under the command of Colonel Marshall have volunteered to take part in our expanded research."

"Why would you do that?" I asked Preston in a sharp voice. I hadn't meant to be so blunt, but I was baffled by the potential sacrifice that this would mean for him. The staff sergeant shifted his gaze only slightly until his eyes met mine. His hard stare made me feel as if I were about to be chastised, but the man kept his mouth shut. I couldn't decide if the chastising might have been worse than his silence.

"You have been on this base for a while now and outside information has been slim," Marshall started to explain. "At least, it has been for you."

She shuffled through some papers inside a folder laid out before her and picked up a sheet. "Your only outside contact has been with FBI Agent Rodrigo Marsden, his family, and Ms. Rebecca Reed."

"Ash," Angie and I both chimed in unison. Marshall glanced up at us and quirked the tinniest of smiles.

"Of course. Ash," she added. She placed the sheet of paper on the table as she continued. "Ash's information of the outside world had been limited as well, and we have instructed Agent Marsden, including his family who she resides with, to keep it that way. We didn't want you to worry."

"How bad is it?" Angie asked, straight to the point.

"It's bad," Dr. Chen answered. "That is why we have sped up testing on human subjects." His use of the word *subjects* brought a nasty taste to my mouth, and I had to bite my tongue from verbally abusing the short man sitting across from me. Dr. David had used that phrase as well, and I couldn't stand the word. My hands gripped the armrests of my chair, and I squeezed them hard to release some of the tension that seemed to be building inside me. I didn't think it would be a good idea to flip out on these people, and I tried to take calming breaths.

"At this point, the eastern side of the Mississippi border is completely overrun. We have managed to contain several smaller outbreaks in Texas, Colorado, and even Utah," Chen continued, "but time isn't on our side. We need to act."

I closed my eyes at his mention of Colorado and wondered if I had been the one responsible for the outbreak that had occurred there. Trying to escape Warren's men inside Cheyenne Mountain and during a fight with one of his goons named William, I had triggered the change in the big man. I shuddered at the thought of sinking my teeth into William's ear and biting off a decent chunk. At the time, I hadn't thought of the blood flowing from my mouth after I'd received a punch in the face and, with it, had infected William.

The big man had turned instantly and torn through the military facility like a raving lunatic, infecting anyone in his path. Some of those infected could have escaped and caused more havoc in the state of Colorado than I might have imagined. Unwittingly, Chen was trying my nerves by raking up all these memories I was hoping to forget.

I didn't know whether Angie noticed, but she shifted her arm to rest against mine as if offering a sign of comfort. Fortunately, Marshall took over from Chen.

"So far the results from Staff Sergeant Preston's inoculation and his two colleagues look promising, and we want to expand the field of testing," she said.

I raised my eyebrows. "Oh," I said. I didn't like where this was going, although it was to be expected. Dr. Chen was right, we were running out of time and I guessed the more unconventional options might be in order. I didn't have to like them, though.

"A group of people have taken refuge in a distribution center just outside Maxwell Air Force Base in Alabama, and we haven't been able to extract them," Marshall said.

"Why not?" Angie asked.

"Because we don't have the resources. They are spread thin as it is, and we can barely even supply the soldiers and civilians remaining at the base," Marshall explained. As if knowing we would have more questions she added, "Most of our troops have been relocated to secure the border along the Mississippi. The ones remaining in the infected parts of the country provide the help they can, but the infection rate is too high, and for most people, it is too late."

It was evident in her voice that the situation hadn't left Colonel Marshall untouched, but I also sensed that she was someone who was capable of doing what needed to be done. This made me kind of dread what her next words would be.

"We want you to fly to Maxwell Air Force Base in Alabama and head out to distribute Divus serum to the people inside the DC."

I wanted to say something but sensed my mouth was hanging open.

"Wait, what?" I managed to say.

"How does that make sense?" Angie said, sitting up and leaning on the table.

"With 'you,' I'm hoping you mean the guys trained to do this, right," I said, pointing a finger at Preston. He didn't seem to take offense.

"You won't fly those distribution center folks out, but you're willing to fly us in," Angie said with disdain in her voice.

I was still trying to figure out whom Marshall meant by "you," and it took me a moment to pick up on Angie's comment, but it made me wonder if they didn't want to rescue these people.

"There are over fifty people out there," Marshall said. "We just don't have the resources to fly them out."

"Then get them to—what was the name of the base?" I said.

"Maxwell," Angie replied.

"Maxwell's current situation prohibits any form of extraction, but I'll be honest with you," Marshall said, "this DC provides an opportunity."

"Here we go," Angie said.

"You have to understand that if this works, it might save us all, and you of all people should know how careful we have to be with our test groups," Chen said. "And this DC is remote, and we would be able to monitor them from Maxwell."

The pieces started to come together, and I did understand their need to distribute Divus into a broader group of people, but this left those particular people without a choice. Divus would effectively turn them into virus incubators. They wouldn't turn into a zombie, but they would be able to infect others. This would mean isolation for the rest of their lives unless they decided to inoculate the entire world, but maybe that was the plan all along. I wasn't sure I would mind that. Mars could get inoculated, and that would mean I didn't have to worry about killing him with a simple kiss.

"Injecting these people with Divus makes them Mortem virus incubators," Angie said, "a situation like that might be impossible to control."

"We are looking into ways to circumvent that, but that is also a reason why we need to expand testing," Chen said.

"These people will be overrun by the infected," a low voice said. All our heads perked up in the direction of Preston, whom I hadn't heard speak yet. "There are too many infected, and Maxwell troops won't be able to stop them. If this serum works the way I've been told it does, then we should be able to just drive up to the DC and knock on their door—right?"

He looked up at Angie and me in search of conformation. I nodded. He was right: the zombies wouldn't look or sniff twice if they saw us. I didn't want to say that they might follow me around like lemmings. That was what they had done the last time I had encountered them. I didn't know if it had something to do with what Warren had done to this new version of zombies the fact that I had been the cause for the outbreak in the first place.

"Then why are we discussing this?" Preston continued. "These people are isolated as it is, and this serum might buy them some more time—time Dr. Chen here can use to perfect the solution." Preston closed his mouth and then shot an apologetic glance at Marshall.

She waited a moment, maybe to see whether any of us wanted to add something, and then said, "Thank you, Staff Sergeant. The decision has been made; you will leave first thing tomorrow."

Her eyes shifted from Angie to me, and I felt the blood drain from my face. I hesitated before I stuck a hand in the air and asked, "Could you clarify who it is you mean when you say *you?*"

8

Ash

"Get in here," I said, grabbing Luke's shirt as he was about to step off the porch. A gun went off, followed by a loud cry.

"Ash, let go," he said, sounding annoyed. "I need to check what's going on."

"If that is what I think it is, then you need to get back in here," I replied and tugged harder. "Let's check the back door." Unable to break my hold on him, he relented and followed me inside the house.

"Lock the door," I said, "and stay with Rowdy."

Pushing hard, I rolled down the hallway and into the kitchen. I barely kept myself from slamming into the back door and then locked it, but held a hand on the lock in case I needed to unlock it fast. I held my breath, chanting the word please inside my head repeatedly. A couple of muffled screams reached me from beyond the door.

"Please, please, please," I started to whisper as I eased the curtain covering the small window in the backdoor. The window gave a partial view of the garage door and a side door—both stood open.

A trail of blood started inside the garage and colored the white pebbles, decorating the drive a crimson red. A shoe I didn't recognize lay halfway up the trail, but I couldn't see a body. Another blood trail led to the back door, but again I didn't detect any movement.

I had to expect the worst and told myself to do so, but that tiny flicker of hope that still lived inside me couldn't draw the curtain close. In my mind, I knew the chances for Mr. and Mrs. Marsden to come out of this unscathed were nonexistent, but my heart told me I might be able to help. After all, the zombies wouldn't come after me; I might be able to help.

From out of nowhere, a body slammed into the door, cracking the window and pulling me from my futile thoughts. Miller's bloodied face pressed against the glass with eyes nearly bulging from their sockets. Blood gushed from a deep gash in his neck as he pounded a fist against the wooden frame of the door.

"Let me in," he shouted. "Let me in!" Footsteps came up behind me.

"Let him in," Luke said as he pulled the curtain open more widely and gasped. Releasing the curtain, he took a few steps back and sounded as if he were clearing his throat. Glancing over my shoulder, I saw him standing bent forward with a hand over his mouth.

"Tell me you have seen this before," I said in a harsh tone. Luke nodded.

"Just not this up close," he said.

"So you know we can't help them."

He nodded again without the reply.

Shifting the curtain, I returned my gaze outside. Miller had disappeared from sight, although I heard an eerie scratching sound at the bottom of the door. A woman stumbled into view as she exited the garage. Her feet shifted on the gravel, and she slowly turned as if she were finding her bearings. The back of her dress was torn and hung loosely off her body. Her gaze shifted to the house as her head tilted backward, and she sniffed the air. It wasn't Mrs. Marsden, but I recognized Mrs. Johansson, one of the friends who had followed Mrs. Marsden inside the garage. As a low growl exited her throat and my peripheral vision caught some additional movement behind her, I dropped the curtain. I didn't have to see the Marsdens to know what had happened to them, and I preferred to keep them in my memory as they were.

I turned to find Luke, and I found him still standing by the table. My eyes took him in and then veered to his sides and the kitchen floor.

"Where's Rowdy?" I pulled back from the door and swirled around. As I passed the kitchen table, I shot Luke a look. "Don't open that door!"

"As if," I heard him say just before I entered the living room. My heart stopped at the sight of the empty room.

"Rowdy," I said while I rolled around the couch, "where are you, little man?" My voice wavered, and my breathing was heavy as I heard a small whimper. I spotted Rowdy hiding underneath the coffee table.

"Hey, little man," I said in a soft voice, trying to coax him out, "you can come out now." He hesitated, looking up at me from underneath the table, and my heart broke at the sight of his tear-streaked face. "It's okay. I've got you."

He crawled out from under the table and straight into my lap. Arms wrapped around my neck, and his body shook as he started to cry again.

"It's okay," I said in an attempt to comfort him, but I knew that it was anything but okay. Patting Rowdy's back, I called for Luke. He stepped into the living room, looking a little less green then he had before.

"What?"

"I need you to check the downstairs windows," I said. "Make sure they're all closed. We can't let them smell you." He nodded and started to move.

"I've got one dead elderly woman lying in the drive," he said as he went from window to window. "That agent from the back door is now lumbering across the front lawn."

As Luke left the room, it went quiet for a while except for Rowdy's whimpers. The little guy's agony brought tears to my eyes. As I wiped my eyes with the palm of my hand, I stared at the door. A strange combination of fear that zombies would break it open and snatch Rowdy from my arms and the futile hope that Mars would come bursting through at any second kept me frozen in place. That and the fact that I didn't know what to do.

"Dammit," I said under my breath. Mars had gone back to Monterey Regional Airport, and I wouldn't be able to count on him, but I should know what to do: I'd been in situations like this before. On my lap Rowdy stirred and looked up at me in shock.

"You said a bad word," he said, barely audibly.

"I know, kiddo. I'm sorry," I said, matching his tone of voice and wiped at the tears rolling down his cheeks. His face was a mess of tears and snot, and I rolled us to the couch to set him down when Luke came back into the room.

"I've checked the entrances and the windows; all are closed. From what I can tell, there is only the one body, one person is roaming around the house, and that could mean five are on the move. We need to call this in."

"Phone is in the kitchen," I said. "You need to press zero for an operator." Ever since the outbreak, phone use had been restricted. If you wanted to make a call, then you had to get permission through an operator. It was as if the country had regressed back to the nineteen fifties.

I spotted the stuffed panda bear on the floor and picked it up. Rowdy crawled into the corner of the couch, and I handed him the stuffed animal.

"Here you go, buddy," I said. "Hang on to Pan. I'll be right back."

"Where are you going?" he asked, sounding worried.

"I'll be in the kitchen for a second and be right back," I replied. "You can see from here, okay?" Rowdy nodded reluctantly, and I took the opportunity to leave him.

Luke was already on the phone and tapped an impatient foot on the floor. I grabbed some paper towels and a glass of water.

"See if you can contact Mars," I said as I rolled past Luke to make my way back into the living room. He nodded slowly as his eyes went wide, and he pointed at the phone. It usually took a while to get through, but still I hurried to get back to Rowdy.

If Luke managed to get Mars on the phone, then I would have to talk to him myself. I wished I didn't have to do this on the phone, but I wanted him to hear about his parents from someone familiar, and unfortunately, that would be me.

I swallowed hard at the memory of Mr. and Mrs. Marsden, but I couldn't change what had happened, and I needed to focus on what was to come.

Rowdy took a few swallows from the glass of water that I handed him before I started to wipe at the snot and tears that coated his face.

He looked up at me with those big eyes as he asked in a small voice, "When are Grandma and Grandpa getting home?"

I held his gaze for a moment but had difficulties forming the words. Mr. Marsden had been in the garage for a while. Rowdy must have thought he had gone out, and I guessed he hadn't heard Mrs. Marsden come home. How was I supposed to tell a child that his grandparents had turned into zombies?

"I don't know, kiddo," I said, opting for the easy way out, "but see Luke over there?" I pointed at Luke who seemed to be in a heated conversation on the phone. He looked a lot more freaked out than he had before, and I hoped he'd be able to keep it together. It hadn't been that much of a joke when I said he looked like a twelve-year-old. Standing at the door earlier, it had seemed as if he had come here straight from boot camp with a serious lack of experience.

Rowdy followed my finger with his gaze until it hit the young man in uniform. "That man is a soldier, and he is here to protect us," I said. Rowdy nodded but then turned a questioning gaze in my direction.

"He doesn't have big guns," he said in a whisper.

"No, he doesn't," I said as I eyed Luke with exaggeration. "Maybe he has hidden them in his back pocket."

Rowdy raised an eyebrow. "That won't fit, silly," he said and giggled a little. I smiled at him and rubbed a hand over his head, relieved that the kid was sort of okay. Luke entered with the cordless receiver in hand.

"Mars wants to talk to you," he said.

I grabbed the phone from Luke's hand and gestured for him to stay with Rowdy as I rolled into the hallway. Tears sprang to my eyes as I heard his voice on the other end of the line.

"Ash," he said, "you there?" I pressed a hand to my mouth until I reached the end to the hall and swallowed hard. A lump in my throat prevented me from talking, so I cleared it before I spoke his name.

"I'm so sorry, Mars," I said. "I don't know what happened, I—"

Mars cut me off as he addressed me with a firm voice. "Listen to me. Luke already explained what happened," he said, "This is not the time—just know that this is not your fault." I nodded like an idiot as if he could see me. "I'm on my way along with containment teams. I need you to stay inside the house. Stay away from the doors and windows. Don't let them see you or let them smell the others. Got it?"

"I know the drill," I said, but I didn't hear the confidence in my voice as I had hoped to expect from myself.

"Just give me an hour," he said and paused. "Ash," he added in a questioning voice.

"An hour," I repeated more firmly this time and nodded again. Mars excused himself for a moment, and I heard him shouting at someone. I took the time to collect myself and then started rolling down the hall back to the living room.

"Ash," Mars said in a soft voice as he came back, "could I ..." He didn't finish the sentence, but I could guess what he wanted to say.

"I haven't told him yet," I said and swallowed

down another lump.

"That's okay," he said. "I'll talk to him after I get you out of there."

"Yeah, sure," I said as rolled into the living room and approached the couch. "Here he comes."

"Ash," he said again, more firmly. I returned the phone to my ear and felt the nerves unsettle as he began to speak.

"That is my boy," he said, "if anything were to happen to him ..." The silence that followed the deep exhale probably told me more than his words would have.

"I've got him," I said, "you just get here." I pulled the phone from my ear and held it to Rowdy's.

"Hey buddy," I said, trying to sound light, "your daddy's on the phone."

Rowdy's face lit up as he gripped the device with two hands and called out, "Daddy!"

Luke gestured for me to follow him. I checked Rowdy, who was listening intently to his dad over the phone, and I rolled to the kitchen where Luke waited for me with a concerned look on his face.

"What?" I asked. His eyes flickered nervously from me to the living room where Rowdy was still talking to Mars.

"I'm worried," he said.

I shook my head in disbelief. "We're all worried," I said.

"No, I mean, I'm worried he won't be able to come."

I frowned, not exactly sure what he meant by that.

"That's his son," I said incredulously. "Of course he's coming."

"I'm not saying he won't try, but with three more outbreaks surrounding this area, I'm worried he might not be able to," he said.

I glared at him in shock.

"And he didn't tell you. Great!"

I turned my chair and rushed into the living room. Just as I had reached the couch, Rowdy pressed the button to disconnect.

"Shi—" I started to say, but stopped myself as I noticed Rowdy's eyes on me. I took the phone from him and tossed it at Luke. "Get him back on the line."

Meanwhile, Rowdy got to his feet, standing on the couch. I was about to grab for him as he let himself fall into my lap. He landed with a thump. I didn't feel him hit my legs, but I was pretty sure he'd just left me with a nice bruise.

"Daddy said to stick to you like glue," he said.

"He did, huh?" I said.

"Yep."

The distant sound of tires screeching followed by a crash had me drawn to the window. Someone must have wrecked a car. I pulled the curtain aside but couldn't detect any movement. The agents' black sedan stood parked right in front of the house and blocked most of my view of the street. Those zombies would have wandered off if they didn't find an immediate snack in the direct vicinity, but that didn't mean they couldn't be close. I didn't need to see them to know this was about to get out of control, and considering multiple outbreaks in the surrounding area, I tended to agree with Luke. Mars might not be able to get here in time.

My eyes veered across the lawn, and I spotted a handgun in the middle of the driveway. Must have belonged to one of the agents or that soldier who had come along with Luke. I glanced back at the sedan, wondering if there'd be more weapons inside. Movement inside a neighbor's house across the street caught my eyes. As I watched Mr. Jackson's place for a moment, nothing seemed to stir, and I wondered if I'd imagined it.

Then I saw it again and gasped. This time it was hard to miss. Bloodied hands clawed at the window from the inside. Having seen enough, I turned my head. Besides, Rowdy didn't need to see that.

"Hang on, buddy," I said as I rolled us back to the kitchen. As he saw me, Luke shook his head in an emphatic no.

"Agent Marsden left and they cannot reach him," Luke said. I sighed and refrained myself from cursing. Rowdy was sitting on my lap after all. I glanced down at him, and the PJs he wore. It was time to get him dressed and ready in case we had to move.

"Can you keep an eye on things?" I asked Luke. "I need to get some stuff and change." Without waiting for a reply, I rolled my chair along with my passenger from the kitchen and headed to my room.

9

Mags

My butt ached as I sat up in my chair and shifted to get a better look down the row of seats. Beside Angie, who sat next to me, only three other seats inside the small plane were occupied. Staff Sergeant Eric Preston sat on the first row on his own. Two rows behind him sat Corporal Tom Harding, a stocky guy who talked as if he had seen too many Rambo movies, and next to him Chase Gibson, a combat medic.

Preston had introduced us just before we'd boarded the small plane bound for Alabama. After our chat with Colonel Marshall, we had received another briefing where Preston had shown us maps and details of what we were planning to do, but my attention had kept slipping.

A low sounding growl came from my left as I shifted in my chair again.

"Stop fidgeting," Angie said. "I'm trying to get some sleep here."

"Sorry," I whispered as I slumped back in my chair.

Preston had also told us that as soon as we landed at Maxwell Air Force Base, we'd be heading out, and he had suggested we take a nap on the plane. That just seemed impossible to me.

"What am I doing here?" I said under my breath. Angie groaned and sat up. "I'm not a soldier."

"You've said that already," Angie said. "Several times in fact."

I had tried to bring my point across to Colonel Marshall, but the woman wouldn't relent. Only three men had volunteered to be injected with the serum, and she countered that she needed Angie and me for the team to succeed. That didn't make sense to me, and it felt I'd be more likely to endanger the mission with my lack of experience in just about anything.

"Your instructors tell me that you performed adequately in the basic training that you've received and that your gun handling was even above adequate," she had said. When I'd flat-out refused, she had pulled the one card that I couldn't counter —Ash. The bitch had actually threatened to keep Ash away from me. My assertion that Colonel Lauren Marshall would do what it took to get the job done had become evidently clear to me then, and the rest of the conversation had become a lot less civil. Angie had to drag me from the room after that.

"How did I get here?" I said, starting to sound like a broken record.

"You decided to take a vacation in the Big Apple, and then after it became too crowded with zombies at the airport, you took a left and headed into Brooklyn," Angie said. I lifted an eyebrow and glared at her. She grinned in return.

"Look at it on the bright side," she said.

"Which is?"

"You won't be cold in Alabama."

I groaned and sank further down in my seat. At that point, there was some movement at the front of the plane, and two men started to approach our seats.

For a moment, I hoped they would pass us to maybe check our gear or something, but it became evident that we had been their targets as the medic, Chase Gibson, moved into the row of seats in front of us and Corporal Tom Harding took the seat next to me across the aisle. I cleared my throat as I gazed up at the men. With my mood, I didn't think I'd be good company, but I forced a friendly smile on my face anyway.

"What's up, guys?" Angie said.

"We thought it would be polite to get to know

one another a little better before we land and start slicing and dicing," Tom said. Chase shot Tom a look of disapproval and slightly shook his head.

"We heard you were awake, and we thought we'd come say hi," Chase added.

"Hi," Angie said. When she didn't say anything else the men kind of glanced at each other as if they were asking each other now what? I grinned at the blank expression on Angie's face.

"Chase, wasn't it?" I asked.

"Call me Gibs. Everyone else does," he replied. Figured, most people I had met over here either used a nickname or some abbreviation of their real name. I turned to Tom questioningly, wondering if he had some altered version of a name.

"Tom," he said and shrugged.

"So," I said after a moment of awkward silence, "what's up?"

"We were wondering if we could do a little background check of sorts," Gibs said hesitantly. His eyes flickered from Angie to me and then to Tom as if he needed some confirmation.

"We wanna know if you can kick ass," Tom said. "You know, if we can count on you to have our backs."

Gibs shook his head again and added, "I probably wouldn't have put it that way, but that's basically what it comes down to. Except for the medical stuff, there hasn't been that much info in the briefing on you two." Gibs voice was soothing, and I imagined he'd be great at reading audiobooks.

At my side, Angie grinned and I figured she appreciated that the men inquired after our skills instead of presuming that we'd be useless in the field, or was that a sexist thing to assume that a man would think that? Still, I doubted I'd be insulted if they had thought that, but that wasn't true in Angie's case.

"My background is with the FBI," Angie said, "and I've seen my share of zombies."

Gibs nodded while Tom asked with a cheeky grin on his face, "So you know how to fire a gun?"

"That I do," Angie replied.

"And what about you?" Tom said, pointing a finger at me.

"I … uh…" I started to mutter before Angie took over.

"Mags here was smack in the middle of the outbreak in New York where it all began."

"Nice," Tom said. "What was that like? Must have been crazy out there."

I nodded in agreement. It had been crazy. Images of my friend Emily with those white, foggy eyes, sitting on a gurney in an infirmary at JFK along with the chaos that had ensued inside the departure hall flashed across my mind.

"It was," I said in a low voice, "and at the time, I had no idea what I was dealing with. It was crazy."

Both men looked at me as if I had something stuck to my face.

"They hadn't told you that you'd be dealing with the undead before they sent you out?" Tom asked, sounding incredulous. He must have thought I belonged to the military or some agency, because the look on his face was one of disgust. Gibs narrowed his eyes and watched my exchange with Tom carefully.

"What's with the accent?" he finally asked.

Angie grinned and grabbed my arm.

"Oh, I forgot to mention, my friend Mags here is a tourist from the Netherlands who missed her flight when the shit hit the fan, but don't worry— she'll have your back," she said as her eyes twinkled with mischief. Both men frowned and glanced at each other in disbelief.

"I need to talk to Preston," Tom said and climbed out of his seat to walk to the front of the plane. Gibs's gaze turned from Tom's back to us.

"Sorry about him," he said and paused as he glanced at the front of the plane. Then, he added, "Excuse me." With that, he hurried after Tom.

I shoved an elbow in Angie's direction and caught her in her upper arm. Her face sat buried in her hands as she tried to muffle her laughter.

"Thanks for that," I said and once again sank down in my chair.

Angie was still grinning as I felt the plane start its descent. I tried not to think of what was expected of me and the fact that at some point these people might have to rely on me. My heart hammered in my chest and only seemed to increase in speed when I felt a hand on my upper arm.

"Don't worry," Angie said as I gazed into her confident eyes. "You've got this."

Even decked out in full assault gear, I didn't feel the confidence that Angie seemed to have in me. I looked down at the pixelated tiger-stripe pattern that covered my uniform and shook my head. It had been less than an hour since we had landed, and after the plane had stopped rolling, Preston had ushered us out. On the tarmac, a truck had waited for us in what seemed like the middle of nowhere. A lot of empty space surrounded us, which ended at a fence with a wooded area behind that.

Even though the sun had set, movement along the fence caught my eye. Fortunately, the figures had been too far off to recognize any details, but a cold shiver ran down my spine nonetheless.

"We have to hurry, ma'am," an airman had said as he came up beside me. "We don't want to lure too many of them out there. The fences might not hold."

I just nodded and followed him to the truck that stood ready to take us inside the compound.

Riding the truck, we passed several layers of defenses in the form of fences, and the headlights of patrollers guarding those fences. That same airman from before explained that the remainder of the troops stationed here had set up a defendable perimeter using the area's natural surroundings. The Gun Island Chute had become a primary part of that perimeter.

I didn't want to come across like an idiot and therefore didn't muster the courage to ask, but what I determined from the airman's explanation, it had to be a body of water or a river of some kind.

Inside the compound, we were brought to a small hangar where two other airmen greeted us and directed us inside. After unloading several duffel bags and a couple of hard-shelled cases, we started gearing up.

I zipped up my load carrier vest and clicked the buckle at the top to close it. I glanced over the table to see whether there was something I'd missed, but all the ammo pouches sat securely weaved onto the vest along with the cantina covers and all the other stuff I had to carry around.

Angie had been right about one thing though: this place felt a lot warmer than Alaska. She came over to where I stood by the table and trailed her eyes over me.

"Looks good," she said and tugged on the vest. I stuck up my right hand and looked at it with a goofy expression. A thumb and two fingers filled the glove that covered my hand. The empty pinky and ring finger just flapped around as I waved it. Angie rolled her eyes and grabbed my hand.

"Come here," she said and pulled me after her to the end of the table where she found a roll of duct tape. As Angie started peeling off strips of tape, Tom sauntered in our direction. His eyes narrowed as he watched Angie tape up my gloves.

"What happened there," he asked. I looked at him and shrugged.

"Zombie ate my fingers," I said. A disgusted look morphed his face, but then his eyes widened, and he exclaimed, "Cool, I guess that serum actually works."

As if he realized his remark might have been insensitive, he added, "I mean, sorry about the fingers."

His eyes drifted to the table with the weapons sorted out on top of them.

"You can still shoot, right?" he said as his gaze returned to me.

"I can," I said and added as a reassurance, "I'm primarily a lefty, so it's not a problem." Tom's eyes shifted down where my gun holster was strapped to my left thigh. He didn't seem convinced, and Angie noticed.

"Don't worry," she said. "We can handle zombies. They don't even like our taste, and it's not as if they'll return fire."

"As long as you don't stick a finger into their mouths," he said.

"Maybe you should stick a finger in your mouth and shut up now," Angie retorted.

"Are you offering?" Tom said in a bold voice and even batted his eyelashes at Angie. With more force than I would have deemed necessary, Angie tore off the roll of tape and released my hand. She slowly raised her head and narrowed her eyes as she gazed up at Tom with one of her hard stares. The cheeky grin on his face faltered for a moment but didn't relent.

I eyed the exchange with interest, wondering about Angie's next move as Gibs showed up behind Tom and smacked him on the head.

"Hey," Tom called out.

"Behave," Gibs replied and pointed a finger at Tom. "We're about ready. The sarge wants us over there." Then he grabbed Tom's arm and dragged him in the direction where Preston stood talking to an African-American male in the same fatigues as we were wearing. He was of average height, but he had the width of a bodybuilder. His hair had started to turn gray, though, and it added to the seniority that he conveyed with his posture. So I guessed him to be a little higher up on the ranking scale.

I glanced out the open hangar door into the darkness. Lights lit up a couple of buildings standing in the distance, but I couldn't see any activity. The base in Alaska had been gutted of its manpower because of them being deployed elsewhere, but it still felt occupied. This place looked dead. Of course, we might have just been dropped in a spot where no one came because of whom and what we were. Although part of a potential solution, we also represented a threat as the five of us carried the virus that, if exposed, could easily overrun this base.

Angie shoved a helmet into my hands and forced me to make eye contact.

"You okay?" she asked.

"Just peachy," I replied. She narrowed her eyes

and gave me one of her hard stares. "I'm okay."

I tried to sound convincing, but I doubt she bought it. I didn't buy it myself. Nerves rattled my bones, and I felt somewhat eager to get a rifle shoved into my hands just so they would have something to do besides shake.

We walked over to Preston, and he introduced us to Colonel Kenneth Eaves. My hand just about disappeared in his as Eaves shook it.

"I have been fully briefed by Colonel Marshall," he said in deep rumbling voice. "I won't bother you with the facts of why I have my doubts about this mission, but the decision has been made—desperate times and all." He gauged all five of us for a moment, making eye contact with each as if he were looking for something. Maybe he was looking for signs of dead, mindless eyes with a hint of white fog wafting over them. That was one of the first signs that person had become infected with the Mortem virus.

Seemingly satisfied, he said, "We lost many men during the first weeks of the outbreak, and now we have a hell of a time protecting this base. I cannot afford to lose anyone else, and we have to consider the civilian population that has settled here." The airman who had escorted us from the plane, whose name I had never asked, had told us as much. The base had taken in many people fleeing their homes after the first zombies showed up.

"We need to preserve our resources, and that's why I've kept all aircraft that we have left on the ground. Who knows how long we have till we run out of fuel and we need our vehicles to run in order to get the guards over to the fences. The distribution center you're looking for is about ten miles out, and the land between here and there is saturated with the infected," he said as if he felt the need to explain to us why they hadn't been able to reach or help the people hiding out inside the distribution center. "Besides, we couldn't take the risk of bringing back any infected."

"We understand the situation," Preston replied. "May I ask what type of transportation you can afford us?" Preston had barely uttered the words when two Hummers came driving up and stopped outside the hangar door. Colonel Eaves gestured at the vehicles.

"These should carry you and your crew without problem, but when it comes to transporting all of the survivors back here, you may have to make two trips."

I eyed the vehicles that didn't look like the standard Hummers that I had seen before. The trucks had an open back that seemed to fit at least eight people.

"Why don't you guys get loaded up while I finish up with the colonel?" Preston said. He pointed a finger at a hard-shelled case that still stood on one of the tables. Besides weapons, we had also brought our own stash of Divus serum—courtesy of Dr. Chen. The case held everything we needed to inoculate everyone staying at the DC and then some. I glanced at Angie, and she shrugged before turning and headed for the table. I followed.

10

Ash

As Rowdy waited in my room, I snatched a few items of clothing from his, along with the picture of his mom that he kept on his nightstand, and some other trinkets. Then, I got him changed out of his PJs and into a pair of jeans, a T-shirt, and the cutest black hoody with the words *Tough Guy* written on the back in bold white letters. I tossed some additional clothes of my own into Mags's old backpack.

I opted for a pair of dark green cargo pants with a black long-sleeved shirt and a black hoody.

"What do ya think?" I asked Rowdy as I spread my arms. He noticed the similarities between our clothing and grinned.

With all the curtains drawn, we couldn't see outside, but that didn't stop the noise from getting through. It hadn't been much until then, but it seemed the disturbances outside had started to pick up. Glass shattered and the loud clank of what I decided to be a garbage can tip over had the hairs on my neck stand up straight. Tension sat in the air as I waited for the bubble to burst and chaos to ensue. I wanted to spare Rowdy from that as much as possible and tried to distract him where I could.

I grabbed the picture of him and his grandparents off my desk and removed the frame. Along with clothes, a toothbrush, and my phone, I shoved it in the pack. I didn't own much stuff, and even in the time I had spent with the Marsdens, I had only got some new clothes. It could be that I wanted to protect myself from the eventual loss, or that I knew it just to be unimportant stuff, but I'd always had this feeling that I wasn't supposed to stay here for long.

Rummaging through my desk, I found a pocketknife and shoved it into one of my pants pockets along with the baton. I glanced across the room and found nothing left of value except for the kid sitting on my bed and the panda bear clutched in his tiny hands. I rolled to him, grabbed his legs, and pulled him closer so he sat facing me. I had to swallow as the little guy stared at me with those big eyes and wondered for a second how and when I had turned into this softy.

"Hey, buddy," I said. "I have to talk to you about somethin'." He must have sensed my earnestness, because he gave me a very serious look, and I was almost tempted to smile at the sight of the frown on his face. "Listen, there are some things goin' on out there that I don't have any control over, so that means that I basically have no idea what's about to happen."

Rowdy nodded emphatically as if all I'd said made sense to him, but how could it? He had no idea what was going on out there. His grandparents and dad had protected and shielded him from seeing the horrors that plagued this world. And I couldn't get rid of that sinking feeling that I would be the one to introduce him to all that mess and ruin his life forever. I still had some hope that Mars would come to get us, but like Mags had once told me, hope killed.

"If anythin' happens or if I tell you to," I continued, "then I need you to close your eyes and just hang on to me, okay?" As he gazed up at me, I couldn't tell whether he looked worried or was mulling it over, but eventually he nodded.

"Like glue," he said.

"Yeah," I said, "just like daddy said—like glue."

A knock on the door brought my attention to Luke, who stood leaning in the opening.

"It's getting rougher out there," he said.

"Yeah, I heard."

"There's something I'd like you to see," he said. The crease that formed on his forehead distorted his baby-face features and had me a little worried.

"Okay," I said as I grabbed the backpack and fastened it to the back of my chair. Rowdy climbed onto my lap, and just as I was about to follow Luke, I noticed a baseball cap sticking out from underneath the bed. I grabbed the cap with the Brooklyn Nets logo on the front that Mr. Marsden had given me and placed it on Rowdy's head. The cap was too big, but maybe that could be an advantage because he could use it to cover his eyes.

"Hang on to that for me, okay?" I said.

"Okay," he replied and pulled it firmly over his head.

I rolled us down the hall and found Luke in the living room, sneaking a peek out of the window facing the street.

"What's up?" I asked after depositing Rowdy on the couch. Luke made room for me to look beyond the curtains without moving them too much. I looked up at him for a second, curious to what had him look so worried.

"Do you see?" he asked as I peered out the window. I glanced down the drive and past the cars in the street. The opening in the curtains was small, and it took me a moment to take everything in, but then I gasped at the sight of the white unmarked van. A man wearing a red baseball cap sat behind the steering wheel with the window rolled down. He didn't seem impressed by the shell of the woman who lumbered by his vehicle. From her shuffle, she was clearly infected but hadn't yet obtained the corresponding zombie look.

He blew smoke at the woman from inside the vehicle as she passed. She shoved her nose in the air and sniffed. As her whole body shuddered from the unappealing smell, she moved on.

I closed my eyes as the pieces of the puzzle started to fall into place. Mr. Marsden had come inside to fetch the box before he went back to the garage. The same box that had been delivered the day before by that same guy in that unmarked van.

"The delivery guy," I muttered.

11

Mags

For the first fifteen minutes of the trip or so, I had wondered what the hell the deal was. After we exited the final gate that separated Maxwell Air Force Base from the rest of the world, we steered our way in the direction of Air Base Boulevard. Preston sat behind the wheel of the first Hummer, with Tom riding in the back. Gibs followed in the second, with me and Angie riding in the back. Where it touched my face, the wind felt a bit brisk, but it was nothing to what I had gotten used to in Alaska. With every other part of my body covered, I actually felt somewhat hot.

Although it could be that the night provided camouflage for most of the walking dead, the streets around us looked deserted and displayed the usual that I had come to identify with the zombie apocalypse. Cars stood abandoned by the road. Some had been trashed, some had crashed, and others just stood there. We passed houses with boarded-up windows and houses that had burned to the ground as well as looted stores and gas stations.

There wasn't anything I hadn't seen before. Even the occasional zombie roaming the street didn't make me look twice. The last part of the trip took us along a stretch of highway, and for as long as it lasted, it seemed as if someone had exaggerated the situation, until we started to near our destination. Except for some trees lining the highway, we had a pretty decent view of the massive building, the surrounding parking lots and open fields behind it, but it had been the smell that caught my attention first along with the low hum of murmured moans.

Angie pulled up her nose, and must have caught a whiff the same time I had. She grabbed a railing and pulled herself from her seat. I followed her to the front. Holding on to the driver's cabin, I gazed to my left as we passed the large stretched out building, until Preston in the lead vehicle slowed to a stop and Gibs pulled up alongside him.

"That is just ..." Angie started to say, but she didn't seem able to finish her sentence. Not even the dark could hide the overwhelming sight, and the moonlight only added to its eeriness.

"Fucked up," Tom said, finishing it for her. He slammed his palm on the top of the cab a couple of times and then called out, "I told you we should have brought RPGs, Sarge."

Preston remained silent as he took in the sight.

He had led us to a stop near an exit road at a safe distance from the building but close enough to realize this wasn't going to be easy.

The fifty or so people who had kept themselves alive these past months and had even been able to maintain contact with Maxwell had done so tucked away in a distribution center. Most of the survivors had probably attempted to leave the state and were heading to Montgomery Regional Airport or had come from there when they had gotten themselves stuck inside that large building.

It had been their luck that the DC held tons of cargo, including food and water. What worked against them, though, was that apparently every zombie in this area and beyond had found their way to them. The L-shaped building measured over two hundred thousand square feet and from this angle looked to be completely surrounded by zombies.

Gibs stepped out of the truck and walked around it to where Preston hung out the open window.

"Now what?" he asked.

"Do we have any idea where these people are holding up?" Angie asked.

"From what Eaves told me, they've moved to the second floor after the fence collapsed, taking whatever supplies they could," Preston replied as he stepped from the truck and climbed into the back with Tom. He pulled out a pair of night-vision goggles and peered at the building.

"Is the building compromised?" Gibs asked.

"It hadn't been the last time they called in, but that was a couple of days ago," Preston replied.

"But they know were coming, right?" I asked, feeling anxiety creeping up on me. "Because I don't want to get shot or something by accident."

Gearing up, we had decided not to fit the heavy armored plates into our vest, because zombies didn't carry guns. I was beginning to doubt that decision.

"Maxwell has transmitted that we were coming, but they haven't received a reply," Preston said. "Eaves didn't seem worried about that. It appears they've had trouble with their equipment before."

"I say we run them down like bowling pins," Tom suggested.

"Yes, that's why you're not in charge," Preston said as he jumped from the truck. He pointed a finger in the direction of the building and started conversing with Gibs. I couldn't make out what they were saying and figured I'd hear it later.

Feeling the need to release my eyes from the enormous number of mutilated corpses lumbering around, I sat down in my seat.

"Remind me why I'm here," I said. I looked up

at Angie who was still peering out over the cab. She shook herself and then sat down next to me.

"I'm not so sure about that myself," she said in a low voice. "I can't imagine surviving in there for all that time."

"If someone is in there, then Divus would probably be their only way out," I said. "There is no other way to get around those masses."

"All right, ladies. Listen up, here's the plan," Preston said in loud voice. We both stood and lent him our full attention. "We're gonna drive around the back and enter where the loading area used to be and where the fence is breached. Then we split up. You'll stay close to give us cover fire until we can drive ourselves up close to a fire escape. If we can bypass the zombies, we should get close enough to park the Hummer underneath the ladder to pull it down. Once we're up, the rest of you follow."

My eyes shifted from Preston to Gibs and Tom. They both nodded in agreement.

"That's all the plan there is?" I asked, surprised.

"What more of a plan you want?" Tom added. "We go in, we kick ass, and we go home."

Annoyed at his bravado, I narrowed my eyes and zeroed in on Tom.

"Aren't you just a tad bit stereotypical?" I asked, raising my brows. Tom's eyes didn't waver from mine as he shrugged and loaded a bullet into the chamber of his weapon.

"The way I heard," Angie said, pulling me from my staring contest with Tom, "was that we enter without stirring the zombies too much." She glared down at Preston, almost daring him to contradict her.

"I agree," Preston said, raising a sharp eye at Tom. "We can't be sure there aren't any zombies inside, and I don't want any of them to go all crazy on us. With the amount surrounding the building, God, what'll happen if they are to find a way inside? Inoculating those people might take a while, and we still have to find a way to get them out."

Tom didn't argue. Instead he lifted his arm in salute, but with the wink he gave Angie, it didn't seem all that convincing.

As planned, Preston and Tom drove their Hummer around the distribution center. With that, they caught some attention from a couple of zombies that seemed intrigued by the movement and probably the engine noise. Gibs kept our truck at a low speed and at some distance from Preston's. We had taken the exit road that eventually paralleled the DC until we hit an access road that led to the loading docks. An open field stretched out behind the building, and I assumed that would have had something to do with the approach trajectory of the planes heading to the nearby airport.

A couple of zombies heading in the direction of the DC shuffled across the road. They seemed intent on joining the others in crowding the building and perhaps the hope of a midnight snack. Preston didn't stop as he caught them in his headlights and slammed into them head on.

Tom, who stood in the back, dropped to a crouch, hiding behind the driver's cabin as one of the zombies slammed into the Hummer's grille. I couldn't hear him, but from Tom's fist pounding on the rearview window, I could imagine the curse words that would have parted from his lips.

Gibs followed Preston as he took a turn that would lead us to the loading docks before he slowed the vehicle. As Preston kept moving closer to the loading docks, Gibs stopped.

"Get ready," Angie said without taking her eyes of the other Hummer approaching the DC. I lifted my rifle on top of the cab and settled in comfortable position. Peering through the scope and adjusting it accordingly, I felt grateful for the familiar M4 in my hands. I had a considerable amount of experience with this weapon and wouldn't have wanted to familiarize myself with something else at this point.

At my side, Angie did the same as we watched the lead Hummer maneuver through the first line of zombies. The vehicle shook and shuddered as it plowed over bodies. The truck did a good enough job, but I would have preferred to be driving a Knight XV, like the one Mars had confiscated at Warren's lab in Florida to aid our escape. I had always regretted abandoning the massive tank-like vehicle. That truck had been a home to Ash and me for several weeks after we'd escaped the Florida lab and would have easily disposed of the zombies now faced by the smaller vehicle.

My thoughts started to drift, and memories of hanging out at the beach with Ash threatened my concentration when a burst of static in my ear brought me back to the present.

"It is getting pretty thick out here," Preston said over the com link. "They don't seem that interested in us, but they don't seem to wanna move either."

"At least we now know for sure that the serum works," Tom said as he stood in the back of the Hummer, gazing over the bodies milling around the truck. With the night-vision scope, I could clearly see his discomfort by the grimace on his face. Talking about kicking ass was one thing, but it wasn't easy staring down into the glazed-over blank eyes of so many people who might as well be dead.

Even a hard ass like Tom couldn't deny that.

Tom lunged forward as the vehicle came to a sudden stop, but he managed to steady himself on the driver's cab.

"What the hell!" he shouted over the earpiece. I grabbed my ear as if that would protect it from the loud noise.

"This isn't going to work," Preston said. His voice remained pretty much what it had always been—calm and collected. Zombies pressed against the hull of the truck from all sides, and it seemed the Hummer sat stuck in the mud. "There is at least eighty feet of zombies between us and that fire escape. We won't reach it like this."

"You want us to distract them?" Gibs replied.

"How do you wanna do that?" Tom said.

"We just need to make some noise," I said. "I've done it before." A zombie attack while we were having a pit stop at a gas station had forced Ash and me to help out some of the locals. All it had taken was some loud rap music to distract the zombies surrounding the car occupied by the chief of police and his deputies. After that, I only had to run them over. Of course, then I had my iPhone available with a considered amount of high-strung, bass-thumping songs to choose from. Not that I had taken the time to choose an appropriate song, although I didn't think a ballad would have cut it. Ash had always been in charge of the entertainment, and I had even given her my phone before I'd left for Alaska. The kid would have gone crazy without her music.

"Why don't you take a couple of shots at them?" Preston said.

"Is that wise?" Tom countered, "I mean, I'm sitting right here in the open." With an exaggerated gesture, he tapped a hand on top of his helmet as if he needed to remind us he was still standing there. Ignoring him, Angie and I both lined up our sights.

"Is the safety supposed to be up or down?" I said over the com link. On the truck, Tom threw his hands up in an *I-don't-believe-it* gesture. I grinned as Angie pulled the trigger and shot a zombie in the back of the head. Brain matter splattered the other zombies as its body crumpled down after it.

"Take a couple near the back," she said. "Let's see if we can trigger their interest."

I followed her example and pulled the trigger. Three bullets and three permanently dead zombies later, none of the others took the bait. We had hoped the sound of gunfire might draw their attention toward us. Unfortunately, that tactic failed.

Tom threw his hands up at the ineffectiveness of our efforts. It wasn't enough to kill them. The infected showed no interest in us. They shared only one common interest in finding their next meal. To find that next meal, zombies primarily used their sense of smell, but that didn't work with us anymore, so we needed an alternative to attract their attention.

"I have another idea," I said as I lined up my sight through the scope. My finger hovered over the trigger for a moment until I found my target. The bullet slammed into the zombie's shoulder, and the force of the impact spun it around. "Now take out your flashlight and wave at it."

Angie hesitated for a moment but then seemed to pick up on my thinking.

"Gibs," I said, "honk your horn and flash the truck's lights." Waving her flashlight, Angie shouted at the zombies to come get us as I shot two more of them. One just tumbled over, but the other spun in a similar fashion to the first one. Whether because of Angie's waving or Gibs's honking, the zombie kept its gaze in our direction. It took a moment for the few remaining gears inside its head to start spinning, but then it moved its feet and headed our way.

"Keep at it," I said as I fired another shot.

Once a couple of them headed our way, it seemed more of them decided to follow. I stopped firing and stood to wave my own flashlight in the same manner as Angie. Fortunately, we stood up wind and the zombies couldn't catch our scents.

As the zombies had drawn their attention from one Hummer to the other, Gibs started the engine and eased us into reverse. It wasn't a pretty sight, watching the undead after all those weeks, and time hadn't done them any good. The limp forms struggling to make their way to us didn't own any recognizable features. As they came closer, I couldn't tell whether I was looking at a male or female, even in the truck's headlights, although their clothes sometimes betrayed them. But it wasn't as if I wanted to see them as the human beings they had once been. It was better to view them as the things they had become.

To do that was easier with these zombies than those that we had encountered in Cheyenne. With these, I didn't have to fear their pleading gazes as if they knew what had happened to them. The zombies walking toward us had that fogged-over, blank glaze in their eyes that made it a lot easier to take them out for good.

The mass of zombies on the left side of the building started to thin out as the amount of zombies that followed us grew. When the number of zombies surrounding Preston's Hummer had decreased, he moved backward, running over a couple. With that he managed to draw the attention of the zombies still clawing at the building. As soon as the remaining zombies noticed their peers were leaving, they followed in the hope of an easier prey. Preston took advantage of the situation and parked the truck underneath the fire escape.

| 12

Ash

Mars hadn't shown up an hour later. In fact, it had been several hours, and he still wasn't there. The sun started to set, and the number of zombies roaming the street had increased. The delivery guy with the red baseball cap still sat undeterred in his van as the pile of cigarette butts on the ground next to it grew higher.

"What is takin' him so long?" I muttered as I peered out the window.

I was starting to get frustrated with Mars for taking so long and with myself for having waited this long. With every minute, the number of zombies outside increased, and if we had left earlier, we might have been able to evade them. But as I glanced over my shoulder and watched Rowdy fast asleep on the couch, I knew I could never have left the house with him—not with the zombies roaming outside that viewed him as a mere snack. Besides, I didn't know the intentions of the guy in the van, and I would never have been able to climb the fence surrounding the backyard, not without attracting a whole lot of attention from either zombies or the guy in the van.

I cursed my inability to use my legs and the fact that I was the reason that guy sat out there in the first place. He must have been sent by Warren, and that also meant I was to blame for the outbreak. I was the reason Rowdy's grandparents were dead and the reason he and Luke were now in danger.

"What do you think he's waiting for?" Luke asked from the hallway. He had taken up position at the front door to watch the delivery guy and keep an eye on the roaming zombies. Now and then he would walk around the house to check the windows and doors, but our main focus was the guy in the white van.

"I don't know," I said in a whisper.

"I mean," Luke continued, "this whole outbreak was probably meant as a diversion to create time for whatever it is he has planned, and it appears to be working, because from what I could tell of our short conversation it seemed Agent Marsden was pretty determined to get here, so if he didn't ..."

His words faded as if he had suddenly realized the implications of what he was saying, but it wasn't as if I hadn't thought about it. Something could have happened to Mars—something bad. I didn't want to think about it and rolled my chair away from the window. I yawned, and my back ached as I straightened.

"Why don't you take five?" Luke said as he watched me from the hallway. I nodded and rolled my chair between the couch and the coffee table. I grabbed one of the energy bars off the table that we had dumped there and stuck it between my teeth. Hefting my body from the chair, I slid onto the couch and then grabbed the fabric of my pants to hoist my legs up onto the wheelchair. Finally, seated, I leaned back and took the energy bar from my mouth.

My movements hadn't been subtle and were enough to stir Rowdy. He lifted his head, and sleep-filled eyes peered up at me. I smiled as he scooted closer and laid his head on my lap.

"Hey, buddy," I said, caressing his cheek, "want something to eat?" He shook his head, let out a deep sigh, and fisted the fabric of my hoody before he drifted off to sleep again.

I knew we had to act. We couldn't just sit here and wait for the inevitable. That man out there was waiting for something, or worse, someone, and I had a distinct feeling I knew whom. There were just too many coincidences that made it all seem deliberate: the delivery of the package, Mars's warning that Warren was nearby, and now the deliveryman sitting out front waiting. What was worse was that he repelled the zombies just as much as I did. They didn't attack him, so that would mean he'd be able to walk straight up to the house without a zombie sniffing twice about it. So what was I supposed to do if Warren showed up before Mars?

I lifted my gaze from Rowdy and caught Luke staring at me from out of the hallway. He seemed to have his eyes fixed on my legs resting on the wheelchair. This stirred some annoyance inside me, but I could understand the worried look on his face.

"You don't have to worry about me," I offered. "I can handle myself." His eyes widened as if he were embarrassed to have been caught staring.

"I ... uh ..." he started to say, but stopped himself. He leaned against the doorpost, abandoning the window and the delivery guy for a moment. He inhaled sharply as if to compose himself and said, "I'm sorry. I didn't mean to stare, and Agent Marsden has told us as much during the briefing before he sent us out. It's just ..." He paused and his eyes drifted to the ground.

"It couldn't have been easy out there, you know, during those first days," he said. "Agent Marsden has told us some of what had happened in New York and Colorado." He looked up to face me, and I didn't know what he saw there, but he quickly added, "No details, but just the idea of being out there and not being able to, you know ..." Luke gestured at my legs and then fell silent. I peeled the wrapping from my energy bar and took a bite, mulling over his question.

It hadn't been easy, but it could have been so much worse if Mags hadn't found me inside that hospital. Still, it wasn't something I wanted to dwell on.

"Where were you when it happened?" I asked, steering the subject away from me. Luke grinned sheepishly, almost embarrassed even.

"In school on this side of the country," he said as I took another bite.

I narrowed my eyes at him, wondering if my assessment of him coming straight from boot camp hadn't been so far off.

"So how did you end up here?" I asked with a mouth full.

"I wanted to help and signed up," he said. "It seemed the right thing to do."

The loud rumble of a big engine pulled Luke's gaze from me back into the hallway.

"What is it?" I asked with a mouth full of calories and carbohydrates. I didn't have to wait long for my answer. I had barely finished my energy bar when Luke tapped the door.

"A truck just stopped in front of the house," he whispered.

"Shit," I muttered and lifted Rowdy from my lap. I shifted back into my chair and reclaimed my spot at the window where, lo and behold, I saw none other than Dr. David Warren step out of a large truck that blocked the entire street, strolling in the direction of the delivery guy.

"Son of a b—" I started to say, but swallowed the last word as a cold shiver ran down my spine.

"Is that who I think it is?" Luke asked.

"I don't know," I said. "Who do you think it is?"

Luke stood at the doorway, pausing to take another peek through the front door window and then stepping back to stand at the doorway to the living room, gaping at me.

"That's Dr. David Warren," he said, sounding stunned.

"Then you are thinkin' correctly," I said. I bit my lower lip in the hope it would bring on some profound idea, but nothing happened. They had us trapped in here.

Warren glanced around and took a step aside to let an approaching zombie pass. It looked as though he had finally figured out the serum and found a way to duplicate what had been working for Mags and me for all this time. He had managed to make it so that a human would not be of interest to the zombies. But if he had done it, then what was he doing here? He wouldn't need me for his research anymore; he had fixed the problem.

Still, he was here, and with his wavy black hair, he looked as smug as he had the day he'd appeared at the house where Mags and I had sought refuge. He even wore a similar-looking leather jacket. I supposed I should be grateful that he had shown up that day and that he had fixed my leg after a zombie had taken more than a mouthful, but it was kind of hard to feel that way as the memories of what had happened later inside that lab in Florida seeped into my mind. I shook my head as if that would drive the memories away.

Warren stopped at the van and kicked at the pile of cigarette butts on the ground. Then he got himself into an animated conversation with the delivery guy. They both pointed fingers at the house, and Warren didn't seem pleased, because he shook his head.

I pinched the bridge of my nose, trying to think up a course of action, but none came. It seemed that Mags was usually the one to come up with the ideas. Although a bunch of them hadn't been the brightest of ideas, they had worked out and I wished she were here.

Another man came around the truck and joined the conversation. He looked like one of those apes that usually hung around Warren. I'd seen them in Florida and in Cheyenne—broad shoulders, thick neck, and a bald head, wrapped in a suit and tie that didn't look comfortable. I wondered how anyone would even want to be associated with Warren. Unless, of course, endless amounts of money were involved. It seemed money really did make the world go round if people could lend themselves to do the dirty work of a man like Warren.

As the delivery guy stepped from his van, Baldy pulled a weapon from a holster tucked underneath his armpit.

"Uh-oh," Luke muttered, and I heard him pull his own weapon from his holster. "I think they're planning on coming in."

Once again Warren forced my hand and left me with little choice. On the couch, Rowdy had woken and sat up as he watched me with those big brown eyes. The sight of him only strengthened my resolve —I couldn't let them get in here. From what I had witnessed before, Warren wasn't averse to some collateral damage. He had made that clear from the moment he had started to accelerate his testing inside that lab facility he had in Florida. Warren didn't care who died or got infected—he just cared about the result. So who knew how he or those goons of him might react. At the sight of Luke, they might decide to shoot up the place. Rowdy would not get hurt because of me.

"I'm goin' to face him," I said rolling my chair to the hallway, but Luke blocked my way. "Move!" The word came out harsh, and I heard a little gasp coming from Rowdy behind me.

"You're not going out there," Luke said. He stepped back to press his body against the front door and peeked out the window.

"Oh, so you're gonna take on three men with guns," I said, trying to shove him away from the door, "with a kid, and a cripple to back you up. And let's not forget about the zombies." I shoved him again when he didn't move. "It's me he wants, and Rowdy will not get hurt because of it." At that, Luke knelt by my side, a firm hand pressed against the door.

"How do you know that?"

"I do—trust me."

Luke glanced past me, at Rowdy no doubt, and then shot a quick look out the window.

"They're gesturing for one of them to go around back," he said. Without hesitation, I shoved Luke again—harder this time. It tipped him off balance. As he released the door to catch himself from falling, I grabbed the handle and opened the door.

"Warren!" I yelled. The door stood open a crack, and through it, I could see all three men pause.

"Don't do this, Ash," Luke said as he pulled himself to his feet.

"They'll leave once he has what he wants," I said, hoping my voice sounded firm. "Stay here, wait for Mars, and keep Rowdy safe."

"Ms. Reed." I shuddered at the sound of Warren's voice. "What a pleasure to see you again." I pulled the door open and rolled the chair through the opening while Luke stood behind me. "I see you have company."

Warren stood in the driveway, flanked by his two goons. The delivery guy had his weapon pointed my way, but Baldy didn't seem to bother. Warren shoved his hands in his pockets, and a smirk formed on his face.

"I'm guessin' it's me you want," I said, more as a statement than a question. Warren sighed shifting his gaze to the sky before lowering it and shrugged.

"Not exactly, but you'll do for now," he answered. *What did that mean? What else could he want?*

Mr. Fletcher, who I recognized by the hideous

flower shirts he used to wear, hobbled across the path between us. His face was bloodied and unrecognizable. He stumbled and fell flat on his face, crushing what was left of his nose on the gravel. The delivery guy pulled a face of disgust, and Baldy held a hand to his mouth. Warren didn't even feign interest.

Finding some leftover courage, I rolled forward and said, "If you promise to leave peacefully, I'll come willingly." Warren shot me a look of surprise.

"What," he said, "don't have enough soldiers in there to fight for you?"

"In fact, the soldiers are eager to pull their triggers," I said, keeping up the ruse Warren had created himself by implying others were inside the house, "but I don't want anyone to get hurt because of me."

Warren tilted his head as if considering my words or perhaps calculating the chance of more soldiers being inside the house, or worse, wondering what else might be of his interest. I needed to get him out of here. "Do we have a deal?"

Warren paused and eyed me thoughtfully. I thought he was ready to comply when Rowdy burst outside. He grabbed my arm and pulled it against his chest.

"No, Ash, no," he said, whining the words.

Tears streaked his face, and the sight of him made my stomach drop. I placed my hand on his cheek and kissed the top of his head.

"Go inside, Rowdy, please," I said softly.

"No, Daddy said to stick like glue," he replied.

"Rowdy, please," I said more firmly and looked to Luke for help. He didn't hesitate and grabbed Rowdy around the waist. Luke hoisted him off the ground and placed his own body between Rowdy and the men. The little guy was still crying as Luke stepped back until Rowdy disappeared into the house.

"How interesting," Warren said. "I'm thinking that must be Agent Marsden's boy."

"He has nothing to do with this," I shouted.

Warren pulled a hand from his pocket and tapped a contemplative finger on his cheek. Then he waved me over.

"All right, come on then," he said. Fortunately, Luke held Rowdy from view as I glanced reluctantly over my shoulder. I didn't know whether I'd been able to go through with it if I had to face Rowdy's pleading eyes, but I also knew I didn't have a choice. Luke cocked his head as if to ask whether I was sure of what I was doing. I nodded my head as if I knew I was.

I eased forward until I reached the edge of the

steps and started to balance on my rear wheels. Rolling forward, I eased off the first step and held fast at the next. Taking my time, I took the last one and dropped the front casters to the ground. As I rolled closer to them, Warren's goons stepped away from his side to circle me. Somewhere in the distance I heard the rumble of an engine and the fast-paced rat-a-tat of machine gunfire, but with the men closing in on me, I couldn't focus on the sounds. My heart seemed to have taken up residence inside my head as it pounded away, drowning out all other sounds. As I came closer, Warren gestured at the delivery guy to move me along. He came around me and started pushing my chair. I bit my lip to keep myself from lashing out at him.

"Why don't you see who else is in there?" Warren said to Baldy as the delivery guy wheeled me past him.

13

Mags

My arms started to hurt from waving them over my head. Gibs had turned the truck and pulled it back onto the road, heading south away from the DC. We hadn't moved far at our slow pace and I could still see the building in the distance. Two figures stood on top of the roof: Preston and Tom had made it.

I pointed the two out to Angie, and she stopped waving. Instead, she slammed the palm of her fist on the top of the cab and yelled, "Time to go back."

We had managed to lead quite a trail of zombies behind us and away from the DC, but there were still plenty of them milling around the building. There must have been thousands in total, and these hundred or so hobbling behind the Hummer had been just enough to get Preston moving again.

Gibs steered the truck in a lazy circle until its nose pointed at the DC. With their focus fixed on the moving vehicle, it wasn't hard to imagine the zombies would just keep on following us back, and so they did.

"Now what," I asked Angie, pointing a finger at the ongoing parade behind us. "If we stop near the building, these and the others will just box us in."

"We shouldn't stop then," she said and pressed the button to activate her radio. "Gibs, just stop long enough for us to hop onto the other vehicle and then move the truck to a safe distance?"

"You think they're gonna surround us again?" Gibs asked. Angie didn't need to answer as Preston's voice came over the radio.

"I agree with Ms. Meadow. Don't stop."

I grinned and mouthed *Ms. Meadow*. Angie rolled her eyes at me.

"I respond better to Angie," she added, "and if you want tall and mean over here to move, call her Mags."

Gibs did as he was told. He pulled away from the zombies trailing us by placing his foot on the gas. Then he stopped next to the other Hummer, and as soon as Angie and I had exchanged trucks, he sped away.

I followed Angie up the ladder and found Preston patiently waiting for us, while Tom let out a breath in exasperation as if he'd been waiting all day for us. Kneeling beside the others, I gazed over the roof. A variety of exhaust vents poked up from the flat surface, and four little sheds with exit doors stood scattered across the roof.

"Wouldn't there be someone here to greet us?" I asked, peering at the closest structure and its closed door. "I mean, someone must have heard or seen us."

"I was kind of wondering the same thing," Preston said.

"So," I added.

"So either they're dead or they're hiding," Preston said.

"Wouldn't that be great," Tom said. "Getting shot because they think we're looters?"

"I guess we'll find out," Angie said.

"Okay, here's how it goes," Preston said. "Tom and I have the lead. Mags, you follow, and Angie will have the rear."

In a line, we moved to one of the small structures with a door that would lead us inside the building. Within seconds, Tom had it open, and we peered into a black hole. With the aid of flashlights, we moved down the steps until we reached a landing. The narrow steps, with barely room for one person, should have led further down if they hadn't been dismantled. Shining our flashlights into the depths of the staircase revealed the concrete floor and the metal frame of what had been stairs. Although we couldn't see them, we heard the low moans that could only have come from the zombies. Fortunately, we didn't have to go any further, because the people had moved up to the second floor.

With our weapons at the ready, Preston opened the door to exit the landing. One after another, we filed into a dark open space illuminated by the flashlights we carried. I tried to get my bearings, swinging my flashlight back and forth. The floor underneath my feet seemed to be made of some metal mesh while a railing mounted on one side prevented us from falling. I gathered we stood on some kind of walkway. My flashlight wasn't strong enough to punch a dent in the darkness that lay beyond. I could make out the tops of containers and racks that nearly reached the roof of the building.

A punchy and putrid smell rose from the darkness underneath our feet along with the moans of the undead. The sound of a strange rustle raised the hairs on my neck. I tried to shake it off and swirled the flashlight to my left where the beam bounced of a wall. That end of the walkway was a dead end. There was only one way to go.

Preston led the way, moving with determination, but cautiously. I tried to be as quiet as possible as I followed in Preston's trail, but I couldn't seem to take a step without that damn metal walkway clanking underneath my feet. The moans in the depths below grew louder, and I cursed myself for my inability to move as stealthy as the others.

The walkway ended at another set of stairs, and Preston stopped after he'd led us down.

"This should be the second floor," he said. "From what Eaves has told me, the remaining survivors are on this level and have barricaded themselves inside the offices and lounge."

I glanced around with the help of my flashlight, trying to ignore the strange sound that gave me the chills, and I noticed the walkway at the top of the stairs was just that, a walkway—a metal construction appearing almost suspended high above the ground. It was probably meant as an emergency exit. To my left there was another railing, but it ended abruptly, leaving a gaping hole between it and the wall. As the others took their first steps down the hallway, I paused to raise my light to the opposite side and moved closer to the railing. I pointed my light down and gasped. The light hit a forklift with a crate suspended in midair surrounded by zombies.

Shifting the light revealed more zombies. Every inch of the place sat packed with the bodies of the infected. Foggy eyes peered up at me as the light skimmed their mutilated faces. Smears of blood stood out against the yellow paint of another machine that had probably been used to haul around goods but now sat stuck among the countless bodies. Everywhere I pointed, my light fell on walking corpses, barely recognizable as the humans they once had been, while they shuffled among the debris of fallen crates and boxes.

I stood there frozen as the thin beam of light fought a path past the aisles filled with the walking dead. Chills rose up my spine as the moans along with the snapping of teeth grew louder with every passing of the flashlight.

The moans echoed hollowly in the large space, and I jumped as Angie came up beside me.

"Guess that explains why the others couldn't get in," she said as her own flashlight bounced across the racks and then veered over to a large space packed with zombies. One of the loading bay doors stood halfway open, but the number of bodies pressing their way inside had kept us from noticing. The large space sat packed with so many bodies that there just wasn't any room for the ones left outside. "Why haven't they moved on?"

Angie's words were barely audible as if she had asked the question for her own consideration.

"What the fuck," Tom said, trailing off as his gaze swept over the gruesome display.

Preston didn't say anything as he thoughtfully shifted the helmet on his head.

"It's like those parades I've encountered with Ash," I said somewhat to myself but also as a reply to Angie.

"What do you mean?" Preston asked. A bit shocked, I looked at him. It felt as if this was the first time he had addressed me since our meeting in Marshall's office. I shook myself, trying to regain my thoughts.

"Out on the road," I said. "A few months after the initial outbreak, Ash and I encountered these large groups of zombies. They were enormous, and they stuck together as if something told them to do so."

Preston nodded in understanding, but I doubted anyone understood.

"Guess this explains why Eaves had been so reluctant to send anyone in," he said.

"And why they sent us in," Angie said. "If Divus can get these people out, that would make a solid case for dispensing it."

"Come on," Preston said as he turned. "Let's find these people first."

Without hesitation Tom followed him, but I still

stood frozen as my eyes lingered over the open space.

"Mags," Angie said in a soft voice, and she placed a hand on my shoulder.

I steeled myself ready to follow as the light from my flashlight bounced off metal on the ground just below us. Among the stumbling bodies, I recognized the stairs that once probably fitted between this railing and the wall.

"Somebody's been busy," I said pointing my light at the jagged and, in some places, melted edges of where the stairs used to fit.

"Smart," she said, "isolating themselves from the zombies—they must have used a cutting torch."

"Ladies," Tom called out in a loud whisper. Angie and I looked over our shoulders and saw Tom standing with his hands on his hips as if he'd been waiting for us while we were shopping for clothes or something. His rifle hung across the middle of his chest, and his helmet sat high on his head.

I steered my light to his face, and he released an instant groan.

"Hey, stop that." Tom raised his hand to shield his eyes and added, "The sarge is waiting, c'mon."

We followed Tom down the corridors and

caught up with Preston. My hand had held a firm grip on the gun handle, and I released it to clench and unclench my fist. The sight of those zombies had gotten to me, and I had no idea how anyone could have stayed alive inside this place. There had been contact with the survivors a few days ago, but I couldn't help wonder if we should fear for the worst.

Preston sat in a crouch, peering around the corner. Tom raised a finger to his lips as we stopped behind Preston with our backs against the wall.

"What is it?" Tom whispered. Preston made a gesture with his hand near his ear, and then he tapped his helmet. Tom turned to us pointed a finger and then balled his fist. Angie nodded.

In a practiced move, both men eased themselves around the corner and disappeared from my view. Angie moved around me and edged closer to the corner.

As she peered around it, I whispered, "Not fluid in hand speech, but I'm guessing they're checking on something Preston heard and we're supposed to stay put." Angie nodded her head in answer.

I eased further from the wall in an attempt to peer around Angie to see what was going on. Preston and Tom moved down a hall with doors lined on either side. The place was still dark, so I couldn't make out Preston or Tom that well, but I could see the beams from their flashlights.

For a moment, the lights halted before one of them pointed in our direction and shifted from left to right.

"We're up," Angie said. Without looking back at me, she stood and stepped forward. Shifting my weapon to aim at nooks and crannies and from door to door, I felt as if I were back at that gun range, and I expected a cardboard figure to pop up at any second.

Angie's flashlight acted as an extension of her rifle as the light veered from left to right. In a fluid motion, she moved down the hall, shining her light around corners of intersecting hallways and doors we passed. I followed close on her heels. Ahead of us, Preston and Tom disappeared around another corner, and it started to make me wonder just how big this place actually was.

A moment later Preston's voice came over the radio.

"We've located survivors. Hang back a moment while we make contact."

Angie shrugged and moved a few steps further down the hall.

"I guess we wait," she said as she leaned against the wall. Ever so vigilant, she kept bouncing the light from left to right so she could keep an eye on things.

I stretched my back, and my bones cracked loudly. The sound made Angie sweep her light over my body.

"Sorry," I said in a low voice.

"Having fun?" she asked as I stepped closer.

"Tons," I replied, shining my flashlight down the hall. The truth was that this place gave me the creeps. It felt haunted, and as the thought crossed my mind, I heard the creek of a door.

For a second, I froze, but then I swirled around until my light and the barrel of my gun aimed at a door that stood ajar. I couldn't remember if it had been like that as I had casted my light across it before.

"What is it?" Angie whispered as she raised her weapon at my sudden movement. I also couldn't remember an appropriate hand gesture, but I figured Angie would know what I was doing if I slowly approached the door, gun raised.

My heart rate had gone from pretty excited to out of control within seconds, and I tried to slow my breathing as I edged closer to the door. I pressed my hand to the door and pushed slowly.

"Who are you?" a tiny voice called out. I whirled around, shocked at the sound. Moans, growls, I had been expecting those, the voice of a kid not so much. The young boy had appeared in the hallway behind me, seemingly from out of nowhere. In my clumsy attempt to turn, I hit the doorpost with my back, and the door I had been wanting to ease open before swung open.

Angie had her flashlight on the young boy, but I had barely time to make him out as another voice spoke up.

"Jimmy, you're not supposed to show yourself to strangers."

"Goddammit," I called out after being startled for the second time within two seconds and pointed my light in the direction from where I thought the voice had come from.

Shock riddled the girl's face. Her dark eyes were wide, and her mouth stood open.

"You used a bad word," the girl said in a tiny voice. Her mouth hung open, and as the expression brought a smile to my lips, it also managed to calm my racing heart. I turned my flashlight to Angie who had knelt beside the boy as she talked to him. Footsteps down the hall drew my attention and saw two lights bumping up and down.

"It's Preston and Tom," Angie said. Blowing out another breath, I shifted my weapon to point it at the ground and turned to the girl. She stood next to a bunk bed, holding a teddy bear in her arms.

"Hey," I said as I kneeled to be closer to her level and removed my helmet. She stood frozen in her spot. I cleared my throat and pointed a thumb over my shoulder.

"I'm sorry about the bad word back there," I said, "but you kind of startled me." She closed her mouth but didn't say anything, so I added, "Are you okay?"

Slowly her head bobbed forward. I guessed her to be around five, maybe six years old, and she must have been terrified.

"My name is Mags," I said in my most reassuring voice. "What's yours?"

The young boy popped his head inside the door as the girl continued to stare at me.

"It's okay, Joanie. They're here to help," he said. The boy stepped inside the room. He looked a bit older than the girl and seemed to radiate confidence. He stopped in front of me and stuck out his hand.

"I'm Jimmy," he said as he shook my hand.

"Mags," I replied.

"Nice to meet you," he replied. "This is my little sister Joanie—she's a bit shy."

"I'm not," Joanie replied in a tiny but loud voice. Still, she remained in her corner beside the bed clutching her teddy bear.

"Who's that big guy?" I said and pointed at the bear in an attempt to make the girl feel a little bit more at ease. Before she could answer, a frantic female voice called out down the hall.

"Jimmy, Joanie, where are you?"

I stood and turned to the door opening and found Preston leaning against the post. A woman burst through the door past him, dropped to her knees, and threw her arms around Jimmy. She reached out a hand to Joanie.

"Come here, baby. It's okay. Mommy's here," she said. The girl didn't hesitate and reached for her mother's hand. I moved around them and looked to Preston for answers.

"These are the kid's quarters," he said. "The rest of them are held up down the hall, and I have to say they were pretty surprised to see us."

I stepped out into the hall and found several people had come to greet us.

| **14**

Ash

"What? No!" My voice was shrill and urgent. I blocked my wheels with the brakes, and the delivery guy bumped into me. He braced himself on my shoulders, and I took the moment to unlatch the brakes and pulled away from him. I turned to see Baldy standing with his gun raised, pointing at Luke, who had his own weapon aimed at the bald man's chest. Luke held his weapon left-handed and had his body pressed against the doorframe, no doubt holding Rowdy around the waist with his other. At this point, the kid was screaming, and I couldn't take it anymore.

I reached for the baton in my pocket, unfolding the stick in one swift motion, and swung it at Warren, who was still within reach. The metal rod connected with his upper arm, and Warren let out a shriek of pain. Before I could raise my hand to smack him again, the delivery guy hit me on the wrist, and the baton fell from my hand. He shoved me hard, causing me to tip over, and I landed hard on my shoulder.

Looking up, I saw Baldy's attention shift from Luke to Warren and then behind him. I glanced in that same direction but couldn't see over the hedge from my position on the ground. It didn't prevent me from hearing the rumble of an engine, and it sounded close.

I tried to push myself up, and although I knew how to get myself righted again, I also knew it usually took me a minute or so.

"Fuck," I muttered as I saw Warren and Baldy heading my way. At the sound of automatic weapons firing, they picked up their pace and almost seemed frantic. I hadn't seen the delivery guy was already hovering over me as he gripped my arm and roughly jerked me up. I couldn't help crying out at the pain that shot up my arm, but that didn't stop me from lashing out with my other. Baldy stopped my attempt midswing and held my arm tight.

With both of my arms trapped, it was easy enough for them to hoist me backward. I barely heard Luke shout my name from the porch, between the increasing gunfire, and I craned my neck to see him. He took a step forward but hesitated at the edge of the porch. Rowdy clung to Luke's chest, his face contorted from crying as the two men dragged me to the van. Just before they jerked me around the back, I saw a green army truck pull up behind the truck that Warren had left to block the road. Shots rang out, and I twisted my head in an attempt to get a glimpse of what was going on. Soldiers standing on the army truck fired their weapons at the surrounding zombies as I heard the familiar voice.

"Secure the house!"

"Mars!" I shouted as loud as I could, but the gunfire was too deafening. A sense of relief filled me at the knowledge that Mars had finally come. I knew he would, but it would have been better if he hadn't cut it this close.

Baldy opened the back door of the van, blocking the situation even more from my view. One of the men released me and stepped around the opened door. From the closeness of the shots, I assumed he returned fire. With one arm free, I swung a fist at my remaining assailant. It was Baldy, and my fist might as well have collided with a wall. He grabbed the wheels of my chair and lifted me off the ground. He tossed me in the van as if I were a toy. I landed on my side, all the while I screamed for help.

The doors closing muffled the sounds of gunfire around me. A jolt of fear reared up inside me as the engine of the van came to life. The darkness that surrounded me grabbed me by the throat as if it were choking me, but that didn't stop me from shouting.

"Get me the hell out of here, Mars!" I shifted to the side of the van, dragging my chair, and started banging on the metal. Panic set in as the van started to move. This couldn't be happening. Mars was right there. Why didn't he come get me? Reflexively, I wrapped my arms around my head as bullets struck the van.

"Go! Go! Go!" someone shouted, and I suspected Baldy, because his was the only voice I'd never heard before. The van picked up speed, and my stomach dropped. In the darkness, I searched the inside of the van for a latch, anything to get out of there.

The van must have hit something hard, because the vehicle jolted, and the impact lifted me off the floor before I landed with a thud. I grabbed my elbow as pain shot through it, but a sharp turn had me grabbing for something to hold on to. Finding nothing, I skidded across the floor, smacking hard into the side. Another sharp pain jabbed at my skull. I tried to blink, but I couldn't even tell whether I had as my consciousness slowly faded into oblivion.

"Please tell me that you didn't kill her." I was pretty sure I heard Warren's voice, but a thick fog seemed to cloud my brain functions. Fingers stabbed at my throat, and I flinched.

"Nope, still alive," a vaguely familiar voice said as the fingers stopped poking my throat.

Slowly my memories started to return—Warren and his men, the van. An overwhelming *oh-shit* feeling started to take me over as I felt a pair of hands grab me. I kept my eyes shut, and pretending to lull my head wasn't a problem. I didn't think my neck would work anymore. The pain that shot through my skull was excruciating.

Whoever had grabbed me set me down on my wheels. I slumped forward, and that wasn't even on purpose.

"Ugh," the man who I presumed to be Baldy said disgustedly.

"Let me see," Warren said and tilted my head. I groaned and jerked my head as he poked at it, but that sent even more pain through my skull. "Stitches will have to wait; put some gauze around it. Should be fine."

My eyelids refused to work as I tried to open them. I heard someone move away from me and fuss around before footsteps came closer again. A hand grabbed my head and jerked it up. My eyes shot open at the sudden motion.

"Ooowwwww," I wailed, sounding like a small

child. "Watch it." The big bald guy stood before me, looking down at me as if I were some bug that he was about to crush.

"Don't be a baby, kid," he said as he grabbed my head and started wrapping gauze around it.

"Stop it," I said as I tried to swat his hands away, "and I'm not a goddamn kid."

"You sound like one," Baldy said as he finished and slapped a piece of tape to my head so the gauze would stay in its place.

"Well, we'll talk again when someone grabs you from your home and bashes your head in."

Baldy took a moment to think about that and shook his head as he weighed the thought inside that thick skull of his.

"Okay, you win," he said. I glared at him. He just shrugged and walked away.

With my eyes working again, I glanced around. I sat in the corner of a barn of some kind. The building was made of wooden planks that, in some places, allowed slivers of moonlight to penetrate the space. The doors stood wide open, but I couldn't detect any lights in the darkness outside.

A big eighteen-wheeler truck, not unlike the one that had blocked the house in front of the Marsden home, stood in the center of the space. I squinted at the all-black vehicle that somehow reminded me of the Knight Rider. I forced a disturbing image of David Hasselhoff from my mind and focused on my surroundings. Baldy walked around the truck as if he were inspecting it. He didn't seem to pay much attention to me.

I glanced at the doors, but there weren't any guards. Straw and dirt covered the ground. This could be a problem in gaining speed, but I felt confident I could outride Baldy. He didn't seem like the athletic type, except maybe in the lifting weights department. I spotted Warren as he walked to the back of the truck and climbed inside. If there was a good moment to try to get the hell out of here, it would be this one.

I hesitated as I peered out the doors and then back at my surroundings. This place definitely looked like a barn. What if they'd dragged me to some farm or something that was surrounded by farmland? How the hell would I be able to wheel my way out? But even farms had roads, which would give Warren and Baldy over there the perfect opportunity to pick me up again in their van. Besides, I hadn't spotted the delivery guy yet, so he could still be out there.

My hands hovered over the push rings. *What did I have to lose?* I was pretty sure Warren's plans wouldn't be the kind that had me doing a happy dance. I'd rather be dead than end up on that man's cutting table again. At least Rowdy was safe. Even when Mars hadn't been able to get to me out, he would have gotten Rowdy and Luke out.

I pushed the rings. Something clinked and rattled before the wheels locked in place. Glancing around me, I noticed the chain holding me in place. Baldy looked up from what he was doing and chuckled.

"You didn't think I was that dumb," he said. I stared at him and narrowed my eyes. If looks could kill, Baldy would have been a bleeding mess on the ground.

"Actually I did," I said in a venomous tone.

Baldy scowled and turned back to what he was doing.

"Don't worry, Ms. Reed," Warren said, poking his head out the opening at the back of the truck. "It'll be your turn soon enough."

I tried to keep my face deprived of emotion; I wouldn't let that bastard see how much he got to me. My hands clamped around the push rings so tight that my fingers started to cramp, but at least it kept my body from shaking, as a cold chill ran through it.

"Ah, bite me," I said, sounding more confident than I felt.

"Be careful what you wish for," he replied.

| 15

Mags

Dire would definitely be a term that would come to mind in describing the situation that these people had found themselves in. On the other hand, I was somewhat amazed at the way they had managed to survive all these months. Six kids, fifteen women, and twenty-two men had carved out a spot for themselves on the second floor of a distribution center. Considering the fact that this had also become zombie Grand Central, it was even more impressive.

Everyone we had talked to inside the DC credited Bob as the man who had saved them. Apparently, Bob had been one of those survivalists or preppers or whatever they were called who had been hauling up supplies to his cabin in the woods for as long anyone could remember. Unfortunately, on the day that all hell broke loose, he found himself at the airport, waving off a friend.

After realizing all his efforts had been in vain, I guess he must have thought that the DC would serve as a worthy replacement. It held all the stuff and supplies that he would have collected at home, probably more.

From what I had gathered, he had taken charge after survivors had taken shelter inside the building. The zombies must have sensed their presence because the building had become surrounded right from the start, and they hadn't left since. With preparation running through Bob's blood, the group took on the task of hauling as much equipment, water, and nonperishables up to the second floor as they could and then securing it by removing all the stairs. After that, they had made use of pulleys, rope ladders, and the massive racks to get around inside the DC.

Angie had inquired about the reason that the ground floor sat infested with the undead, but none of them seemed eager to answer. One of the men, a burly fella named Marcus had said, "Let's just say that it all went to hell." He stared at the ground for a moment after that. I didn't think it wise to ask any further questions, and apparently neither did Angie. It seemed obvious to me something had gone terribly wrong because that half-opened loading bay couldn't have been opened by the zombies.

Preston had informed the bunch that we didn't expect any backup, because there was just none to give. Some of the men had scoffed and cursed so much that little Joanie had run and fled into her mother's arms. It had been Bob who had calmed them down. He had spent the past hours in his office with Preston and Tom, who no doubt were informing Bob of our great plan. Apparently, it took time to convince Bob—lots of time.

I was sitting on a desk in a corner of the room and took in the activities inside the lounge. The kids played in the middle of the room with one of the adults by their side. A couple of others had made themselves useful in the small kitchen. I had no idea where the others had gone, but considering the late hour—or perhaps I should say early hour—I presumed they had retreated into the offices that they had turned into somewhat private quarters.

Angie sat at a table across from me and peered out of the window, which looked over the ground floor area of the DC. I had no desire to watch the zombies stir about and had turned my back on it.

"What the ..." she said, but trailed off as she pulled her feet off the chair that they had been resting on. At the frown on her face, I turned to look over my shoulder. I could only see the darkness that lay beyond the window. I turned back for a second, but Angie's eyes sat fixed on the window. Again, I followed her gaze and then saw it.

I lifted my but off the desk and maneuvered to

the window where I placed my hands on the glass to peer through it.

"You saw that, right?" Angie asked.

"Yeah, but what was it?"

There was another burst of light, longer this time. A moment later, two shorter bursts followed as if someone were signaling with a flashlight.

"I have a bad feeling about this," I said, glancing over my shoulder. Angie's frown had deepened, and a dark veil had fallen over her eyes. I didn't need to ask whether she thought someone was out there; her expression confirmed it.

"Let's take a closer look," she said and moved for the door. I paused and glanced around the room, but no one seemed to pay attention to us. We took a right and ended up on a balcony that stretched out alongside the second-floor structure. It gave me a better view than I would have liked of the flesh-eating crowd downstairs. There was another flash, and I had to swallow hard. It came from one of the racks dead center in the middle of the DC.

Without warning Angie veered left, jogging down the balcony. I quickly followed.

"Hey," she said as she came to a stop. The balcony was too narrow to stand alongside her, so I peered over her shoulder.

"Hey," a boy of about ten said. I reached for my

flashlight and flicked it on. "Turn that off." At the frantic tone in his voice, I quickly extinguished the light. He used his own light to flash a couple of times and then apparently waited for the answer that came from the person on the racks. He sighed after a couple more exchanges.

The boy sat on a barrel and leaned on the balcony's railing as he peered over the zombie-filled space at the rack. From the brief instance that the light had been on the boy, I had noticed straight, black, shoulder-length hair that stuck to a face with a slightly darker complexion. It gave me the impression that he might be of Hispanic descent. He looked severely malnourished. The dark rims under his eyes expressed he hadn't had much sleep either.

Angie kneeled by his side and placed a gentle hand on the boy's shoulder.

"What's your name, kid?" she asked. The kid's head shifted before he answered.

"Toby, ma'am," he said.

"Yeah," Angie replied, and I could hear the delight in her voice. "Well, I'm Angie and the tall one behind me is Mags." Having spent a lot of time with Ash, we weren't that used to polite kids anymore.

"Hi," I said along with a wave of my hand.

Angie's tone returned to serious as she asked, "Who's out there, Toby?"

It wasn't hard to hear the despair in the boy's voice as he answered, "That's my sister."

Toby's seventeen-year-old sister Savanna had been stuck on a rack raised high over a sea of zombies for nearly four days now. Toby had been communicating with her by light signals all that time.

"Are you using the light so you won't rouse the zombies?" I asked as I leaned against the railing peering out into the darkness in the hope of catching a glimpse of the girl.

"No," he replied in a shy voice, "she's deaf." Eyebrows raised, I glanced over my shoulder. My eyes had somewhat adjusted to the dark, but I could still only make out the silhouettes of Toby and Angie, who had taken a seat beside him.

"That couldn't have been easy, running from zombies," I said. The girl wouldn't even hear them approach.

"I don't know," Toby replied, "but I think she might have developed a sixth sense or something, because she always seems to know when there's trouble." The kid's voice sounded brighter as he started to explain.

"She knew something was up even before most others knew. We'd been waiting outside in our dad's truck, watching one of the planes take off. I couldn't believe it as in midclimb the plane's wing started to tip, and it came crashing back down." Toby paused and took a breath to gather himself. "Everyone stood aghast as they watched the black smoke billow up in the distance, but not Savanna. Her gaze sat fixed on the opposite direction over the field and at the airport. Soon after, she was pulling me by the collar inside this place."

"What about your dad?" Angie asked hesitantly.

"I don't know," Toby said, sounding sad. "I never saw him again. I think he might be down there, and I've looked for him, but ..." The boy fell silent. At that point I felt relieved that the kid hadn't found his dad's face gazing up at him with those foggy, dead eyes.

"How has she gotten herself out there?" Angie asked.

"Because she's an idiot," Toby replied in a harsh tone.

"Hey, don't be like that. She's your sister," Angie said.

"She always thinks she needs to prove herself."

"Because of the hearing," I said.

"Yeah," Toby said, and I could still hear some

of that anger lingering in his voice. "She volunteered to get stuff from out there to back here, but one of the men fell, and she tried to help him. The zombies almost got her before she managed to back up." The boy's voice cracked and we waited patiently for him to continue. "They thought she might have been bitten, and Bob ordered the others out there to cut the ropes so she wouldn't be able to infect others."

"Why would he do that?" I asked.

"Because they didn't trust her to stay over there and wait to see if she were infected," Toby said.

I bit my lip to prevent myself from saying something I might regret. These people had been stuck here from the beginning; they might not have known that the virus worked fast and that the girl would have changed within minutes. And with her brain quickly reduced to mush, she wouldn't have been able to shinny those ropes.

"Have they tried to get her back over here?" I asked. Toby didn't answer aloud, so I turned to see his head shaking no.

"Bob thought it to be a lost cause," he added.

"Excuse me!" I said. A sudden rush of anger flashed through me and felt a need to vent it. I was ready to open my mouth when I felt Angie's boot kick me in the shins.

"What!" I said appalled.

"They haven't even tried?" Angie asked in a much calmer voice than mine.

"We wouldn't know where to begin," Toby said.

Overhead light started to filter inside the distribution center though the glass domes mounted on top of the roof. The sun had begun to rise. It shed a light on the terror that lay underneath my feet one story down, and I tried to ignore it as I leaned over the railing. My eyes searched the outer rim of the balcony and found the spot where another set of stairs would have been mounted. The ground floor continued underneath the balcony and revealed more of the undead. It wouldn't be easy, but it could be done.

"What are you doing?" Angie asked as I heard footsteps approach.

"Mags, Angie," Preston said before I could answer Angie, "I'd appreciate it if you two would let us know before you wandered off."

"Yeah, we almost left without you," Tom added.

"Tom, you wouldn't last a minute if you didn't have one of us to hold your hand," Angie said.

"Oh yeah," Tom uttered, "Well, let me——"

"What did Bob say?" I asked. The words came out sounding a bit condescending, and I cleared my throat. "I mean, how did he react?" Hearing that they hadn't even tried to get the girl had rubbed me the wrong way, but I wasn't in any place to judge.

Preston cocked his head, and I was sure he'd be giving me a look I wouldn't have appreciated, but fortunately the sun hadn't risen enough for me to see it.

"They are talking it over now, but I'm not sure Bob believed me," he said.

"That's not hard to believe," Angie said.

"Maybe we can show them that it works," I said.

| 16

Ash

Stuck in the back of an eighteen-wheeler truck tracking across country or wherever it was they were taking me, I sat tucked behind dozens of boxes holding God knows what, my chair bolted to the truck, my hands zip-tied to the armrest of my chair, and duct tape covering my mouth. This was turning out to be a bad day.

My backpack lay at my feet with most of the stuff that had been inside scattered about. Baldy had seemed very amused at the toddler-sized jeans that I was still carrying around. I had almost forgotten about the backpack that I had fastened to my chair.

I shivered and glanced at the discarded clothes on the ground. Moonlight filtered inside through the air grilles that allowed the temperature inside the truck to lower significantly. That extra sweater tossed on the ground looked very enticing at this point.

Wriggling around only made the zip-ties cut deeper into my skin, and I sighed. Fresh tears stung my eyes, but I noticed crying only made breathing harder with a piece of tape stuck over your mouth. It also didn't help the throbbing in my head, and I squeezed my eyes shut tight to force them down.

Opening my eyes, I noticed the small bulge on my left thigh. Baldy had checked my bag for stuff that I could use as a weapon, but he hadn't checked me. That guy actually was an idiot. A tiny sliver of hope lifted my spirits as I wriggled my hand below the armrest. I bit back the pain as plastic cut into my wrist.

Once my hand hung underneath the armrest, I stretched my fingers to reach the fabric of my cargo pants. Luckily they had a wide fit, and I tugged at it with two fingers until I managed to grab a handful of fabric.

It took some effort, but eventually I managed to take a hold of the pocketknife that I had snatched from my room. With the click on a button, it was easy enough to extend the blade, but cutting the zip-tie turned out to be a bit tricky.

"Son of a bitch," I called out as the sharp blade cut into my flesh. My hand shook, and I took a moment to calm my nerves. Steadying the knife, I continued to saw at the plastic.

Relief washed over me as the tie gave way, and I quickly freed my other hand. I closed the knife and stashed it back into my pocket. With a tentative finger, I poked at the bandage wrapped around my head and winced. My fingers came back dry, though, so the wound didn't seem to be bleeding anymore.

As I rummaged through the clothes, I found another black long-sleeved T-shirt and that sweater. Shivering all over, I removed my hoody, slipped on the extra T-shirt, and then put my hoody on again. The sweater was a bigger size, and I slipped it on over everything before extracting the hood and pulling it over my head. I instantly felt better, but I wondered if it would be enough.

It crossed my mind that I was probably lucky that this wasn't Alaska. I would have frozen to death already. The thought made me wonder what Mags was doing right now, whether she and Angie had been sent on their mission yet. *Would she know what had happened to me? Would Mars tell her?* Probably not. He hadn't told her about Warren in the first place. Boy, was she going to be pissed at him when he did. Usually, I wouldn't want to be in the room when that happened, but this time, I kind of hoped I would be, because that would mean everything had turned out okay.

The truck shook and groaned as it carved a way across the roads. There was no way I was getting off the thing at this speed, but that was a problem for later. First, I had to free my chair. I undid the strap that held me seated and then did the same for my legs and slipped out of the chair.

Inspecting the undercarriage, I noticed a chain wrapped around the axle between the frame and the rear wheel. Realizing the simple fix that was needed, I smiled. I should have known I could count on Baldy to take the easy route as he had he fastened the chair. This meant I only needed to remove the wheel axle bolt, remove the chain, and reattach the wheel. The action was simple enough. I had done it before, changing tires. I reached for the small tool pouch mounted underneath the seat and got to work.

I had my chair unchained, and the wheel reattached as I noticed the truck started to slow. Then I felt it turn a corner. Could it be we were leaving the freeway—if we were ever on it? Quickly, I gathered my stuff that was still scattered across the floor and shoved everything inside my backpack.

Something slipped from my grasp as I picked up a pair of Rowdy's jeans, and it thumped to the ground. It was Mags's phone. I lifted it from the floor and pressed the button. As the light flashed on, I smiled at the picture of Mags and me wearing aviator glasses and silly smiles plastered on our faces as we sat behind the wheel of the Knight XV. Those freaking tears started to sting again. This was getting ridiculous. I'd been in tougher spots before and came out of it okay. Except those times I hadn't usually been alone. Mags had been there, and no matter how bad the situation, she'd been a comfort to me. Guess I would have to do it on my own this time.

I checked the nonexistent signal on the phone, and considering it a bust, I shoved the phone in my pack. After I had climbed in my chair, I fasted the straps and made sure they were extra tight and secure. The backpack returned to its spot on the back of the chair. I rolled back and forth a couple of times to check the chair, but everything seemed in order. Now came the part of escape, but I had no idea how to do that.

A bunch of boxes surrounded me, maybe even hiding me from view in case the truck was stopped and maybe inspected. I managed to turn in the small space and rolled to one of the sides of the truck. Through a fissure between the boxes and the truck wall, I managed to see beyond the narrow space.

What looked like work tables stood bolted against the walls on either side of the truck. In the dark it was hard to see the equipment standing around, but the gleam from the stainless steel tables pretty much divulged their purpose. It seemed as if Warren had fashioned himself a miniature lab inside this truck, and I wondered if this wall of boxes was just a facade to keep me out of sight.

A tensioning belt held the boxes in place, and I reached up to release it. My fingers grazed the metal latch, but I couldn't find purchase. The chair tilted slightly, and I finally got it. The latch released, and in the same instance, the tower of boxes came crashing down on me. This wasn't exactly what I had hoped for, and I braced myself for the impact. Fortunately, the boxes were empty.

I just prayed the driver hadn't heard any of that as I shoved at the boxes. A couple of them I had to pick up and toss them aside, but soon I had a decent path to the back of the truck. As I neared the rear, the truck started to slow again and nearly stopped. My heart rate picked up. *Had we arrived? Had all this been for nothing?* I reached the door and grabbed the latch. Able to push it up, I felt relieved that door wasn't locked. I opened it at a crack and gasped at the distance I'd needed to bridge in order touch the asphalt. As the truck sped up again as it eased into a turn, I closed the door and pulled the latch down.

Still, this could be my window of escape, if I

could only find a way to lower myself. I inspected the door and noticed a horizontal rod that seemed to aid the locking mechanism. I spun around and rolled to the front of the truck where, hidden underneath the boxes, I retrieved the chain Baldy had used to tie up my chair.

Back at the door, I tied the chain to the horizontal rod and prayed it would hold me. After that there was nothing I could do but to sit and wait patiently. That and summon the courage to actually go through with it.

I had opened the door twice but chickened out. Inside, it seemed the truck slowed, but as I opened the door and watched the asphalt speed out from under the rear, I was certain I would break my neck. I wondered if that would be so much worse than what Warren had planned for me. Be careful what you wish for was what he had said after I called him out to bite me. *Could that be what he had planned? Was he going to feed me to the zombies?* A broken neck would surely be better than that scenario.

As the truck began to slow again, I figured this had to be it. I had no idea how far we'd traveled and how far there was still to go, but the longer I waited, the worse my chance of escaping would get.

The engine sputtered and the rig shook as the wheels came to a halt. Figuring now or never, I pushed up the latch, swung the door open, and held onto the chain. The momentum of the door pulled me along easily, and I rolled off the truck bed. I dropped hard and felt a jolt reverberate through my arms as the chain strained tightly.

As the truck pulled up, it triggered a motion that started me swinging. I had been working out to build up some arm strength, and I was pretty sure I had succeeded, but this was too much. I knew I wouldn't be able to hang on for long, and I moved my hands along the chain to lower myself. My wheels touched the ground, and still holding onto the chain, I was pulled by the truck. I released the chain, letting my momentum slow before I grabbed the push rings and then stopped altogether. The truck kept going and pulled around another corner. I let out a sigh of relief as it disappeared from view.

It was only then that I took a moment to see where I had ended up and froze. Slowly I moved my head from left to right as my eyes met with each of the five soldiers who stood before me.

17

Mags

We had explained the situation to Preston and Tom. The people occupying the distribution center who had been awake at this early hour had all gathered inside the lounge and were still conversing about our proposition to inject them with Divus. With nothing else to do, we figured it wouldn't hurt to try to rescue the girl in the meantime. Besides, retrieving the girl might aid in the decision-making process. It could be the thing that tipped their choice in favor of Divus.

The plan was simple enough. One of us would walk through the crowd of zombies, get to the girl, inject her, and then walk back with her. But as with most plans, it seemed simple enough as you say it aloud. The risk involved was one I preferred to avoid. Large crowds of zombies were unpredictable, and if something happened to agitate even one of them, then our immunity wouldn't be enough to get us out alive.

I shed my load carrier and M4, but kept the handgun strapped to my thigh. Preston handed me a little black box that held the syringe needed to inoculate Savanna, and I shoved it into one of the pockets of my pants.

"Here," he said, handing me a bandana, "you better tie that around your neck, so you can cover your mouth. It's bound to smell bad down there."

"You mean, worse than it does up here?" I asked and brought a smile to Preston's face. Maybe he wasn't such a hard ass after all.

"And why exactly is it that you're the one who has to go?" Angie asked, sounding not too happy. Enough daylight filtered in through the glass domes overhead now that it was hard to miss Angie's glare and the scowl on her face.

"Because we might need the guys' strength to pull us up if I get the girl back here, and because I have the most experience wandering among zombies," I replied, and to emphasize my point, I stuck my right hand in the air. Angie didn't seem impressed by my gloved hand wrapped in tape. She narrowed her eyes and cocked her head. I shifted uneasily as I tugged on the harness I would use to lower myself. My answer clearly hadn't satisfied her, and this was her way of sharing that. She was right, of course. Angie had the same if not more experience roaming around zombies.

"Besides, I'm taller," I blurted out. "I'll be easier

to spot when you need to take out zombies."

The expression Angie's face softened in what I was hoping would be resignation as she shook her head.

"Ash will kill me if anything happens to you," she said. I stopped pulling the rope through a loop and gazed up at her. In truth, I hadn't thought about that, and I probably should have. It wasn't just the idea of not being able to see the kid again, but she had lost so much already, and I didn't want to add to that pile. My gaze shifted to the other kid leaning over the railing flashing his light at his sister, and I knew Ash would want me to try to help them.

My eyes returned to Angie, avoiding looking at the zombie mass between her and the rack.

"It'll be okay," I said, hoping that I sounded more convincing than I felt. She threw her hands up in defeat and gathered her M4 from where she had placed it against the wall.

"Okay," she said and gave me a reassuring nod.

Tom stepped closer to Toby and placed a hand on the kid's shoulder.

"I didn't know that they teach kids Morse code in school anymore," he said, sounding impressed. Toby glanced up shyly at the rugged soldier and shrugged.

"My sister taught herself and then me," he

replied. "It's how we talked at night when we were supposed to be in bed. Our rooms sat opposite from each other and this way our dad wouldn't find out."

"Pretty smart," Tom said and watched how the kid continued to signal his message. A moment later he stopped and peered out at the rack in wait for a reply.

"Excellent," Tom said, having deciphered the returning message. "Now get back from the edge. You're freaking out the zombies below us, and we can't have them rattled." He pulled the kid away from the railing and ushered him further down the balcony.

Preston came up to me and checked my harness. He tugged on it so hard that the straps dug into my thighs.

"Thanks," I muttered. He looked up at me and held my gaze.

"Are you sure about this?" he asked. His voice held concern, and I appreciated the gesture.

"Not really," I replied honestly, "but I'm ready."

"All right then," he said and nodded. "Let's do this."

I walked up to the railing but stopped as Angie stepped in front of me. She glanced down over the railing and grimaced, but quickly hid it as she looked up to face me again.

"Be careful, okay," she said and pulled me into a hug. A bit shocked at the display of affection, I stiffened, but then hugged her back. For a moment I thought of the things that I wanted her to say to Ash, Mars, and even my family back home if I didn't make it out of that zombie pit, but I figured she would know.

"Thanks," I said instead. Angie released me, and I stepped forward, almost slamming into the railing at the heavy pat on my back. I gripped the iron bar and looked up the find Tom standing next to me.

"All in a day's work," he said as he attached the rope to the railing and threw the rest over the side. He steadied me as I climbed over the barrier and then checked the rope. "All clear."

I glanced down although I had promised myself not to, and swallowed hard at the sight of what awaited me at the end of this rope.

"Just take it easy," Tom said. "You'll be fine." I raised an eyebrow and grinned.

"You're not getting soft on me, are you?" I asked playfully.

"If you want me to push you, I'll gladly oblige," he replied, but he couldn't hide the kindness in his eyes.

"I'll remember that," I said and was ready to

lower myself as I heard commotion further down the balcony at the entry of the lounge.

"What do you think you're doing?" a large man called out.

"Bob," Preston said, quickly turning to the man and effectively cutting off his access to where the rest of us stood.

I heard Preston starting to explain our plan, but Bob seemed appalled by it.

"Are you people insane?" he said as he pointed an angry finger at Preston. "If you think we'll let your subordinate up here again, then you are mistaken."

"Please, Bob," Preston said, "just give us a chance to prove to you what this serum can do."

I watched as the men argued until Angie came up to me and squeezed my arm.

"Just go and don't worry about big Bob," she said. "If it comes to it, I'll kick his ass."

"And I'll be standing right behind her to cheer her on," Tom said.

Unable to help it, I chuckled. Bob was about my height, and I figured all four of us could fit inside him.

"Go slow, okay," Angie added.

"Yes, ma'am," I replied and stepped off the ledge.

Tom's pace in lowering me down was agonizingly slow. I wasn't sure if that was a good or a bad thing. This pace would probably keep me from arousing the zombies too much, but it also gave me time to think about what the hell I was doing. With every inch that Tom lowered me, I felt my nerves rise up.

I gazed up and saw the DC people watching me from the far left. Preston must have kept them at a distance so their scent wouldn't rattle the zombies. Above me, Angie peered over the railing, her eyes dark and focused. Tom stood by her side, his muscles straining and his face tight from the effort of lowering me.

"Pull your legs in," Angie said. Her voice was low, and I probably wouldn't have heard her over the groans and moans of the zombies below my feet, but her words sounded clear over the radio stuck in my ear.

My head shot up to face her and then down to see that the tips of my toes had almost come within reach of the outstretched arms of a zombie. Movement must have caught its attention. Most of the others still bumped and grinded against each other, not giving any indication that they had noticed or smelled my presence. That was the point, though. That was one of the things Divus did besides protecting you from the Mortem virus and keeping you from turning into a zombie—it repelled them.

"Pull them up, and Tom will lower you some more. Then you can ease your legs down at your own discretion."

The idea was sound, and I pulled my legs up as high as I could. The zombie that had raised his hands up groaned. I kept an eye on it as Tom lowered me again. Its irises swam behind a thick, milky fog. Eyes that seemed to track my movement otherwise looked abandoned and dead. The flesh on its cheeks was long gone, and I got a good look of its working jaw as it snapped its teeth. Its head started to sway a little before the zombie lifted its nose and sniffed. As if it had smelled something foul, it shuddered, lowering its arms and its gaze shifted down.

I took that as a cue to ease my legs down. A shudder similar to the one I had just seen ran through my body from the tips of my toes until it raised the hairs on my neck as the mutilated bodies bumped into my legs. Swallowing hard, I raised the bandana tied around my neck so it would cover my mouth and nose. Finally, I stuck a finger in the air to signal Tom to lower me the rest of the way.

I had stopped breathing by the time my feet touched the ground. The floor was slick, and I nearly slipped on something that felt soft and mushy underneath my boots, but I managed to steady myself on the rope that Tom had, thankfully, kept taut.

Eyes closed, I tried to find my bearings and forced myself to breathe. I needed air in my lungs if I wanted to do this. Bodies pressed into to me, and I wished I could banish the sensation of the decomposing corpses touching me.

"Mags," Angie said in a tentative voice, "you still with us?" I nodded my head vigorously as if Angie could see. The bandana did nothing to hide the putrid smell, and it was as if the taste of death lingered inside the back of my mouth. My heart pounded inside my chest as my body trembled, and I couldn't seem to get my eyes to open.

"Mags," Angie said forcefully, "just breathe." My eyes shot open at her loud voice, and I did as she demanded. I stared at the back of someone's head. Hair had been ripped from the scalp, leaving it bald in certain places, but it was better than glancing into those milky eyes.

"I'm okay," I said over the radio. "Just getting my bearings." I tried to sound more confident than I felt, but I knew Angie would see straight through it.

Knowing that if I didn't act soon, Tom would start to pull me up, I started to unhook my harness. From what I was seeing, I knew I'd have nightmares about this for the rest of my life, but if I didn't do this, then someone else might have them too.

Immediately after the rope released, I eased forward. I kept my hands to my side as I maneuvered through the sea of bodies as if I were attending a rock concert or something. The motion felt the same, although navigating though the decaying, near-stationary corpses didn't appeal as much as a bunch of people sweating and drinking beer. Still, I kept that thought in my head and even started thinking of songs to distract myself by remembering the lyrics. It seemed that the lyrics to "Sympathy for the Devil" were destined to run on repeat inside my head at that point. But it helped to focus as I tried to avoid looking at the faces in the crowd around me.

"You're doing great," Angie said over the radio. "Keep to your left."

From overhead, Angie had a better grasp of the situation, and I needed her to guide me through this. For all I knew, I was walking around in circles.

It started to get harder to push through the bodies without disturbing the zombies too much. They all stood too close together, and once in a while, I needed to shove my way through. I was breathing hard, but it wasn't so much out of fear than it was from the effort. The fear was still there, plenty of it, but every step seemed to cost more strength.

"How ... far?" I asked between gasps.

"About sixty feet," Angie replied. I tried to do the math as I pushed past another zombie. Its head snapped in my direction, teeth bared and jaw stretched open to its limit. Only one eye remained, leaving a black hole on the left side of its skull. I flinched as I saw something move inside it and jerked back. Tumbling backward, I collided with the zombies pressing at my rear. Some of them swirled around, flailing their arms, and I ducked. I ended up in a crouch facing the zombies at butt level. Their bodies started to crowd me, and I stretched my arms out to keep them at bay. Fortunately, the zombies directly crowding me all wore pants. Grimy, bloodied and disgusting pants in different sizes and shapes, but definitely pants. I heard Angie's slightly frantic voice over the radio.

"Mags, Mags," she called. "Where the hell did you go?" Before I could answer, she added, "You better get off your butt now so I can see you, or I swear to—"

"I'm here," I said.

"Well, I still don't see you." On hands and knees, I pushed past the legs, desperately trying to ignore the substances that saturated my pants, and I felt an undying gratitude for the gloves covering my hands.

A little to my left I noticed a bright yellow color peek between the forest of legs and moved toward it.

"Sixty … feet?" I asked, panting harder than before.

"What about it?" Angie asked. I wriggled past the last few pairs of legs and grabbed a hold of the yellow panel that belonged to a forklift.

Pulling myself to my feet, I asked, "How far was that again?"

"Jeez, there you are," Angie said, and I could hear the relief in her voice. "Well, it's more like sixty-five now and that's what"—she paused as if she were checking with someone—"about twenty meters. You know, you Europeans should think about losing your metric system."

I climbed onto the forklift until I reached the roof of the cabin and sprawled on top of it with my legs dangling over the side. My limbs burned from the effort, and my breathing came in ragged huffs as I stared up at the ceiling of the large building.

"Are you still alive up there?"

Angie's voice slowly filtered in, but it took a second, for the words to translate. It seemed that the situation that I found myself in kept my brain from functioning properly. I threw up an arm and waved in a big arc before I gathered my strength and managed to sit up.

I blinked as I tried to focus, and I noticed Angie and the rest standing on the balcony as if suspended over the crowd of zombies milling around like ants. My gaze shifted, and just as Angie had said, the rack that towered over us stood only meters away. A grim, streaked face peeked out from beside a couple of cases, staring at me with wide eyes. The young woman looked terrified, so I raised a hand and waved. She eyed me warily for a moment before she raised a trembling hand and waved back.

18

Ash

"Hi," I said as I raised a tentative hand. That must have adjusted their perceived threat level because all five of them lowered their weapons. I took the opportunity to glance around and found myself surrounded by tents—a lot of them.

Giant green tents that did not seem appropriate for a standard camping trip stood back to back. It looked like one of those refugee camps that the news used to show in places like Syria or somewhere in Africa. That thought rang a bell and reminded me of what Colonel Cornwell had talked about back at Cheyenne. He had mentioned these kinds of refugee camps. These places were meant for people who had fled across the Mississippi border to escape the zombie horde. He had even threatened to place me in one of those camps until Mars intervened and offered me a place with his parents. I bet he wished now that he hadn't done that.

Ignoring the shiver that ran up my spine, I glanced right, noticed stands rising beyond the tents, and figured it to be a stadium—maybe soccer or football.

Except for the soldiers, there weren't many people out, but then the sun had barely shown its face as it hovered on the horizon. I wondered if I could make a run for it. With all the gear the soldiers carried, I'd bet I'd be faster, but where would I go?

"Jesus, kid," one of the soldiers said as he took a step closer, "that was quite a stunt you pulled back there." Instinctively I gripped the push rings as the man drew closer and eased back. The soldier stopped, raising his hands in surrender, and smiled. "Easy," he said as he knelt in front of me and cocked his head. "Welcome to Salinas Sports Complex. My name is Sergeant Townsend. What's yours?"

"Ash," I said, keeping my guard up, "and I'm not very good at sports."

Townsend grinned. "Well, you could've fooled me."

He pointed a finger at my head as he said, "Do you mind if I get my friend Mike to take a look at that—he's a medic." I raised a hand to touch my head as if I needed to check what Townsend was pointing at. As soon as my fingers brushed the spot, I felt the pain flair up and I decided I wouldn't mind someone taking a look at it. My eyes shifted to the remaining soldiers standing behind him. They all looked alike to me—big, decked with gear and shaved heads, but it wasn't hard to spot Mike. He was the only one of the four who had a white band on his arm with a Red Cross on it, and even I knew what that meant.

Mike stepped closer and knelt at my side. He kept a little distance, and I wondered if that was for my sake or for his.

"Let's see what we've got here first," Mike said and clicked on a flashlight that he had retrieved from a pocket. Instead of pointing it at the top of my head, as I would have expected, the light flashed right into my eyes. I winced and shut them.

"I'm not a freaking zombie," I said, sounding agitated.

Mike grinned. "Sorry, kid, but you can't blame a guy for checking."

"Yeah, well, you could have warned me, and don't call me kid."

Mike cocked an eyebrow at that, and as his eyes ran over me, I knew what he must have been thinking. I was smaller than most others of my age. That had a lot to do with the drugs doctors had pumped into my system and the procedures that had been done to my body ever since I was a little kid. I wished I could have said it been worth it, but then my sister Alison would still have to be alive.

That didn't take away the fact that I loved my sister and had enjoyed every moment I had gotten to spend with her, so maybe it had been worth it. Besides, it hadn't been just the actions to save my sister that had kept me small. The cancer and the coinciding treatment that had started to ruin my body at a young age had its part in it, but I had hoped that would right itself after being exposed to Divus serum. Unfortunately, it wasn't showing yet.

Mike shook his head and reached up to remove the bandage.

"Stop," a loud voice called out. Mike froze on the spot and turned his head to see who was shouting. The other four including Townsend did the same. None other than Dr. David Warren stood behind them, in a military uniform no less.

I jerked my wheels to get out of there, but Mike stopped me.

"Please," I said to him. The pleading look that Mags used to joke about was definitely sincere this time, and the tears that sprang in my eyes couldn't be otherwise interpreted than the fear that I felt.

"Major," Townsend said as he sprang to his feet and jogged to Warren. As they spoke, I vigorously shook my head at Mike.

"He is not a major. His name is Dr. David

Warren."

"Mike," Townsend called out, "step away from her. She's infected. The rest of you guard her." My heart rate tripled as the remaining three soldiers raised their weapons and pointed them at me. In a reflex, I grabbed Mike's arm. He looked down at it and spotted the blood on my wrists from where I had cut it with my pocketknife. He jerked away from me, but stayed on his knees by my side.

"If you don't believe me," I said, "call Agent Marsden of the FBI—he'll vouch for me." The desperation was evident in my voice, and I hoped it wouldn't leave the young soldier untouched.

Warren waved around papers that seemed to have been enough evidence for the sergeant. I shouldn't be surprised; Warren would have his shit together.

"Soldier, step away from her," Warren said as he came closer. Mike glanced at his shoulder and then gave me a questioning look. I wondered if Warren had made the same mistake I had made with Luke. Perhaps Mike served as an airman and was expected to be called as much by a major.

"Please call Agent Marsden," I said again, but at a whisper so Warren wouldn't hear. Mike didn't give any indication if he would or not, but he rose to his feet and took a step back.

Baldy came running up behind Warren, also dressed in a uniform. The idiot actually wore a captain's insignia as if anyone would ever grand him that rank.

Instead of continuing my plea, I sought eye contact with Mike. Pleading wouldn't do me any good. Besides, Warren would probably be able to counteract anything I said with paperwork. I just hoped Mike would see the truth in my eyes as Baldy grabbed my chair started to push me to where I had seen the truck disappear around the corner. As we passed Warren, I kept my eyes on my lap. I couldn't handle seeing the smirk that would surely be plastered on his face.

| **19**

Mags

As I took a moment to compose myself, I glanced at the zombies between Savanna and me. The remaining bunch separating me from the girl seemed solidly packed together. The closest ones to Savanna stood clawing at the boxes stacked on the shelves underneath hers and from the looks of the damage to the boxes they had been doing that for a while.

A sense of dread collected in the pit of my stomach at the thought of getting back into the mix of zombies. The thought of climbing a rack that looked to be as high as a two-story building didn't appeal to me either.

I hadn't brought a rope, which I might have been able to use to climb over to her, but then I wasn't a cowboy, and I doubted I'd be able to throw it within her reach.

"What's the hold up?" Tom said over the radio, and I glanced in their direction.

"There is no way I'm going to get through that," I replied in an exasperated voice.

"So," Tom said. Along with the exhaustion, I started to feel annoyed.

"I'm open to ideas," I said, "or maybe you might want to get over here and show me." My tone was harsh, and I regretted it the moment the words left my mouth. Savanna was still watching me, and I tried to give her a reassuring smile. I felt glad that she wouldn't be able to hear the desperation that would have accompanied the anger in my voice.

"I have an idea," Tom said. There was mischief in his voice, but I felt too tired to counter it.

Instead I asked, "What?"

"Look down," he replied. I closed my eyes a moment to brace myself before I did as he asked. All I could see were the greasy and ragged heads of the zombies swaying from left to right as they shuffled an inch forward and then back again.

"I've got nothing," I said.

"You're sitting on it, for Christ's sake," Tom said in a raised voice.

"He means the forklift," Angie interjected. "You might be able to use that." I glanced down at the machine and then at the large crate that rested on the forks, but I couldn't see the forks themselves.

"Hah," I muttered.

With no better ideas springing to mind, I climbed off the top and eased myself into the driver seat of the machine. Seated, I could still see over the bumping heads, and it made me doubt that this machine could carve itself a path through the mass.

I eyed the controls; they looked familiar. At one of the warehouses that my dad owned, they used similar machines, although those were a bit smaller. I had worked in the family business for as long as I was able, and although the last few years it had been behind a desk, as a kid I used to work the floor. Usually that meant stuffing things into boxes, but occasionally it meant driving around in one of these things.

"You do know how to drive shift, right?" Tom asked. I was guessing Tom didn't know that in the Netherlands, and I was pretty sure in most of Europe, people primarily learned to drive using a gear stick. But, unwilling to answer him, I flicked the key that fortunately enough sat in the ignition, and the forklift rattled to life. I couldn't find any descriptions on the levers, so I tried them until I found the up and down one for lift. Before shifting into gear, I lifted the forks a little to raise the crate off the floor. This gave me some disapproving growls from the zombie onlookers. Ignoring them, I eased the machine forward.

This wasn't the Knight or even a Hummer, so I figured brute force wouldn't work with this thing.

Therefore, I eased it forward—nudging the zombies instead of ramming over them.

It worked, and I raised the lift when I thought it would be close enough to the rack where Savanna was. After parking, I climbed out of driver seat and onto the roof. In my head, it had seem a lot simpler to climb the side of the lift. There were plenty of handholds, but the crate stacked up on top of the forks turned out to be more of a box and less solid than I had hoped.

Clambering over the box, I place a foot on each fork. Forcing myself not to look down, I checked the rack for the best way to climb over to it. In doing so, I noticed Savanna shifting back against a box in the furthest corner she could find. Her wild eyes stared back at me, and she shook her head vigorously. She looked like a deer in headlights.

Afraid Savanna would freak out on me and cause me to fall, I paused and leaned against the box.

"What's the hold up?" Angie asked over the radio.

"I don't know, but she seems scared shitless," I replied. "She's acting all frantic."

"So get in there and knock her out," Tom said.

Ignoring him, I raised a hand palm out in an

attempt to calm the girl, but she kept shaking her head and pointing down.

"Nooo, you ... will ... turn," she said, stretching out all the words in an almost singsong voice.

"Savanna," I called out and then realized she wouldn't be able to hear me and started to wave before I pointed at my mouth. I spoke her name again but made sure to exaggerate in articulating the word with my mouth. Convinced I had caught her attention, I patted my chest and then made a motion that I would stay put. That seemed to calm her down.

"I think, she thinks that I'm going to turn into a zombie," I said. "I thought the kid had explained it to her."

"How much explaining can someone do using Morse code?" Angie replied.

"I guess," I muttered and then added more firmly, "Can you see if the kid can signal her some more?"

"Right," Angie replied.

I watched the movement of people up on the balcony, but from the corner of my eye, I noticed Savanna eying me suspiciously. Turning to her, I pointed a finger at myself and said, "Mags, my name is Mags."

The girl nodded that she understood.

"Nice … to … meet … you," she replied. I smiled at her and then glanced around.

"Just wished it had been elsewhere," I muttered. Savanna's brows furrowed and shook her head. She hadn't been able to decipher the words from my lips. I felt the heat crawl up my neck and flush my cheeks as I considered the rudeness of that. I pointed a finger down and made a swirling motion to indicate the zombies without looking down.

"Bad timing," I said. Savanna nodded in agreement and even threw me a little smile. A moment later her head shifted, and she crawled to the other side of the rack toward the balcony. I followed her gaze and saw the light of Toby's flashlight blink on and off.

It went on like that for quite a while, and I eased my butt up and onto the box. The material dented underneath my weight but otherwise seemed solid enough, and I relaxed my muscles.

The flashing continued as my legs dangled over the heads of too many zombies. The term *ridiculous* came to mind as I shifted the bandana across my nose. I had already tried to rub my gloves clean on the box, leaving streaks of blackened goo all over its brown surface. My pants saturated with the same stuff stuck to my skin, and I shuddered each time I thought of it.

"Is he reading her *Gone with the Wind* or something?" I said exasperated over the radio.

"Let me check," Angie said, which was an answer I hadn't expected. A moment later, her voice came over the radio again. "No, I think it's Harry Potter."

"It's *Harry Potter and the Sorcerer's Stone*," Tom said.

"You are not being funny," I said in a harsh tone. "Besides, it's *Harry Potter and the Philosopher's Stone*."

"It is not," Tom said appalled.

"Yes, it is," I said, pretty sure of my statement, because I owned hardback copies of all seven books.

Before our debate could progress into an argument, the light flashing stopped. Savanna slid back in front of the opening where I could see her, but her demeanor didn't tell me anything. I raised my shoulders questioningly, but she just pointed in the direction of the balcony.

"What?" I asked over the radio.

"Short version," Angie replied. "They know it takes time for the virus to take hold of a body, and she wants you to wait for a while to make sure you won't turn."

"Oh, come on," I said with a groan and almost ran a hand through my hair but stopped myself in time after seeing the smudges on the glove.

"Just give her a minute to convince herself you're not a threat," Angie said.

I huffed out a breath and leaned back on my hands, ignoring the groaning of the box underneath my weight.

Ash

They took my chair. I couldn't believe the bastard had taken my chair. They'd left me in a room the size of a closet with something you could barely call a mattress and a pillow. My backpack was gone, and even the pocketknife had been taken from me. The room was bare except for the sunlight that greeted me through a small window too high for me to reach without any aid.

After the effort of escaping that truck to end up in here, I couldn't stop the anger building inside me as it slowly morphed into rage, but there was no way to vent it. Punching the wall hadn't helped and had only left me with a bruised hand. Screaming hadn't helped either. I grabbed the pillow and whacked it against the wall again and again. I hadn't meant to unleash the near-primal roar that exited my throat, but it seemed to help as I felt my arms grow tired.

The door to the small room opened, and Baldy stuck his head inside.

"Uh," he said, looking at me dumbfounded, "everything all right."

I grabbed the pillow and launched it at him. Baldy didn't even try to duck and caught the soft material in the face. He glanced at the pillow for a moment as it lay at his feet before he turned back to me.

"Go away, Baldy," I said as I let myself fall over on the mattress.

"Sure," he said. I poked my head up to look at him.

"Hey," I said, feeling a bit calmer. "What's your name anyway?"

Baldy looked to be surprised at my question but opened his mouth to answer. "Chester."

My mouth fell open; I couldn't help it.

"Chester," I said, hearing the incredulity coming from my voice. "You're an evil badass and muscle for hire named Chester."

"I'm not an evil badass," he replied. Apparently, that being the only thing he had taken away from what I'd said.

"You're not?" I asked with surprise.

"Warren has presidential orders."

I glared at him. "Orders from the president?" I said.

Chester nodded emphatically.

I had nothing further to say to that and fell back on the mattress again. The door clicked shut, and I closed my eyes. That throbbing in my head had returned with a vengeance and I would have loved some pain medication right now. I pinched the bridge of my nose, hoping that would help, because I wasn't expecting any of those pain meds anytime soon.

A moment later, I raised my head as the door clicked open again. Chester stuck his head in the opening.

"I thought this might make you feel better," he said with a sheepish look on his face. It crossed my mind that maybe this guy really wasn't such a badass. He held out my backpack and swayed it back and forth. I sat up as he stepped inside and handed it to me.

"Thanks, I guess," I said as I looked up at him. He showed me some teeth, and I assumed it to be a smile before he turned and headed for the door. He stopped for a moment, grabbing the pillow I had thrown at him off the floor and tossed it back to me. Then he left, closing the door behind him.

There wasn't much inside the bag that could help me. I didn't think I'd be digging a hole out of here with a toothbrush, but still, the familiarity of the stuff gave me little a comfort. I was still wearing the extra sweater that I'd put on inside the truck. Fortunately, the temperature inside this closet was warm, so I pulled it over my head and shoved it in the bag. My fingers traced the hard plastic of its cover, and I pulled out the phone. A mixture of excitement ran through me as I switched it on, but as soon as the photo on the lock screen appeared, it faded instantly. I didn't have to unlock the screen to see there was no signal—not a cellular, GPS, or Wi-Fi signal anywhere. For good measure I held the phone higher, but to no result.

At that point, it was as if the energy drained from my body. I felt tired, but most of all helpless, and I hated it. With force, I grabbed my legs one by one and deposited them onto the mattress. Meanwhile, I cursed the unmoving limbs. I punched my left leg for good measure, grabbed the pillow, and crashed on the mattress. Intellectually, I probably knew my legs had nothing to do with my situation. This could have also happened if I'd been able to walk—maybe I just needed something to blame.

To distract myself, I grabbed the phone and opened the photo app. The recent additions were mostly of Rowdy doing the most stupid things, like trying to stuff a carrot up his nose, and the most adorable things, like handing his grandfather a hammer as he helped to remove the threshold at the backdoor. I quickly skimmed through the pictures of

Mr. and Mrs. Marsden as the pain of their loss was still too fresh and I couldn't mourn them now, not here. A close-up of Angie sticking out her tongue made me smile. The next one was a picture of Mags kissing Mars as they said good-bye before Mags left for Alaska. It looked like one of those pictures that came with a new frame as if it were staged out there on that airfield with the sun falling behind them. I think they didn't even know I had this or that it existed.

Behind me, I heard the door open and figured it to be Chester. But then I flinched at the voice as Warren spoke up.

"I see you've gotten yourself comfortable." I jerked up, hiding the phone underneath my pillow and shifted so I nearly sat on top of it. "Chester, would you come in here for a second?"

Warren crossed his arms over his chest as he waited for Chester to appear. The big man eyed Warren questioningly as he pointed at the backpack. "Is that one of your brighter ideas?" Warren said. Chester shrugged.

"It's just some clothes and some knickknacks, nothing than could help her. I've checked," he said. "I thought it might … just … you know."

"I don't know," Warren said. "Now take that and go get a chair."

Chester shrugged again and gave me an apologetic look as he retrieved the bag and stepped from the room. Warren narrowed his gaze at me, and I swallowed hard as he closed the door.

"Now, sit still," Warren said as he lifted my chin. Chester had moved me into a chair and had tied my hands behind my back before he had removed the bandage from around my head. Blood had coated the rag and clung to my head like a Band-Aid. Apparently, Chester did not have the sense to rip it off like a Band-Aid, and it had hurt like hell as he slowly peeled it from my head.

Warren pulled my hair back as he hovered over me, and I felt the first sting just below my hairline. I squeezed my eyelids shut as tears sprang to my eyes, and I strained my jaw to keep my mouth shut. He took his time pulling the thread through the skin, and it felt like torture. I squirmed in the chair, wishing I could wriggle out of there, but the restraints kept me firmly in place.

"Hold still," Warren said sounding agitated. "You didn't act like such a child when I stitched up your leg all that time ago."

"I was sort of unconscious then," I said through clenched teeth.

"And I used a sedative now," he said.

"Well, maybe you should have used some more," I said and hissed, as I felt him poke my skin again. I internally cursed Warren for taking his time as if he were deliberately prolonging my agony.

"There," he finally said, "all done with only four stitches. Those head wounds always look worse than they are." He stepped back to admire his work before he plastered some gauze on my forehead with tape.

I blinked the residual tears from my eyes as Warren turned his back to me to pick up the small black pouch that held his medical supplies. He took out a pill bottle and shook out a tablet. He returned the pill bottle to the pouch and exchanged it for a bottle of water.

I bit my lips, holding them shut as he attempted to shove the pill in my mouth. He arched an eyebrow and shook his head before he held out the pill for me to see. I read the tiny letters on the pill and blew out a breath—Advil, maybe there was a God. I hesitated a moment longer but figured that if he wanted to drug me, he would have others ways to do that, and I opened my mouth to accept the pill.

Water trickled down my chin as he offered me the bottle. I wiped my mouth on my shoulder and eyed Warren suspiciously as he placed the bottle in his pouch.

"There," he said as he moved around me, "all done and I doubt it'll leave a scar." I felt that the bindings restraining me loosened and once released pulled my hands upfront and rubbed my wrist.

"What do you care?" I said. He grinned, looking down at me, and I imagined a sardonic laugh would have completed the picture, but fortunately he deprived me of the pleasure.

"I care for as long as I need you to get what I want," he said. I narrowed my eyes at him, not sure what he meant, but eager to find out. *What possible reason could he have to hold me?*

"Well, it seems you've finally figured out the *zombies-don't-touch-me* serum. So I can't think of anything you would want from me," I said in an attempt to taunt him.

"Yes," he said with a chuckle, trying to disguise the frustration in his eyes, "but that was never the point now, was it?"

I glared at him. "Please don't tell me you're still looking for that super soldier solution," I said mockingly, "because I can't picture you as a super villain. I'm thinking more in the line of the Smurfs and a balding guy named Gargamel."

Warren didn't say anything, but I could see the anger in his eyes. Aggressively he stepped closer, and although I feared he might strike me, I raised my chin. At least I could pretend I wasn't afraid of him. He didn't hit me, though. Instead, he grabbed the back of the chair and tipped me over. I slid off the seat and landed sideways on the mattress with a thump. He held onto the chair as he kneeled in front of me.

"You're actually not that far off," he said in a low voice as he stared into my eyes. "All I need to finish my work is to get my hands on your friend Ms. Vissers one last time, and you're going to help me get her."

"No," I said in a loud voice as I pushed myself upright. "I won't help you with that."

He smirked as he said, "Oh, but you already have. You're doing it right now." He laughed aloud as he stood up. With the chair in hand, he walked to the door and opened it. "Sweet dreams."

"Fuck you," I shouted after him, but the door locked and he was gone. All I could do was sit there and stare at the door as the fact that Warren was using me as bait to get to Mags ran through my mind.

| 21

Mags

Savanna was still eyeing me warily. To let her know I was still me, I had waved at her a couple of times and had removed the bandana.

I glanced at the watch on my wrist and realized I had been sitting there for half an hour. That word *ridiculous* crossed my mind again, but then I couldn't blame Savanna for being cautious.

She caught me eyeing the watch, and I shrugged. I didn't want to push her, but I was getting tired of sitting on this box. Luckily the box sat mounted on a pallet or else I might have been freaking out. I had made quite a dent in the material. Savanna bit her lower lip, clearly not sure of herself as she scrutinized my face. Determination crept into her eyes as her lips pulled into a thin line. Straightening her shoulders, she nodded her head.

Finally, crossed through my head, but I plastered a smile on my face as I placed a foot on each fork and stood. My smile faded at the sight of the distance I had to breach and the zombies that I would have to hop over. Fortunately, I had long legs.

Shifting over to the right fork, I stretched out my arms for balance. I reminded myself to take it slow and then edged forward on the narrow fork. Something metal clanked, and my heart jumped. My eyes shot to the machine that was supposed to carry my weight. The fear of it not being able to jolted me out of balance, and I waved my arms to gain it back.

I managed not to fall and stood still for a moment as if waiting for the machine to tip over. It didn't and it felt solid underneath my feet. Shaking off the idea that the lift wouldn't be able to hold me —which seemed ridiculous anyway—I focused on a spot to grab hold of the rack. I edged as close as I could, and then let gravity do the rest.

My right foot caught the ledge I was aiming for, and my hands gripped for the ledge above. Hanging off the side of the rack between two shelves, I edged sideways to the opening between the boxes on the shelves where Savanna sat waiting for me.

This climbing was harder than it looked, and my muscles started to tremble with the effort. I lost my grip with my right hand, which wasn't that surprising considering the missing fingers, but it took me off balance in the middle of taking a step. The ledge seemed to have vanished as I searched purchase for my left foot, while I felt my right starting to slip. Panic set in at the thought of tumbling down into the midst of the zombies below my feet. I doubted they'd be as forgiving if I came crashing down on them, and I imagined being eaten on impulse even if they didn't like what they were snacking on.

In the middle of that thought, I felt hands wrap around my waist and holding me steady. Savanna had come out of the depths of her hiding spot and tried to pull me in. I swung my body and let her reel me inside.

Our bodies crashed on the wooden shelves that had been Savanna's sanctuary for the past few days. The moment after crashing safely to the floor, Savanna pulled away from me and ducked into a corner. I just lay there panting from the effort while my heart pounded in my chest so loud that it made me think the people standing on the balcony could hear it.

"Jeez, Mags, you okay?" Angie called out over the radio. Gasping for air, I wasn't exactly able to answer, but I clicked on the mic anyway.

"Are you auditioning for a service that provides phone sex?" Tom asked.

"Shut ... up," I wheezed and turned my attention to Savanna. "Just ... gotta ... catch my breath." I waved a hand in the air as if that would explain it all and sat up straighter.

The fear in Savanna's eyes was evident, but she stayed in her spot, although she had some room to maneuver. The small space could barely fit two people but seemed to be Savanna's main hangout. A blanket lay at her feet while a couple of empty cans and candy wrappers lay in the corner. A couple bottles of water stood neatly in another corner. A narrow opening that she must have created by shoving boxes to a side and most likely off the rack ran as far as I could see toward the other side of the distribution center and probably went as far as the rack would allow it. The space reminded me of a tree house, but not one that one would want to spend days in—especially not with all the zombies milling around it.

Without taking her eyes off me, Savanna shifted and reached for the corner with the bottles of water. She grabbed one and then tossed it to me. I nodded with a smile, mouthing *thank you* to her, and then drank it eagerly.

As my heart rate calmed and my breathing evened out, I sought a comfortable position to sit. I didn't know what she had learned from all the light flashing, but I felt the need to explain it to her myself. It didn't seem wise to pull out the box with the needle and just stick her with it. She needed to understand the consequences, and I knew it wouldn't be easy to explain, especially the technical medical bits. Those would be hard to understand even without her hearing disability, but I would certainly try.

Savanna's focus didn't waver from my mouth as I spoke. It felt a little animated at first, but I soon realized Savanna was pretty skilled at reading lips, so I only needed to use the exaggerated mouth thing with the bigger technical words.

"You ... have ... in you," she said in her singsong voice as she pointed at the black box that I had removed from my pants pocket.

"Not exactly," I said. "It sort of came from me."

Her eyes widened at my statement, and she opened her mouth as if to say something, but then closed it. She narrowed her eyes and cocked her head before she said, "So ... you can make ... zombies."

It wasn't as much a question as it was a statement, and it made my stomach churn. I dropped my eyes and found myself staring at the gross stains on my pants. This information wasn't new to me, but hearing it said aloud triggered a gut-wrenching feeling. It made it that more real.

I hadn't answered Savanna's question, but I

guessed my body language had said enough.

"Sorry," she said in a soft voice. I shook my head and then lifted it so she could read my lips.

"It's okay."

At that, Savanna smiled a genuine smile that lit up her beautiful face and said, "Yes, because you're … alive."

It was something in the way she had said it—in a determined way maybe. I couldn't quite place it, but it made me return her smile. She was right of course; anything would be better than death or running around like a zombie.

Savanna started to tug on her shirt that must have been white at some point. She rolled up her sleeve and gave me access to her arm.

"You sure?" I asked giving her a hard look.

She held my gaze as she replied, "Yes."

"Okay," I muttered and reached for the box.

I removed my gloves and used some disinfecting wipes, although I doubted it would be enough to thoroughly sanitize my hands, but they looked clean. Savanna seemed to be hypnotized by the movement, until I realized she was watching my right hand. She winched a little as I held it up as if she were imagining how painful it must have been.

"Zombie ate my fingers," I said in a light tone that was probably fruitless.

"Was this ... when you ... found out that?" Savanna said and hesitated.

"That I wouldn't turn," I said finishing the question for her. She nodded her head. I shook mine and said, "Unfortunately, this was the second time I'd let myself get bitten."

Savanna let out a sigh and shook her head.

"Not ... very smart," she said. I glanced up and smiled as I took the box.

"Nope," I said before I held the box out for her to see. An empty syringe and two small vials sat neatly tucked into the foam that held them in place. "You sure you want me to do that?"

She grinned and nodded a yes in reply.

I followed the instructions, just as Dr. Chen had shown us. The doctor had taught all four of us how to mix the substances and to administer the serum, and soon enough the syringe was empty.

Savanna stared at her arm before turning to me and shrugged.

"I don't ... feel ... anything," she said. Dr. Chen had promised me that he had averted the previous effects of the virus. I remembered far too well when Dr. Matley had tested the serum on Angie. It had been painful, and it still raised the hairs on the back of my neck as I thought of Angie tied up on that bed screaming in agony. Chen said that he had perfected the process, and from what I could tell, Savanna seemed fine.

"How will ... I know ... it works?" Savanna asked.

"Well," I said, with a shrug and crawled to the edge of the shelf. I lay down on my stomach and peeked over the edge. Savanna followed me and lay down at my side.

"They've stopped clawing at the boxes stacked underneath your little hideout," I said but then realized I hadn't faced her.

"They're ... gone," Savanna said, coming to the same conclusion and assuring that I didn't need to repeat myself. "I mean ... no more ..." She broke herself off, extended a hand and mimicked a clawing motion.

Presuming she meant the zombies, I held up my thumb, and Savanna visibly relaxed.

"Now ... what?" she asked.

| **22**

Ash

Sleep didn't come easily that night. At first, my own thoughts kept me from falling asleep, and then the nightmares kept me from sleeping. I sat with my back propped against the wall, waiting for the sunrise to release me from this darkness.

Occasionally I peeked at the time and hoped it to be correct. Assuming I was still in the same time zone, the sun should be coming up soon. I didn't think we had traveled far enough to change time zones. At least I hoped we hadn't. Actually, I had no idea how long we had traveled—not inside the truck and certainly not inside the van. I had missed that trip entirely after I had bumped my head.

I was tempted to look at the phone again, but forced myself not to—afraid they'd see the light and take it from me. I also couldn't put any music on to soothe my mind because I had left the damn earplugs inside the backpack.

"Goddammit," I said aloud, unable to distract my mind. I couldn't stop thinking about what Warren had said, that he was using me to get Mags here. I couldn't let him do that, but I had no idea how to stop him. If Mags knew Warren had me, I was sure she'd come get me. She tended to do stupid things like that.

Warren had also said that I wasn't that far off when I mentioned the super soldiers. That was Warren's idiotic idea that started this zombie situation in the first place. *But what did that have to do with Mags?*

I sighed as I felt the headache return. *Why couldn't that man see what he had done?* Apparently, he didn't care, and it seemed he wasn't finished yet either.

The sound of something scratching pulled me out of my thoughts, and I looked up. It came from the window. I shifted so I could take a better look as the window slid open and someone poked their head inside.

"Who the hell are you?" I asked, unable to recognize the face in the darkness. My heart raced as my hand clamped around the phone.

"Good morning," a familiar voice said and I sat up straighter.

"Mike," I said questioningly.

"The one and only," he replied.

"What the hell are you doing here?"

"Well, and hello to you too," he said. I squinted,

hoping to get a better look at him, but his face remained a silhouette. "I just thought I'd come see how you were doing. I hadn't seen you after your impressive entry." The sound of Mike's voice and his presence at that window let all kinds of hopes and possibilities rise up inside me.

"Did you call Agent Marsden?" I asked hopefully.

"Uh," was the only thing that came as a reply, and those hopes and possibilities threatened to drown.

"Please, Mike," I said, "you have to call him. It's just one phone call."

"Listen, I checked around," he said. "So did Sergeant Townsend. We all found it weird the way things panned out, and Townsend took it all the way up with the base command, but they all said the same thing. This Major—what's his name—is the real deal, and he has permission to keep you here so you can't infect anyone."

"That's bullshit," I fumed. "Why the hell would anyone bring someone that's infected to a refugee camp, because that's what this is, right? That man is Dr. David Warren, and he caused this outbreak in the first place."

"Well, considering the info I got, I think you're wrong about that last bit, but I agree with you on the first," Mike said, "and that's kind of why I'm here."

"Then please call Agent Marsden," I said, sounding desperate. "Tell him Ash asked for him." Internally I cursed the darkness because I couldn't see Mike's face and had no idea of his reaction.

"Listen, kid," he said with a sigh, "I'm not going to go against orders here."

"Calling the FBI is not against your goddamned orders, and don't call me a fucking kid."

The room fell silent for a moment until Mike added, "Okay." He drew out the word, and I closed my eyes, letting out a sigh.

"I'm sorry," I said, hoping to ease the mood. "I'm just a bit desperate here and maybe on the brink of insanity, but that doesn't mean I'm wrong."

A light switched on in the connecting room sending a yellow glow underneath my door.

"I've gotta go," Mike said.

"Mike," I pleaded, "please don't go." The door behind me clicked open just as the window slid shut. I turned to see Chester enter the room. Without a word, he reached for me and grabbed me by the arms.

"Wait," I said, "what are you doing?" He jerked me up, tossing me over his shoulder. "Chester, please wait." My fear was evident from the words I spoke. Rattled by this sudden change in events, I lost the grip on my phone, and it fell with a thump on the mattress. Unceremoniously, Chester carried me outside where the sun had finally started to rise.

I looked up to see the small structure where I'd been staying these past hours. Tents surrounded the place, and a couple of people poked their heads out as I called for Chester to stop.

"Being kidnapped over here," I shouted at them, but except for sharing some confused glances, they did nothing. Two soldiers stood in a pathway that led down the middle of two rows of tents and stared after me. "C'mon, I need help here."

I had barely spoken the words when I saw Mike walk up to them. He pointed at me, said something, and then shrugged.

"Big fat help you are," I shouted at him just before Chester rounded a corner and the men disappeared from view.

Midstride, Chester half-turned—probably to see whether anyone was following him. I bet he wished he had taped my mouth shut. As he did, I saw where he was taking me and swallowed hard at the sight of the massive black eighteen-wheeler truck.

23

Mags

For once things seemed to go my way. The zombies had lost their taste for Savanna, which left the remaining DC people standing on the balcony as an even more enticing snack. The pack that had crowded Savanna's hideout had made a forty-five-degree turn and now faced the balcony, pushing and shoving each other in an attempt to get closer to the people who triggered their noses.

What could only be called a migration opened up some room at the back of the DC, and that was where we were heading. I followed Savanna down the narrow corridor to the far end of the rack. Reaching it, I couldn't help a gag reflex at the smell that made its way up my nose. I pulled the bandana up to cover my nose and mouth and noticed the embarrassed look on Savanna's face. She gave me an apologetic smile before her gaze fell to the floor. It occurred to me that she had reserved this area for toilet use. I just shrugged and squeezed her arm. She had to do her business somewhere.

With the bandana over my mouth, I wouldn't be

able to talk to her, but the smell combined with the stench of decay was kind of overwhelming, so I kept it on. I tapped Savanna's shoulder to grab her attention and then tapped my chest and pointed down.

Fear flashed across her eyes, but I also caught her clenching her jaw, and she gave me a firm nod. I squeezed her shoulder for some final reassurance and then started my climb down.

Savanna gazed down upon me with wide eyes as I hopped off the final ledge and landed next to a zombie. It startled a bit as I hit the ground. I instantly froze and didn't move an inch. From my slightly bent position, I had an excellent view of the hole in its stomach that had some blackened entrails hanging out. I held my breath until the zombie lost interest and started to follow the rest in the direction of the balcony.

I shook my head, but it did nothing to settle the urge to throw up, so I focused on Savanna, who had started her climb down. Just before she jumped the last edge, my hand automatically moved to the gun strapped to my hip.

The zombies stood in little clusters, and some wandered in-between as if on the edge of the crowd of that concert that had sprung to mind earlier. I carefully watched their faces, scanning for that twitch of their heads and the raising of noses in the air. None of that happened as Savanna took the leap of that last ledge.

She hid behind my back as if that would protect her against a zombie onslaught. With her limited height, she could barely see over my shoulder. We stood like that for a long time, just waiting and hoping.

As it became clear that we were of no interest to the unlikely crowd, I turned to Savanna and pulled the bandana down. I needed to be able to communicate with her. Going back the same way I had come wasn't an option for me; besides, I didn't think we'd be able to get past the zombies anymore. Not after the ones here in the back had joined the front—they were packed too close together now.

Grabbing Savanna by the shoulders, I pulled her attention from the mutilated corpses.

"Where to?" I asked. Shocked eyes stared back at me as if she couldn't grasp what was happening, but I needed her to show me the way. From what I had learned before, the group residing inside the DC had used ropes to climb from rack to rack, and they had severed the connection with Savanna's rack so she wouldn't be able to get back. So I gathered that we just needed to find a rack that would get us back to the balcony. It seemed simple enough, if I got Savanna to tell me where to go.

The young woman standing in front of me was a trembling mess. Even with her dark complexion, I could tell all the blood had drained from her face.

"Savanna," I said. She didn't hear me. Well, of course, she didn't hear me. I snapped my fingers in front of her eyes, and she blinked. Focus returned to her dark eyes, and she blinked again.

"There you are," I said. Her head shifted nervously from left to right, and I feared her eyes were about to roll out of their sockets. I squeezed her shoulders again and forced her to look at me.

"Tell me where to go, Savanna," I said. I sounded as if I were addressing a small child, and I didn't like it. Savanna probably had people talking to her like that her whole life, but she didn't seem to mind it this time. She pointed to her right at the large rack parallel to ours.

"That's it," I said with a smile and turned to guide us in that direction.

After we had made our way up, we crawled down a path carved out of boxes and crates on one of the levels of the giant rack. With the use of ropes, we shimmied over to one of the neighboring racks and again followed a path that led us to a gap that had to be at least ten meters and was effectively a dead end. Savanna motioned to me with her arms mimicking a swing. I looked around and found the ropes that she would have likely used before to manage the gap, but unfortunately, they lay in a pile on the other side.

I glanced over Savanna's shoulder in the direction of the balcony and noticed only the group from the DC still standing there. Knowing Angie and the others would probably show up at any minute, I took the time I had to rest my limbs and sat down with my feet dangling over the edge of the rack. Savanna joined me and we sat in companionable silence for a moment until Savanna tugged at my shirt.

"Thank … you," she said. I wanted to say that she should thank me if we made it out of here, but at that moment, the others decided to make their entrance.

"Took you long enough," I called out to beat Tom to the punch. Angie, Preston, Tom, and even young Toby came jogging down the hall. They stopped at the edge, where I couldn't detect any evidence of residual stairs, so the railing had probably been removed.

"You okay," Angie said.

"Just peachy," I replied.

They swung the rope over to us, and about five

minutes later, we stood on the other side, where I wrapped my arms around Angie, relieved that at least this part was over.

"God, you stink," she said as she hugged me tighter.

"Odor de zombie," I said as I released her. Preston patted me on the back.

"Good job," he said, looking at the girl.

"It was decent enough," Tom said with a smirk.

"Coming from you, I'll take that as a compliment," I replied.

"Well, don't let it get to your head," he said before he pointed at the girl. "Who's this?"

"This," I said, tapping Savanna on the shoulder and waited until she released her death grip on Toby, "is Savanna."

I pointed the others out to her and clearly spoke their names.

"She's pretty good at reading lips," I said to the others, but not turning my gaze from Savanna, "so try to face her when you speak."

"We will," Preston said. "Now let's get you guys cleaned up."

"You're stinking up the room," Tom added. I shot Tom a look, but Savanna didn't seem to mind and threw him the biggest smile. I glared at Tom as his face grew bright red.

"C'mon, Rambo," Angie said and grabbed him by the arm. "Let's go."

"Preston," I said, taking a couple of big strides to catch up with him, "any progress with the others?"

He continued walking, but shot me a sideways glance.

"Bob is not the easiest guy to convince," he said. "I'm starting to fear our trip might have been for nothing."

"Well, not entirely for nothing," I said. I glanced over my shoulder where Savanna was holding a tight grip around Toby's shoulders. Preston smiled at that and said, "No, not for nothing."

We rounded a corner, and I almost bumped into Angie who stood alongside Tom with her hands at her side slightly parted from her body. Tom stood in attack position pointing his weapon at Bob, Marcus, and several other men who held guns of their own.

At the sight of them, one of Preston's hands reached for his weapon while he raised the other palm pointing out.

"Whoa, easy," he said. "Everyone relax." His words didn't change anything in the men's positions, guns were still raised, but on the bright side, they weren't shooting each other. "What's going on?"

"Those two are infected," Bob said. "And by

now, you're probably all infected."

"What are you talking about? We're not infected," Angie said.

"We all saw what happened," Marcus said. "That one almost got herself buried under the things." He said those last words pointing a finger at me. He spoke the truth of course, and normally I wouldn't have had a problem with that, but in the way he said it, it sounded as an insult. I stepped around Angie, which inclined the men to point their guns at me, and I raised my hands.

"We are not infected," I said, trying to keep the calm in my voice.

"All right, enough," Preston said. "What is it you're trying to gain here?"

"We want you to leave," Bob said. Shock ran over me in a wave.

"Excuse me!" I said.

"You heard me," Bob replied. He shot me a more than angry look.

"We are the only outside contact you've had in months—military," I said, "and you want us to leave?"

Ignoring me Bob turned, jabbing his gun in Preston's direction as he spoke.

"I don't know what kind of games you're playing, but we want none of it. You can join those ungodly creatures out there as long as you leave us alone."

My mouth had fallen open at that point, and I turned to face Angie. She just shrugged as if she'd seen it all before.

"Fine," Preston said, "if you just point us to the door." He knew perfectly well where the door was, but the fact that five men with guns blocked the hallway that led to it, presented us with the issue of getting there.

"We've already placed the rest of your stuff at the end of the hallway," Marcus said. "Now leave." All five men started to back up until they cleared the hallway that we needed to take.

Tom started to ease his way to our exit but kept his weapon trained on the men. Slowly we followed him, one by one, eyes focused on the men with guns. Bob held his chin up as if he'd been sitting on his high horse for too long. He somewhat reminded me of that father I had met with Ash, which seemed like ages ago. He had a similar way of tending to his flock. The fact that I couldn't remember the rest of the father's name kind of felt reassuring. It made me think that maybe one could get past the nasty experiences in life, or at least forget them.

The rest of the men had eyes big as saucers as if they were high strung on caffeine, and now I started to resent them for not offering us any coffee when we'd first got there. I realized my mind was going all over the place. Must have had something to do with a hell of a crappy day that I'd had to deal with. Fortunately, a voice pulled me out of that haze.

"What about us?" Toby said, his voice a trembling mess. I turned to him unaware that they hadn't followed. It had seemed logical to me that they would.

"You're coming with us, of course," I said. I didn't check with the others for their opinions, because the two siblings were coming with us, but I doubted there would be any objections. Savanna gave me a faint smile as I reached out my arm and signaled her to come. She pulled Toby into her arms and moved cautiously to me. Once in range, I wrapped an arm around her and led her past Preston and Tom into the hall.

The five men remained at the beginning of the hall and stood there watching us while we found the rest of our gear. I released Savanna to collect the rest of my stuff as Angie stepped closer.

"Are you planning to adopt them too?" she asked.

I stood, connecting my M4 to the load carrier vest with a clip before I let my eyes fall on Angie.

She gazed up at me with a goofy grin. "I'm just

asking."

I just shook my head and sighed.

24

Ash

"Strap her in," Warren said after Chester dragged me inside the truck. Chester carried me past the improvised lab tables and sat me down in a corner. To my surprise, I was sitting in my trusted wheelchair. Though the chair was probably chained to the rig again, I couldn't help the sigh of relief that passed my lips.

"I can do it," I said agitated as Chester started tugging at my legs. I grabbed the straps from his hands and fastened them myself.

Chester looked up at Warren, who was peering into a microscope.

"Do you want me to tie up her arms?" he asked.

"No, just keep an eye on her," he said without looking up from what he was doing. Chester shrugged and walked the short distance across the rig and planted himself in a chair.

I was still feeling angry about the conversation I'd had with Mike and his inability to act. That little walk of shame slung over Chester's shoulder hadn't done wonders for my mood either.

"Why the hell does everyone keep buyin' your shit?" I said caustically.

That had Warren look up at me, and he raised an eyebrow as he said, "If you wish to be tied up, that can certainly be arranged." The nasty grin on his face made my stomach churn, but I held his gaze. "If you mean why no one inside this camp questions my actions," he added, "well, then perhaps you should take that up with Colonel Cornwell."

I blinked, remembering that name far too well. Cornwell was second in command at Cheyenne Mountain, but what the hell had he to do with this?

"Cornwell," I said with a little more disdain than I intended. That man and I had gotten off on the wrong foot from the start, and that was kind of how we'd left it. The fact that he had wanted to dump me in one of these camps and threatened to take my friends away still didn't sit well with me. "General Whitfield's stooge."

"He's not so much a stooge if the president has his ear," Warren said. "Well, at least he's not Whitfield's stooge."

"Cornwell is helpin' you," I said, unwilling to believe it, or maybe it was more like hope, because I was pretty sure the man would be capable of it, although I couldn't understand why.

"How did you think I'd gained access to Cheyenne in the first place?"

As I thought back on it, I remembered Whitfield not being a big fan of the president, and I think it was Cornwell who had explained the rift within the government. This had led most of the armed forces to disagree with the president's decisions concerning the Mortem virus.

I had zoned out during most of that briefing, but could it be that Cornwell wasn't on the side that we thought he was? If he wasn't loyal to Whitfield, he could have easily arranged for a free pass for Warren to enter Cheyenne.

"So what," I said, "Cornwell maintains this cover for you, so you can destroy the entire world and not just parts of it?"

Warren shook his head. "Kid, perhaps you're just too stupid to understand any of this," he said.

I didn't like the condescending tone or the fact that he called me a stupid kid, but I managed to keep my voice calm as I said, "Then why don't you explain it so I can understand." He looked up and sat back with a smirk on his face.

"You might think I destroyed the world, and perhaps I did—it was my virus after all, and I released it," he said, "but do you really think I could do this all on my own? The others are all trying to save their own asses now, but I haven't lost sight of the greater picture, and once I have your friend, I'll finally be able to finish this."

I swallowed hard and forced myself to ask the question, "What do you want from Mags?"

His eyes brightened, but he seemed almost shocked at my question.

"Don't tell me you haven't seen it," he said, sounding as excited as a small child. "Don't tell me that you haven't seen how she was able to command the infected."

I remembered seeing the images of Mags getting herself bitten again and how her eyes had changed. The security systems inside Cheyenne Mountain had captured it all, and I had seen the eyes for myself, but I couldn't say that I had seen Mags command zombies. They had followed her around like lost puppies, but that was about it.

"How does zombies' followin' Mags add up to commandin'?" I asked.

"Yeah, I didn't see it either," Chester said from out of nowhere. Warren turned around, shooting Chester a venomous glare. The big man had been sitting silently in his corner on the other side of the rig and hadn't said a word, but apparently he'd been paying attention. "I've seen the videos, but I only saw zombies acting like a bunch of lemmings."

"Well, you're both idiots if you didn't see it," Warren replied.

"So," I said feigning contemplation, "you want a zombie army?"

"Enough of this," Warren said in anger, "let's get this over with. Chester, get me Agent Marsden on the phone—now!"

My eyes widened at Warren mentioning Mars. Was he going to get him on the line?

Warren shot me a look as he said, "Let's see how much you are actually worth to them."

I blinked and swallowed hard.

| 25

Mags

We made a point of not lingering too long after we had gathered our stuff. Preston had decided to leave enough of the serum for at least fifty people with detailed instructions on how to administer it—in case they changed their minds.

Back on the roof we took our time to explain everything to Toby again before he was given his shot. The kid was so glad to have his big sister back that he would probably have let us pump acid into his veins.

Preston had contacted Gibs, who had been waiting for us at a distance. Fortunately, we didn't have the same trouble as we had before. There were now many fewer zombies in the parking lot on the side of the building where Preston had parked the Hummer.

"Took you long enough," Gibs said over the radio as we climbed down the fire escape.

"I blame Mags," Tom said.

"Didn't anyone else wanna come?" Gibs asked, as he must have noticed we had only the two extra passengers. "Or were they the … uh."

"The others decided to stay," I said, removing his doubt that only two had survived.

"Hah … didn't see that one coming," he said.

"Neither did we," Preston replied as he jumped off the ladder and into the back of the Hummer. "What happened out here?" he asked as he leaped from the back of the truck.

"I don't know," Gibs said. "One moment the place was packed, and the next moment they started to make their way around the building. I figure you should hurry up before they change their minds."

Angie was next to jump into the back of the truck, and she helped our two new friends down. She settled them in the back, and as soon as I found my spot at the front, I hit the top of the cab. Preston and Tom were already sitting inside, and only seconds later the engine rumbled to life.

Plenty of zombies still stood around us so that Preston had to bump and reverse a couple of times. The vehicle shook as it ran over the ones that didn't grasp the idea of moving out of the way. Leaning against the cab, Angie and I kept an eye out until we reached Gibs.

He had been able to follow much what had transpired over the radio, but he couldn't have heard everything where it concerned the residents of the DC.

"I'll inform Maxwell that we're on our way back. Base command will want to get briefed," Preston said through the open window. "Then we'll only have to explain it once."

That was fine by me. The day and the events had worn me out, and I wouldn't mind returning to the base. Fortunately, the ride shouldn't take more than twenty minutes. I felt a finger poking me in the shoulder in a repeating pattern and turned to Angie.

"Yes," I asked at her annoying gesture, although the disgusted face she made as I looked at her was probably saying enough.

"I suggest you take a seat with the kids," she said.

Feigning innocence, I said, "But I don't wanna sit with the kids. I wanna be up here with you." The words had barely left my mouth before I threw an arm around her and pulled her into a hug.

"God, woman, get off me," she said close to outraged as she pulled away from me. "You smell awful."

Grinning like an idiot, I moved to the back of the truck and sat down next to Toby and across from Savanna. They were now signing with their hands instead of the flashlights, and it was kind of awesome. They spoke and signed at the same time, which made it easy for me to follow the conversation and participate. Toby explained that he had forced himself at a young age to always sign as he spoke around Savanna. That way she would know whether he was saying something even if he didn't address her.

"That is pretty cool you did that," I said, directing my words at Toby but facing Savanna.

"It comes naturally to me now," he replied. The kids kept an easy conversation going, and time flew by along with the landscape. Talking to them turned out to be less depressing than gazing at the abandoned houses, crashed cars, and roaming zombies that looked even grimmer in the daylight. Before I knew it, the gates to the first layer of fences opened for us, and we entered the base.

Colonel Eaves had carved out an area inside the small hangar for us. It held a several bunks and even a screen to give us women some privacy. It seemed that the colonel wasn't entirely fond of us moving around his base, but if this was what he thought he needed to do to keep the men and women under his command safe, I for one didn't have a problem with that.

To my relief, I wasn't required to attend the debriefing, and I headed for the showers. My body received a thorough, but fast, scrubbing under the stream of cold water. It seemed Colonel Eaves was rationing the hot water, or maybe even the showers were temporary and rigged up just for us. It definitely looked that way. There was, however, an abundance of clothing, and I savored the moment of dressing in my new fatigues.

Upon returning, I found the two kids asleep in adjoining bunks, their hair wet from the shower. From behind me, I heard an exaggerated sniffing sound, and I shifted to find Angie standing by my side, her nose close to my arm. She had taken a shower of her own and followed me out the makeshift shower room.

"Better?" I asked. She pulled a face as if she wasn't sure and then grinned. Her hair hung loose and wet around her shoulders and, for once, wasn't braided into the Mohawk style she usually wore. It made her face look softer.

I plopped down on my bunk and groaned. Every muscle in my body ached.

"Next time you'll be dodging zombies and climbing racks," I said in low voice to not disturb the kids.

"Hey, don't blame me. You're the one who wanted to go GI Zombie on me," Angie replied as she sat down on her bunk.

"I just wished it had worked," I said.

"Well, I would have been convinced by your stunt."

Dr. Chen needed those people as a control group and could have used them to persuade whoever needed to be persuaded to distribute the serum. As soon as that happened, Angie and I could go home, or more exactly, I would have been able to see Ash and Mars again. A thought started to play on repeat inside my brain, and I sat up, suddenly feeling anxious.

"What if they don't let us go? What if they're going to send us out again to find another group, and then another? God knows what kind of people we'll find," I said.

The words spilled out fast and I saw Angie's eyes widen at my what-must-have-looked-like-frantic behavior, but I couldn't help it. Bob's group had reminded me of that Father what's-his-name's group, and although Bob hadn't tried to detain us or handed us over to a mad scientist called Dr. David, I could see the similarities between the groups. Where there were two, there had to be more, and I sure as hell didn't want to meet any of them ever again.

"You guys decent," Preston called out from the other side of the screen. I jumped with a yelp at the sound of the sudden voice, while Angie answered,

"Yeah, fully clothed here." Her voice was still low, and fortunately I hadn't woken up the kids. Angie pointed at them as Preston came from around the screen and nodded in acknowledgement. He nearly whispered his next words.

"We're leaving tomorrow morning at first light."

"Back to Alaska, I presume," Angie said. My hands seemed to fold around the edge of the bunk on their own accord, and I squeezed. I felt less than thrilled to get back there.

Preston nodded. "Yeah, I've talked to Marshall. She expressed their disappointment with the outcome, but Dr. Chen seemed eager to get his hands on the kids."

"What the hell does that mean?" I said, louder than I intended to. Angie shot me a look to tone it down.

"Sorry, wrong choice of words," Preston said raising his hands in defense. "I mean that he wants to monitor them, maybe draw some blood. You know, same as with you."

Same as with you, the words bounced inside my head like a Ping-Pong ball, and I couldn't make them stop. Maybe Preston didn't see it that way, but how could he not? He was in the same boat as us. He had to have seen how the others treated us. It would be the same for him and for Tom and Gibs too. I was tired of being treated as a leper, and if that couldn't be changed, I wanted to be around the people who didn't care about me being a Mortem virus incubator. I huffed out of frustration and let myself fall onto the bunk.

"Get some sleep. We'll need it," Preston said. I glanced up at him, and he caught my gaze. Compassion filled his eyes. It was something I had never witnessed in him, as if for once he had lowered his shield and gave me a glimpse of his humanity. As if it had never happened, his face hardened, but in that fraction of a second, I had seen enough. He hated the situation as much as I did, but he was a soldier, and he would do what needed to be done to make it better.

Although I felt exhausted, sleeping during the day wasn't my thing, and I only managed a couple of hours, but they felt like an eternity. Sleep wouldn't come at first, and the thought of going back to Alaska made my stomach do weird things, and if I thought about it too much, it made me feel sick. I finally started to doze, but woke as I heard whispered voices. I recognized Gibs and Tom.

I sat up and saw Angie staring at me from the other bunk. Her dark eyes bore into me as if she could read my mind. So I found it kind of weird that she asked me the question that she did.

"You okay?" she asked. She propped herself up on an elbow and held me with that intense gaze she had.

I shook my head. "No not really," I said, my voice barely a whisper.

"Figured as much," she replied and narrowed her eyes. "But you're going to be right, because I'd hate to start that orphanage all on my own." A bit shocked at her words I glanced at the kids who looked to be fast asleep.

"Shut up," I said and chugged a pillow in her direction. She caught it and tossed it right back before she flopped back on her bunk in exasperation and said, "Thank God!"

I watched her for a moment as she pretended to wipe sweat from her forehead, and I shook my head in defeat.

"I've gotta pee," I said, grabbed my clothes, and got up.

When I got back fully dressed, Savanna and Toby had abandoned their bunks and so had Angie. I heard voices in what sounded like a heated argument. Grabbing my gear, I rushed outside as I recognized Angie's voice.

"This is not your call to make," Colonel Eaves said, pointing a finger at Angie.

"The hell it's not," she said, fuming. I didn't think I had ever seen her like that. "This is my family you're talking about."

Shock and fear ran through me at the thought that something might have happened to Angie's sister or mother, and I rushed to her side.

"What's going on?" I asked.

"What's going on is that you are leaving for Alaska right now," Eaves said. He sounded almost as angry as Angie. He pointed a finger at Preston, who stood nearby, passively watching the exchange.

"The hell we are," Angie shouted at the man's back. Eaves turned to Preston and started yapping that he should get the people under his command in line. I guessed he had forgotten that we weren't actually military.

"Talk to me," I asked, placing a hand on Angie's shoulder. Our eyes met and the look she gave me sent a chill down my spine in such a way that I even regretted asking the question. Angie wasn't one to beat around the bush, and she wouldn't start now.

"It's Ash," she said. It took a moment for the words to sink in while my vision did some zoom-and-fade-to-blurry thing. I blinked to regain focus.

"But," I said, searching for words and shaking my head at the same time, "Ash is in California, with Mars's parents—"

"They're dead," she said, and reading the shock on my face she quickly added, "His parents, Joseph and Shelley, they turned."

Along with my vision going out of whack, I felt my legs go weak.

"But how ..." I said as my voice wavered. "Where's Ash?" I had so many questions, and I wanted to ask them all at the same time, but somehow my brain muddled them together, and I couldn't even get one out.

"Warren," Angie said. I closed my eyes and steeled myself.

"Does he have her?" I asked. My voice had become so small that it was barely audible, but the grim expression on Angie's face told me she'd heard me, and with it, she had simultaneously given me an answer.

"He wants to talk to you."

26

Ash

It probably wasn't, but it seemed hours after I heard Warren talk to Mars, although I had dozed off for a while. It had taken Warren some time to get hold of him, but the eventual goal was to talk to Mags, and apparently she couldn't be reached. I had wanted to ask Mars if Rowdy was okay and even Luke, but Warren wouldn't let me talk to him, and he also didn't ask himself. It left me feeling like a fool, the way I had pleaded with him, but he had been relentless.

From what I had picked up, he hadn't said anything to Mars about what he wanted from Mags, just that he wanted to talk to her before any deal for my return could be made. Mars promised to make it happen. I had caught that much. There also might have been some cursing, because Warren removed the headset twice, waiting for a second before placing it on his head again. The visual made me smile, but not enough to distract me from the problem at hand. A problem of which I had no idea how to handle.

Warren wanted to use me as bait. That much was clear, and there wasn't much I could do about that. Warren had me, and that meant Mags was coming to get me, right? A smidgen of doubt triggered somewhere in the furthest regions of my mind, wondering if she'd come. But I crushed that doubt immediately after it rose, because in my heart I knew she'd come. Mags had come through for me in the past, and I knew she would again, except this time I didn't want her to. I couldn't let her risk her own life to save mine. Besides, if she came, I wouldn't be surprised if both our lives would be forfeited. Warren didn't seem the type of man who would leave loose threads hanging. If it were true what he had said and cover-ups were being planned, then that wouldn't leave much room for us.

All this was enough to renew the headache that had never left. I leaned forward and stretched my back and neck. Those hours that had seemed to have passed before had definitely passed by now, and I didn't think I'd be able to sit like this for much longer.

I glanced at Chester, who had raised his feet up on a table and seemed fast asleep. Warren was sitting like a statue, staring into his microscope. My own eyes threatened to close, and I fought to keep them open. Every so often my head would loll forward, and I would jolt up feeling a slight rejuvenation that would last only moments.

My eyes fell closed again but shot open at the sound of beeping. At the desk, Warren sat up straight and moved his neck from left to right until bones cracked. The sound sent a shiver down my spine. He let the beeping continue, and I was about to call him out on it when he picked up the headset.

"Ms. Vissers," he said, sounding delighted. He removed the headset and closed his eyes. A moment later, he placed them back, sporting a grimace, and I figured Mags hadn't been done yet. I could only imagine the colorful words Mags was throwing at his head. "Yes, very well, perhaps I should put you on speaker so our main subject of interest can follow the conversation."

Warren flipped a switch and unplugged the headset from the device. The action created a nasty feedback sound that tortured my ears. Then there was silence.

"Ms. Vissers," Warren said again, "can you hear me?" I could hear her breathing over the line and knew she was there. I wanted to shout out to her, to tell her I was here and to please come get me, but I managed to keep my mouth shut. I needed to figure out a way to play this smart, because forasmuch as I wanted to get out of here, I couldn't let that happen at the expense of my friends—especially not Mags.

"I'm here," she said. Her voice was low but steady.

"Excellent," Warren said. "I'll come to business straight away, because you won't have much time, Ms. Vissers. If you wish to see your small friend again, I'll be in Salinas, California, in two days' time, and I'd like to meet you there—alone." A derisive chuckle sounded from the other end of the line.

"I'm in Alabama, Doctor. How am I supposed to reach California in two days? It's not as if I can hop on a charter flight," Mags said mockingly, but I could hear the tiny hitch in her voice.

"Oh, I'm sure your friend Agent Marsden will be able to think of something," Warren said. "I'll be at the Salinas Sports Complex."

The line fell silent again, and I realized I was holding my breath. My knuckles had gone white, holding on to the push rings of my chair.

"How do I ..." Mags started to say, but fell silent again as if she needed it to build up enough courage to finish the sentence. "How do I know Ash is okay, and what guarantees do I have that you'll let her go?"

"I assure you, Ms. Vissers, the girl is quite all right, and there is nothing left in her anatomy that can tell me what I don't already know," Warren replied. "Yours, on the other hand, is a different story entirely."

He grinned at that and glanced my way. From the expression on his face, I could tell that he was already thinking of all the things he needed to do to finish his research, and there wasn't an inch of him that considered what it might cost Mags.

"Prove it," Mags replied. Her tone had shifted to anger. Warren sighed and gestured to me. I just raised my eyebrows and glared at him.

"Well, talk to your friend," he said. Holding his gaze, I kept my mouth shut. It occurred to me that this wasn't one of my brightest ideas, but then what choice did I have? If I could seed doubt in Mags's mind that maybe I wasn't all right and maybe even dead, then she might not come.

Mags had to know what Warren was up to. Even without the details, she would have figured out that Warren wanted her to finish his research, because that's what he did. That's what he'd always done, and nothing good had ever come from what that man had produced. He had created the Mortem virus in the first place, and to make it worse, he had tinkered with the results until it left the infected aware of what they had become. I couldn't imagine a worse fate than to roam around the country feasting on the lives of others, unable to stop yourself.

And Warren wouldn't stop at that. He would take it just that step further where he could control the zombies. We couldn't let that happen—I couldn't let that happen.

There was only one way I could think of that might have the slightest effect to prevent that from happening and that was to keep my mouth shut. It was a slim chance, but it was all I had, and so I stayed silent.

Warren frowned at my silence and then cleared his through. "I'm sorry, Ms. Vissers, but it seems your friend is being a bit stubborn," he said. He snapped his fingers, and Chester looked up from where he hung in his chair.

"Ms. Reed," Warren said questioningly, "do you not wish to talk to your friend? I'm sure you'll have lots to say as per usual."

I slowly shook my head. Warren closed his eyes as if he wanted to tone down the frustration that was obviously building inside him. As he opened them, he pressed a button on the speaker that sat on his desk.

"Do you really think this is going to work?" he said, apparently unable to keep the annoyance out of his voice. His gaze turned to find Chester still sitting in his spot. Warren's shoulders dropped. "Why me?" he muttered to himself. Then he slammed a fist on the table. "Get your ass over here and make her talk."

Chester jumped up from his seat and stepped closer. His shocked expression shifted between Warren and me.

"How am I supposed to do that?" he asked uncertainly.

"I do not care," Warren said with a sigh. "Break her fingers for all I care."

My eyes widened at his words and with a quick glance at my fingers, I balled them into fists. Nope, not a good idea at all, but I was determined. I wouldn't give Mags the incentive she needed to get herself captured by this madman.

Chester stepped closer, and I looked up at him with pleading eyes. I had used that expression numerous times, and Mags had even teased me about it. Usually that look gave me what I wanted, but I had no expectations that it would work on Chester.

"What the hell is going on?" Mags called out over the line. Warren bent over the speaker and pressed a button.

"Just one moment please," he said into the speaker and pressed the button again. He must have been using a mute button that kept Mags from hearing what was going on here.

"Talk to her," Warren said in a demanding voice.

I shook my head. At that, Chester grabbed the back of my neck and rolled me forward. I hadn't tested it, but at least I now knew my chair wasn't tied up, and I could move freely, that is, if I didn't count the two men forceful enough to keep me rooted to the spot.

Chester rolled me closer to the speaker, and I clamped my jaw shut but couldn't keep the oomph from exiting my throat as he slammed me against the tabletop. Pain ripped through my head, starting at the freshly sutured cut. Tears sprang into my eyes, and I was gasping for air. God, this was a stupid plan.

Warren grinned and tilted his head to level with mine. He moved the speaker closer to me and pressed the button.

"We should be ready now," he said into the device.

"Warren, what are you doing?" Mags said.

"Well, I'm only trying to comply with your request," Warren said in an overfriendly voice. As Warren had his attention directed at the speaker, I tried to push myself up from the table, but Chester's grip was too firm, and his strength too much for me to counter.

"Ash," Mags said in a trembling voice. She must have heard my ragged breathing, and I tried to hold my breath, but it didn't work. I grabbed my push ring and tried to maneuver my chair, but something blocked it. Had to be Chester's foot.

Warren stepped closer, and my eyes widened as he reached out a hand. It clamped over my head, and I felt the finger on the bandage that covered the sutures on my forehead. I groaned as he pressed it, and pain shot along my scalp; I couldn't help it.

"Goddammit, Ash, don't let them hurt you," Mags said in a voice fused with pleading and anger. "Don't you hurt her, you fucking bastard."

Warren seemed to enjoy himself, and he pressed harder. I couldn't stop the scream that tore from my throat.

I jerked up one side of my chair, tilted it, and then brought it down hard. Luck had it that it landed on Chester's foot. He cried out, probably more out of instinct than pain, but it did the trick. Chester released his grip, and I pulled at my wheels and bumped the chair into him. Losing his balance, he stepped backward and stumbled. In his fall Chester reached out and grabbed my chair, which wasn't something I had planned for. Not that any of this had been planned.

I careened over sideways and landed with a crash on the floor. With a groan, I grabbed my head and held it tight as if that would let the pain subside. Somewhere above me I heard Mags's frantic voice but couldn't make out the words. Warren replied, sounding calm before the space fell silent.

27

Mags

"Ash," I called out at the sound of a loud crash on the other side of the line.

"Salinas Sports Complex. You have two days," Warren said, and his voice was followed by a click.

"Warren, you son of a bitch, if you touch her, I swear to God." My fist struck the table, and I cursed some more.

"What the hell happened?" I shouted at the young man sitting at my side as only static reached me through the speaker. A hand on my upper arm pulled me away from the table and from the young man operating the radio.

"He broke the connection," Angie said in a soft voice. "C'mon, you're scaring the kid." She gestured at the radio operator who gave us a weak smile. Angie led me from the room through the hallway and took me outside.

"Take a breath," she said as she sat me down on a bench and took a seat next to me.

"What the hell just happened?" I asked, still rattled from the conversation.

"I think Ash was trying to make a point that we shouldn't come after her," she said.

"God, he was hurting her," I said and my blood ran cold at the thought. "She's just a kid." Angie threw her arm around me and squeezed my shoulder.

"Ash is a tough kid, and that last cry wasn't her," she said. "So I'd say she's holding her own." Angie didn't sound very convinced, and from the look that I got from her, I'd say she was as worried as I was. I hoped that last cry wouldn't create any repercussions for Ash. "Warren needs her to get to you, so he'll keep her safe until he gets what he wants, and till then, we still have a chance to get her back."

I jumped off the bench and turned to face Angie. "We have to go get her," I said. I heard the desperation coming from my own voice.

"And we will," Angie said as she stood. Preston exited the building, his expression grim. Angie and I both turned to face him.

"We might have a problem," he said, "Eaves is adamant that we travel back to Alaska."

"But ... how," I started to say. "He just heard what was said in there." My temper flared, though I knew that there wasn't much Preston could do about the situation. He raised his hands in an attempt to calm me.

"Listen, we leave in a couple of hours," he said, "and it's like an eleven-hour trip to Alaska. From there we can still make it to Salinas in time."

I shook my head. "No, you don't understand, I can't take that chance. Not with Ash," I said and felt my voice break. Angie placed a hand on my back as if she knew that I needed the support.

"Hey," Preston said in a soft voice, pulling my gaze to his. "I'm aware of your history, and I think I know what the kid means to you." His eyes shifted to Angie. "To both of you. And we'll find a way to get her back."

"We can't waste time flying to Alaska," I said. "This is Ash's life were talking about, and I'm not going to cut it close."

"Besides," Angie added, "we need to come up with a plan that doesn't include trading Ash for Mags."

"I don't care about that," I said.

"Well, I do," Angie said in a sharp tone and with a look that made me feel about two inches tall. "Furthermore, Ash will kill me if I let anything happen to you, and I'm not even talking about Mars. So shut up about it."

I opened my mouth to reply, but then closed it shut as she held my gaze.

"Okay then, first things first," Preston said. "How are we going to get ourselves to Salinas?"

The doors to the small building swung open, and Colonel Eaves stepped out followed by a small entourage. Among them were Gibs and Tom.

"We just received a call from that Agent Marsden you spoke with earlier," Gibs said to Preston as he came up to us.

"What did he say?" I asked anxiously. All I knew was that Warren had taken Ash and that Mars had lost his parents. I had no idea what had happened or if Rowdy was even all right. The thought of anything happening to the little guy made my stomach churn.

"He and some of the brass have come up with a plan to stop the spread of the virus and they've been working on setting it in motion," Gibs said.

"What kind of plan?" Preston asked.

"He wouldn't say," Tom said. "He's talking to a General Whitfield about it, but apparently, he needs our cargo and not just the lovely Ms. Vissers over here."

Tom meant the hard-shelled case that still held a significant amount of serum, but I couldn't help feel annoyed by his remark, and he flinched a little at the look that I gave him. From the corner of my eye, I could see Angie shake her head at him. It led to

Tom clearing his throat and turning his gaze to the ground.

"Well, then we have to go," I said firmly as I turned to meet Colonel Eaves. The colonel had his back to me and was still in a vivid conversation with one of his men, but at the sound of my voice he tilted his head back and his broad shoulders slumped.

"Isn't anyone listening to what I'm saying?" he said in a loud voice. "As I just explained to your staff sergeant—who I'm sure has relayed the message—you have orders to return to Alaska, and as long as I do not receive orders that dictate otherwise, they stay that way."

A couple of airmen who passed us a second earlier froze at the sound Eaves's thundering voice. I caught their anxious gazes, but I was way past heeding warning signs. I balled my fists and stepped into the man's personal space. Having a couple of inches in height on a person often gave me the illusion of having the advantage, but that didn't seem to work at all with the colonel.

| 28

Mags

"I can't believe Whitfield sold us out like that," I said, still reeling from my confrontation with Eaves. The airplane's engines rumbled all around me, and I couldn't believe I was heading back to Alaska instead of flying to California while Warren had taken Ash.

My body felt wired as if I'd just had an adrenaline fix, and it came accompanied by so many emotions that I didn't know what to feel or how to act. All I knew, while pacing the aisle between seats, was that I was heading in the wrong direction and I couldn't do a damn thing about it.

"I don't think he would do that," Angie said.

"Oh, come on," I said. "Gibs said Mars was trying to convince Whitfield, and we're still flying in the wrong direction."

"I still can't believe you've gotten Eaves so far as to check the story at all," Tom muttered. "Did you hold him at gunpoint?"

"Shut up, Tom," Gibs and Angie said in unison.

"Yeah, and Eaves got a no from Cheyenne," I

said, ignoring the three of them.

"Eaves said he had gotten the no from Cornwell," Preston said.

"That's the same thing, isn't it?" I replied. I was practically yelling now. Angie grabbed my arm in passing and pulled me to a stop. She gave me a look that loosely translated to *calm the fuck down*. I took a breath and closed my eyes.

"Not necessarily," Gibs said. The plane hit an air pocket, and I grabbed two seats as I turned to face him. "It's possible Cornwell kept the request from Whitfield."

"No way," Tom piped up as he stood, dropping to a knee in his seat and leaning over the backrest. "Colonels don't go against generals."

"This one might," Gibs said. "It's not a secret that Cornwell is a big fan of the president."

"And so he would be inclined to defy orders," Tom said. "I don't wanna be the one to break it to ya, but pretty much everyone who joins the military is likely to be a fan of the president."

A sad smile spread across Gibs's face as Angie said, "But times have changed."

"Exactly," Gibs said, "the virus outbreak caused a chasm between different parts of the government, and it's been growing wider ever since."

It had been Colonel Cornwell back at Cheyenne

Mountain who had been asked by General Whitfield to explain the then-current situation in the government. I never had an aptitude for politics or, more accurately, had absolutely no interest in it whatsoever. From what I remember of what Cornwell explained, the cause for these tears within the government had something to do with a pharmaceutical company that may or may not have been to blame for the spread of the virus. The fact that a Dr. David Warren had been on this company's payroll kind of tipped the balance, but that hadn't kept the president from choosing the side of the multibillion-dollar company.

"I thought the military had opted against the president's choices," I said.

Gibs inclined his head before he said, "For the most part."

"What do you mean, opting against the president?" Tom said appalled. Gibs shot him a look and then shook his head as he let out a deep sigh.

"I know for sure Cornwell is on the president's side on this," he continued without answering Tom.

"What makes you so sure?" Angie asked.

"I make it a priority to know these things," he replied.

Despite the vagueness of his answer, I decided to go with it and asked, "So you're saying Cornwell sidestepped Whitfield."

"I think it's possible," he said.

From experience, I knew Cornwell to be, well, basically a jerk. Although I hadn't pegged him as someone who'd go against his commander, maybe in his mind he wasn't doing that at all. It could be that from his point of view Whitfield and all the others disagreeing with the president were at fault. It sounded plausible, but that wouldn't help me. If only I could contact Whitfield directly, he might grant us permission to find Ash and stop Warren once and for all.

I tightened my grip on the backs of the seats on either side of me and squeezed until my fingers started to hurt. There had to be something I could do. Closing my eyes, I lowered my head and clenched my jaw to keep the frustration from rising inside me. Upon opening my eyes, they fell on the holster strapped to my thigh and the gun neatly tucked inside it. My head snapped up, and I caught Angie and the men studying me.

"Mags," Angie said in an urgent voice as I turned on my heels. By the time I reached the front of the airplane, I had released the gun from the confines of the holster and slammed a fist on the cockpit door. Behind me, I heard muffled voices and a distinct, "Oh shit," from Tom.

The door opened, and a clean-shaven face with headphones around his neck stuck his head out the opening. His mouth opened to say something, but he clamped it shut after I placed the nozzle of the weapon under his chin.

"I would like to suggest a course correction," I said.

The young man with the headphones stared at me wide-eyed and the Adam's apple in his throat bobbed up and down as he swallowed hard.

"Captain," he said in a squeaky voice. Up close, I had barely heard him. He must have realized, because he cleared his throat and tried again. The captain glanced over his shoulder, and with one glimpse of what was going on, he jumped up and pulled his own weapon. I hadn't thought of the possibility that a pilot might be carrying a gun, but as he aimed it at my face, I heard Preston step closer as he called for calm.

Although my heart threatened to jump out from my chest and the sound of blood was rushing in my ears, I managed to keep the gun pretty steady. I hoped that I gave the illusion of calm, because on the inside, I felt ready to explode.

"Mags," Preston said in a low voice as he waved at the pilot to back off. "This is not the way——"

"Just stop, Preston," I said, "because I'm not gonna let go of this gun until this plane lands in ... wherever it is that Mars wanted it to land."

I just about had enough of people, and especially military folk, telling me what to do. Ash and I had been doing just fine on our own until we'd gotten ourselves involved in this creating-a-serum-for-the-greater-good bullshit, and it was my own damn fault. I never should've let them coerce me into splitting us up. Mars had intervened with good intentions when he'd offered Ash a place to stay at his parents' home, but I should never have agreed. We should have stayed together.

"Jesus, Mags, you can't do this," Tom said.

"Shut up, Tom," Preston remarked. With a sideways glance, my eyes met Angie's. She leaned against the toilet door inside the small passage leading to the cockpit, and I noticed her hand on the weapon holstered at her thigh. Her face looked placid, but her eyes burned with fire. She gave me an approving nod. Relieved to have her on my side, I returned my focus on the young man with the headphones.

"Preston," I said, "if you be so kind and give these fine men the coordinates of where we would like to go."

"They already have them," he said. I felt a shock

running through me, and I swallowed hard before I turned my gaze to face him.

"Huh?" was all that left my mouth.

"The pilots are informed of a possible secondary location," he said.

"So why didn't you say anything?" I said.

"Because they haven't changed course yet."

"Oh, they're changing course," I said and pressed the gun harder against the young man's chin.

"Just hear me out for a second," Preston said, raising his hands in the air. "I've contacted Marshall about the situation, and she's personally contacting Whitfield. I'm just waiting for conformation."

"That's not good enough," I said.

"Come on, Mags," Gibs interjected. "It won't hurt to wait it out. You know they'll just throw you in jail the moment we land in Cali if you go through with this. Think about it."

I glanced at Angie, who shrugged, but her head shifted, and I glanced over her shoulder. Toby and Savanna stood aghast as they watched the exchange. The kids most have woken up from the ruckus and now looked at me with eyes wide and Toby's mouth hanging slightly open.

"It's worth considering," she said. I silently cursed myself as I pulled my gaze from the kids to the young man whose shirt I clung to and who had eyes even wider than the kids. He was pretty much a kid himself.

"Uh, Staff Sergeant," the captain said, "I've just received information about a revised flight plan."

"See," Gibs said. He gave me a knowing look when I glanced at him and considered his words. He was right; I probably wouldn't have been able to get off the plane before they had someone stop me.

"Let me check the message," Preston said, "and I'm sure we'll be able to convince these nice pilots flying us that you had a bad reaction to stress."

I glared at him, but Preston wasn't impressed. He edged closer and placed his palm on my hand holding the gun. Opening my clenched fist around the fabric of his shirt, I released the young man. He jerked back immediately and all but fell in his chair. I didn't pay attention to his rambling as Preston moved past me and entered the cockpit. I took stock of the others and noticed a mixed response. Tom just looked confused, but Gibs nodded appreciatively. Like most times, I couldn't read Angie's face, but the kids looked shocked.

"Sorry," I said to them. Toby's face seemed frozen, but Savanna gave me an attempt at a nervous smile.

A moment later, Preston stepped from the

cockpit and offered me the gun back. He gestured at it with his head as I gaped at him in surprise.

"You'll need it," he said. "We're heading west."

| 29

Mags

It took me a while to get my butt planted in my seat after that. The combination of fear and impatience along with a pinch of shame kept my nerves strung high. This plane was just moving too damn slow. Fortunately, Angie kept her head cool and even sat down with Savanna and Toby to explain the situation. They seemed understanding, but Toby avoided eye contact the few times that he moved past me to head to the toilet.

I tried to close my eyes, but kept seeing Ash's face, and the sounds from the call played on repeat inside my head. She was hurt—*he* had hurt her. Warren had hurt her and might still be hurting her. The knowledge brought back the memories I'd been trying to forget: the image of Ash's small frame in the arms of a soldier as he carried her back to her cell after Warren had done god knows what to her. I hadn't even been able to comfort her as I'd wanted to because of the bars that had separated our cells. But Ash was a strong kid and I needed to focus on that.

Mars had helped us get out of there, and we had survived. Except for the nightmares that I knew sometimes plagued her, she seemed to have gotten out of that situation okay, and she'd be able to do that again; I'd make sure of that.

I shook my head as my thoughts shifted from Ash to Mars. *How could he have let this happen?* I didn't know whether to feel for him or be angry with him. It had been his idea to let Ash stay with his parents, and now they were dead. I couldn't help wondering whether Dr. David had specifically gone after Ash and if Mars's parents were just collateral damage.

"Hey," a voice said as I stared at the back of the seat in front of me. I looked up and saw Preston gazing down at me. I hadn't exactly apologized to him for my earlier outburst and shifted uncomfortably in my seat to face him.

"Hey," I offered in reply.

"Mind if I sit?"

I shook my head but found it hard to look him in the eye, and I diverted my gaze back to the seat in front of me.

"I ... uh ..." I muttered, trying to think of something to say, but my mind had gone blank. It had worked out, but only because Preston hadn't just relied on orders being orders, and I felt grateful to him for that. That didn't mean that if he hadn't I wouldn't have gone through with it. The anger I had felt and that I still felt would have taken me on a path that pre-zombie apocalypse, I never would have considered possible. Post-zombie apocalypse, I didn't even think that I would apologize for it, although I wished I hadn't scared the kids in the process, and I did feel ashamed about that.

"We both know you're not sorry for what you did, so let's just leave it at that," he said as he took the seat next to me.

I opened my mouth to protest, but considering the fact that I had already decided on the same thing, I closed it again.

"Listen, I've just spoken with Agent Marsden, and he wanted me to give you some details."

I turned my head and stared at him blankly.

"You've been sitting here looking just like that for over an hour," he added.

"You spoke with Mars?" I asked. The slight tremor in my voice had me clear my throat. "Why didn't you come get me?" Preston shifted a little in his seat and cleared his own throat before he answered.

"Because he asked me not to."

"Why?" I asked, unsure if it were shock, disappointment, or anger that made my voice rise an octave.

"Because I had given him the lowdown on what happened before and he figured that, given the information that he needed you to know, it would be better this way," he said. Preston paused a second. "He also suggested I was to disarm you before I said anything."

I blinked at him, unable to find the words for a reply.

"I figured you wouldn't shoot the messenger." Preston shot me a grin and then stuck his hand in the air. "Angie, got a minute," he asked and flicked his wrist to wave her over. Angie strolled over to us, slid into the row in front of us, and leaned on the seat's back.

"What's up?" she said.

"I might need the backup," he said and shot her a half-smile.

"Okay, this isn't funny anymore," I said. "Tell me."

Angie gave me a questioning look and then shifted to Preston as he began.

"Agent Marsden, or Mars," he said with a nod, "thinks he might know where Ash is now." In a reflex, I grabbed Preston's arm.

"Is she all right?" I asked almost breathlessly. This was good news, and I glanced up at Angie to find confirmation, but her gaze remained cool and collected.

"As I was trying to say, he hasn't found her yet, but he has a good indication of where she might be," he said. It seemed Angie's attitude had been the right one to go with. Reclaiming some composure, I asked, "Where?"

"He has received a call from a medic who reported seeing a young girl in a wheelchair," Preston carried on. "She's being held by at the refugee camp where he's stationed."

With every word he said, I felt the blood drain from my face. Angie's, however, flushed a dark red. Somehow we both managed to keep our mouths shut. Preston must have noticed because he paused in hesitation before he continued.

"The medic said that she'd pulled quite a stunt to escape a moving truck." he said.

"Wait. She did what?" I said shocked as Preston's words seeped in.

"I don't know the details," Preston said quickly, "but from what the medic has said she's okay." I shot Angie a glance and found a hint of pride in her expression.

"Then what happened?" she asked.

"A major has claimed her," Preston said, "but not before she'd been very vocal about whom he was and that someone should contact Mars."

"Good girl," I said to myself.

"And this major is …" Angie asked as if she knew the answer to the question already.

"It's not confirmed, but most likely Warren," Preston replied.

"So where are they?" Angie asked.

"They are already at Salinas Sports Complex," he said. I glared at him.

"He's already at the place where he'd said he'd be two days from now," I said. Preston nodded before he added, "And guess who assigned him there."

"Cornwell," I said.

"Exactly," Preston replied.

I rubbed my temples and shook my head. It would take some time to digest the games people were playing with our lives. A heavy silence weighed on me as Preston and Angie seemingly waited for me to say something else.

"How's Rowdy doing in all this?" I asked, hoping for some good news because I could use it.

A reassuring smile grew on Preston's face before he said, "The kid is shaken up but doing fine. He bonded a little with a private named Luke Bennett. He's one of the surviving soldiers of Ash's detail, and he will keep Rowdy company until this matter is resolved. They're in a safe location."

I nodded slowly and felt relieved to hear Rowdy was okay. It must have been a hell of a trauma for the young boy, and I had seen a glimpse of how much he cared about his grandparents. But he was young and kids could forget, right? At least I hoped he could.

"Oh, and Cornwell has been placed under arrest and pending investigation, he's to face charges for his part in this," Preston said as an afterthought.

I nodded, but didn't actually care about what happened to Cornwell. My mind was still processing Preston's earlier words. I shifted to Preston as something occurred to me.

"You said ..." I started but paused, just as much to think of the right words as to get it all sorted inside my head. "Ash was assigned a detail."

Preston gave me a questioning look.

"Why?" I asked.

"Warren," Angie added without waiting for a reply, and Preston nodded.

"When did he show up?" she asked.

"A couple of days ago," Preston replied. My mouth fell open, but I closed it as I shifted my gaze to Angie.

"As in maybe two days before we left for Alabama," I said. From my peripheral vision, I could see Preston narrow his eyes at me. For a second, I thought he glanced down at the gun tucked into my holster, but he had been right before —I wouldn't shoot the messenger.

"Son of a—" Angie exclaimed. I stared at her knuckles as they had gone completely white while she gripped the headrest of the chair. "That video call."

I nodded in understanding. Ash had acted weird the entire conversation, and I couldn't pinpoint why. I guessed this explained it.

"It was him in that room with her," I said under my breath.

"Who? When?" Preston asked, but I ignored him. That strange conversation with Ash played in the back of my mind as it had that night. It hadn't sat well with me, but then all the traveling and the distribution center had happened, and it had sort of slipped my mind. I would have asked Ash about it the next time we talked, but then it wouldn't have mattered. She had lied to me. What was worse was that Mars had put her up to it. Who else could it have been in that room with her? Ash wouldn't have trusted anyone else to sit in on a call with us.

"She lied to me," I said in a whisper, "and he asked her to." I didn't think anyone had heard, but Angie reached out a hand and squeezed my shoulder.

"They didn't want you to worry," she said. I looked up at her and let out a strained chuckle.

"Then why does your head look like a tomato," I said.

Angie shrugged, and as if it were the most normal thing in the world to say, she said, "Because along with understanding, I'm severely pissed, and as soon as this plane lands, I'm gonna find Mars and kick his ass."

Part of me wanted to join in on that, and as soon as the adoption papers were finalized, I would ground Ash for the rest of her life. But as angry as I felt about being left out, there was also Mars's loss that tugged at my insides.

"He lost his mom and dad," I whispered. Angie's face softened as she sighed.

"Yeah," she said, the sadness clear in her voice, "he did."

I had never met the Marsdens in person, except through video calls, but from what I had come to know, they had been the most warmhearted and loving people who cared tremendously about their son and grandchild and had welcomed Ash with open arms.

Preston stood from his seat and offered it to Angie. She dropped herself into the seat with an audible thump as the pilot's voice came over the intercom and announced our approach at Monterey Regional Airport.

"I might hold off on kicking Mars's ass," she said after the pilot finished talking, "but I swear to God, if something happens to that kid ..." I shot her a look, and she refrained from finishing her sentence.

"You're right," she added. "We'll find Ash."

30

Mags

It still took a while for the plane to land at Monterey Regional Airport. This should have given me some time to get my head straight, but it seemed to have the opposite effect. As I grabbed my gear and headed down the aisle, I noticed that my body had turned into a block of tension during the rest of the flight.

As I reached the open door of the plane, it seemed to hit me like the proverbial freight train. On a rational level, I knew Mars would never do anything to jeopardize Ash, and I didn't know any of the details. It didn't stop the rush of anger raging through me every time I thought of Ash. That anger should have been directed at Dr. David, but I couldn't clamp down the aggravation I felt when it came to Mars. He had promised me to take care of her, and he should have told me about Dr. David. *How could he not have?*

It should have been easy to blame Dr. David for everything that had happened to us. He had held Ash and me captive, tortured us and had even stood at the cradle of the Mortem outbreak at Cheyenne Mountain. I was well aware that I had caused those deaths by infecting William, the doctor's aide, but only because of what he had done to me. *So why was it so hard for me to set this anger I felt toward Mars aside?*

On the steps leading from the plane, blue skies decorated with one or two fluffy clouds loomed over us. Preston, Tom, and Gibs had already headed down. About half a dozen men dressed in the same pixelated tiger-stripe pattern we all wore waited for them in greeting.

I watched them walk in the direction of two vans that stood parked a short distance from the plane while I waited for Angie and the two kids. My eyes roamed across the tarmac and the airmen standing around the vans as I searched for the one person I wasn't entirely sure I wanted to see.

Savanna exited first, and she squinted against the sun as she took in her surroundings. Angie and Toby followed, and it was getting crowded on the small platform. I reached out a hand to lift Savanna's chin and guided her head up until our eyes met.

"Stick close to us, okay," I said. "Don't go with anyone." I couldn't help the serious expression on my face and the edge in my voice. Savanna would have to read it off my face, but I think Toby needed both. He had avoided me ever since the gun incident, although he seemed to have bonded with Angie, but I couldn't have him wandering off with someone we didn't know.

"Keep an eye on them," I said to Angie as she and the kids past me and headed down the steps. I'd made it halfway down before I saw him, and the sight of Mars stopped me in my tracks.

He leaned against one of the vans, wearing the same combat fatigues as the others, with a pair of sunglasses bridged on his nose. His frizzy hair was a bit longer, and it looked as if he hadn't shaved in a while. His dark skin stood in contrast against the white van that he seemingly needed to support him.

Despite the anger I had felt before, my body decided on a different reaction at the sight of him. My heart did a double take before it started to speed up. For a moment, I indulged in the mixed signals radiating from my mind and heart, but soon my initial excitement faded, and I found it replaced by a sinking feeling. His shades hid those beautiful jade-green eyes, and there was no smile on his face.

"You okay?" Angie asked, staring up at me from the bottom of the stairs. I slowly nodded and took the last steps without taking my gaze from Mars.

He didn't move from his spot and hadn't given a hint that he'd noticed I was there, but even with his eyes hidden behind shades, I felt them on me. As I came closer, the fact of what the past few days had done to him became clear to me, because they sat edged in his face. With every step, the anger that I had felt before left my body and was gone by the time I stopped a few feet away from him.

He pushed himself away from the van and stood at his full height. I tilted my head because Mars belonged to those that challenged my own six feet. He hesitated as if he was waiting on a scolding or something, and a couple of minutes ago he wouldn't have been so far off from that, but seeing him like this, my heart felt as if it was stuck in a vice.

Mars cleared his throat as he removed the glasses. Those beautiful eyes that always brought a joy to my life with his intense gazes that seemed to touch my soul and the cheekiness that always seemed to hide inside now sat filled with sadness. I breached the gap between us, wrapped my arms around him, and held him tight.

It took him a moment to react, as if my action had surprised me, but then I felt his strong arms weave around me.

"I'm sorry," he said with a voice that sounded like a broken whisper. "I'm so sorry."

The lump that had formed in my throat made it impossible to answer, but I shook my head as I buried my face in his neck.

I didn't know how long we stood there like that, but it didn't seem long enough. Ever since we had said our good-byes in Colorado, I had imagined reuniting with Mars in various ways. This would usually be some PG-13 version of possible events, because thoughts of Ash were never far from my mind. There had been some R-rated versions that usually took place a couple of minutes after our initial reuniting, but never a heartbreaking version like this. I never imagined finding this broken version of Mars, and sitting next to him in this van as he held my hand made my eyes sting all over again.

The tension inside the van was palpable and hadn't just come from me or the others in our group. It was evident on the faces of the men who had joined us after we had exited the airplane. Something was off, and although Ash in trouble would have been enough of a reason for me, I had a feeling it wasn't just that.

After our embrace, the anger inside me had been soothed, but not the fear that had taken up permanent residence inside my chest. My heart raced as I inquired whether Mars had any news of Ash, whether he was sure that she was still at the

Salinas Sports Complex, or whether he had heard anything else from Dr. David. Unfortunately, he didn't answer my questions. Instead, he pressed his cheek against mine and whispered into my ear.

"Not here," he said, "but soon." The intense look that followed had me scared, but as if he could read it off my face, his eyes softened as he spoke his following words. "We'll get her back."

For some reason I believed him, and it stopped me from repeating the questions that I desperately needed to be answered.

Unable to sit next to him in silence, I placed my head on his shoulder and asked, "What happened?" There wasn't a trace of accusation in my voice. I didn't think I could blame Mars more than he blamed himself.

For a moment I thought he might stay silent, but then he started to recite the story that Luke, the young soldier who had been with Ash, had told him. It didn't come as a surprise to me that Ash would pull a stunt like giving herself over to Warren in order to keep Rowdy safe. Despite everything, it filled me with a sense of pride.

"Is Rowdy going to be okay?" I asked.

"I don't know. I've only talked to him on the phone," Mars said. "I haven't told him about his grandparents yet. He was too upset about Ash." His voice never reached over a whisper, but it didn't stop me from hearing it crack as he spoke.

"I should be there for him," he said. I wasn't sure how to feel about those last words. They almost made me feel guilty, because Mars couldn't be with Rowdy and mourn the loss of his parents with his son, but then I felt a flash of anger spark in the pit of my stomach because he should never have left them in the first place.

I closed my eyes at the confusion reeling inside me as Mars continued, "But he told me that I had to go find Ash, and I promised him I would." He squeezed my hand, and pushing my confusion aside, I squeezed back.

As the vans steered across the tarmac along the length of the landing strip, my eyes widened at the bustle of activity that we were about to reach. Several helicopters stood in a line while men and women in green fatigues milled around them. Some occupied themselves with loading gear inside the green flying machines while others seemed to be waiting patiently for what was to come or checked their gear. It looked as if they were getting themselves ready for a war.

We drove past the helicopters and toward a pair of low, white structures with slightly tilted roofs. The vans stopped in front of the buildings, and the other passengers filed out. Mars squeezed my hand as I intended to follow, and I sat back down. Angie, who had taken a seat behind me, ushered the kids out before she faced us. They shared a look as Mars said, "Give us a minute." The words came out as a near plea, and Angie nodded. She squeezed my shoulder and stepped outside.

Angie hadn't asked any questions, although I knew she must have been as eager to know the answers as I was. But she'd worked at the FBI with Mars for a long time and probably knew him better than I did. That silent understanding that they often seemed to have sometimes frustrated me, but after working with Angie these past few months it seemed we'd come to a similar understanding, and I'd come to appreciate it.

Mars shifted in his seat as he held my hand in his. The look in his eyes spoke of the seriousness of the situation, and I swallowed hard.

"We're gonna get her back," he said, "and I know you want your questions answered and to go get her right now—and we will—but something else has happened." He paused, and I couldn't stand it. I couldn't stand the intensity that built around his words. Mars was right: I needed to get out there and find Ash.

"What is it?" I asked impatiently.

"We don't have much time, but you need to know this going into that briefing." His eyes shifted to the building where a small line had formed as the people from the vans filed inside. "There has been another outbreak—a big one." I had a sinking feeling that I knew where this was going.

"And it's …" I said, but hesitated.

"In Salinas." Mars had barely spoken the words, or I shifted to stand, but he pulled me back into my seat.

"We have to go," I said and wasn't able to hide the agitation in my voice.

"They'll tell you she won't be a priority. If you want them to let you go, you'll need to at least pretend that you accept that," Mars said, rushing the words as if he were trying to make sure I'd let him finish. His attempt turned out to be futile as I raised my voice.

"What the hell does that mean?" I said. Angry now, I felt the heat rush into my face. "Not a priority!" I nearly shouted the last bit, and I would have added a bunch of colorful swear words that would have made Ash proud if Mars hadn't placed a hand over my mouth.

"She won't be to you, me, or Angie," he said in a calm voice. "I just need you to keep that in mind during the briefing." His gaze shifted to the door where the line had dissipated. Only Angie and Tom had remained outside. Angie's glances at the van told me she was waiting for us.

As Mars's eyes returned to lock on mine, I felt his calm that always seemed to rub off on me, and I think I knew what he was trying to tell me. I had to see the bigger picture, and with an outbreak in another town in the middle of a safe zone, I knew the focus needed to be on containing the virus. At least the military focus would have to be. A lot more lives were at stake here, and I understood that Ash couldn't be the main focus, at least not for the men and women who had just entered that building. So I did what Mars expected and nodded in understanding. I needed to at least appear to be understanding.

"What's the plan?" I asked.

"Just stay close," he said as a faint smile crept over his face, "and try not to piss anyone off." I frowned at his statement, not sure if I liked his implication. The smile on his face grew, and it brought some of that cheekiness back to his eyes. Despite the direness of this situation, the look on his face calmed my nerves.

"I'll try," I replied with a sigh.

"C'mon," he said as he leaned in and brushed his lips briefly to mine, "let's go get Ash."

As we left the van and neared Angie where she stood waiting for us with Tom by the entrance, she gave me a questioning look.

"What's the plan?" she asked as we came into earshot. Mars shot me a look before his gaze fell on Tom. I realized Mars didn't know Tom as his questioning eyes locked with mine.

"Mars, this is Tom, and he's a pretty decent guy once you get to know him," I said.

"Hey," Tom countered as he reached out a hand to shake Mars', "I'm awesome once you get to know me." He shot Angie a knowing look that to my shock made her face go crimson. I raised an eyebrow, but ignoring me she turned her gaze to Mars in wait of his reply.

"Let's just get in there so you know what they have planned." Mars said in a low voice, "Don't draw any conclusions and stick with me afterward. I've requested that we move out together, but I don't want to take any chances with that."

31

Mags

I followed Mars as we entered the large room. Nothing on his face showed the surprise I felt as I saw the number of people sitting in rows all facing the same way. Soldiers from all the different armed forces waited patiently as two of their colleagues set up a screen behind a row of tables.

All the seats appeared to be filled, and in a single file Angie, Tom, and I followed Mars to where Preston and Gibs were standing at the front. Both of them leaned against the wall as they too watched the screen being set up. Toby and Savanna had found a spot on the floor close by, and they looked up as they spotted our approach. Savanna returned my smile as I gave them a small wave, but Toby just shot me a wary look. The kid definitely had some trust issues, but I couldn't blame him after the stunt I had pulled on the plane.

"I'll be right back," Mars said as he turned. He gestured in the direction of two men in full dress uniform. I nodded and he squeezed my arm, offering a gentle smile before he made his way to them.

After greeting Preston and Gibs, I knelt to check on the kids. I held up a thumb and faced Savanna as I asked, "Are you guys okay?"

"Fine," Savanna replied but, in the same instance, wrapped an arm around Toby and drew him in closer.

"Should they be here?" Angie asked as she looked down on us.

"I tried to get them to go to the commissary, but they wouldn't go with anyone," Gibs said.

"I guess you still hold some credit with them," Preston said. I feigned innocence as I glared up at him. The tiny grin on his face told me he saw straight through me even with my mouth hanging open in dismay.

"Any idea what's going on?" Preston asked in a low voice as he gestured across the room. In this room filled with at least a hundred people, we could only hear hushed murmurs, and it seemed as if even our softest whispers could be heard. Not only that, it seemed as if we'd become the center of attention in the room, and it wasn't because we were standing at the front. These men and women knew who we were. I could tell by the knowing gestures and silent stares. The thought sent a slight shiver down my spine as I stood.

"Outbreak in Salinas, the town where Ash is with Warren," I said.

"Well, that's hardly a coincidence," Gibs said. Angie found a spot next to Tom leaning against the wall.

"And why aren't we out there?" she asked, sounding irritated.

"Well, we're taking your friend's advice," Tom said. "What was it he said: don't draw any conclusions? What kind of crap is that?" Angie shoved her elbow into his side just as the light dimmed. The room fell silent, and I turned to face the screen.

Mars still stood with the two officers as the projector light flashed on and displayed the silhouettes of the three men onto the screen. Moments later he took his leave and joined us at the side of the room.

I drew in a breath and held it in anticipation of what was to come. A protective hand found a spot on the small of my back, and at the warming sensation, I released the breath I was holding. Ignoring the urge to wrap an arm around his waist, I focused on Mars' hand and hoped it would keep me steady during this entire thing.

As an image that must have been taken from a helicopter displayed on the screen, the younger of the two officers remained standing while the other one sat down at the table. The younger man was a bit geeky looking with thick-rimmed glasses bridged on his nose, but it was the senior officer who spoke first.

"My name is Major Franks," he said in that authoritative way that I imagined to be mandatory in applying for a function within the military. "By now you will have heard of the outbreak in Salinas." He sat up straighter as his eyes swept the crowd sitting in front of him. Light from the projector hit the top half of his face and emphasized the shiny bald spot on his head. Even with the lower half of his face obscured by shadows, I could see the muscles in his strong jaw flex. Satisfied with the attention he received from the room, he continued.

"We have reason to believe that this has been a deliberate attack." The room filled with whispers and gasps of shock, but also with an "I-told-you-so" or two.

Major Franks cleared his throat and raised his voice as he spoke again. "We all know the stories that have come out of New York. God knows we have heard enough of the upheaval within the government, and you've all been briefed about the role of Dr. David Warren, but that is not what this is about. This is about saving lives," he said.

By the time he finished his sentence, the room had fallen silent, and he continued in his normal voice. "Nonetheless, taking this second deliberate act into consideration, we have decided on a more direct approach, which will be explained by Lieutenant Romero." The major gestured in the direction of the younger officer with the glasses who waited patiently as he stood behind him.

Lieutenant Romero nodded at his superior officer and turned his back to us as he faced the image on the screen. It turned out it wasn't just his looks that made him appear geeky as he started his presentation.

"Four separate locations have been identified as sources of the outbreak. This led us to the conclusion that this must have been a deliberate act," he said in a nasal voice as he clicked the button on the remote in his hand. The image zoomed in on the city, and three circles appeared, which I presumed to be the locations of the outbreak. The locations surrounded an open area on the map that he pointed out as being the Salinas Sports Complex, and I felt my heart rate pick up as I realized that that was the refugee camp where Ash was being held.

"Additional troops have been sent in to deal with

the initial outbreak and to contain it as much as possible. They are pretty much cleaning house, but that is not what we had in mind for you." The image on the screen changed to two weird gun-like devices. "There are many people in the surrounding area and especially inside that camp, and our goal is to prevent them from getting infected. That's why you'll be sent out with this."

As murmurs had risen inside the room, Romero walked to the table and picked up an actual version of the device displayed on the screen and held it up. I raised an eyebrow as I took in the shape and size of what could have been a miniature version of a staple gun used on construction sites.

"What the hell is that?" I asked in a whisper at no one in particular. I had seen my share of medical equipment over the years but never anything like that. The answer came from Romero.

"This is an intradermal vaccination device that will allow us to inject anyone we come in contact with quickly and easily."

"Inject," I whispered in some compulsive reply as if I needed to hear myself say the word aloud.

"We are going to rid ourselves of that virus once and for all, and we are going to start here," Romero said in a raised voice.

"That thing looks as if it belongs on a

construction site," Angie said.

"That's what I was thinking," I replied. Apparently, we weren't the only ones thinking that, and a voice coming from the back suggested just that.

"You want us to shoot people with a nail gun?" The remark by the unidentified voice was followed by some chuckles, but they were soon silenced as Major Franks cleared his throat.

"This is actually a vaccination tool used at pig farms," Romero continued. My mouth fell open.

"And you want to use that on people?" Gibs asked. Lieutenant Romero's gaze shifted in our direction, but I doubted whether he'd be able to identify who had asked the question.

"This is a needle-free injection tool, and yes, we want you to use it to inject the uninfected with the Divus serum," Romero answered. The six of us shared glances as another voice rose up from the crowd.

"I thought Divus wasn't ready for distribution yet?"

The lieutenant began to explain the story that I was already well aware of, about the Divus serum, its origin. He even mentioned Angie and me by name. He explained how Dr. Chen had been working on it in Alaska and that they've had success in several test cases, including two young children.

At the mention of the kids, my eyes sought out Toby and Savanna where they sat on the floor, and I noticed Toby doing his best to translate everything that was being said to Savanna. They looked to be fine, but I couldn't help wonder about the ramifications of this course of action. This had been the plan all along: to get people inoculated so they wouldn't be able to contract the virus and turn into zombies, but every inoculation meant another virus incubator running around in the world. The Divus serum made sure a person wouldn't become infected, but it considerably raised the chance of them infecting others. I didn't think it'd be any time soon that there would be enough of the serum to inoculate every human being on the planet. How would they even be able to reach everyone?

The thought felt daunting but wasn't even my main concern. I still had to find Ash, and none of the officers at the front of the room had even mentioned her. Not that I thought they would. Mars had warned me about that. This briefing wasn't about saving Ash, but about a desperate attempt to regain some control over the Mortem virus.

Mars shifted at my side, and I gazed up to meet his eyes. He must have sensed my dismay, because his hand resting on my back shifted around my waist. He didn't voice it, but with those intense eyes, he told me to be patient.

Romero continued his briefing by explaining how the device worked, and it seemed easy enough. It worked on a battery, and you only needed to insert a vial at the top, press it to the skin, and shoot.

"Don't worry," Romero said, "you'll all find out exactly how it works when you get your own injection." That mention caused a murmur of hushed voices to rise inside the room and me to look up at Mars. He didn't voice it, but for a second a touch of mischief in his eyes betrayed his thoughts. A faint smile tugged at my lips as Mars gently squeezed my side, but we both knew we had bigger issues to deal with.

Lieutenant Romero finished by divulging their plan of attack, and my blood ran cold as he pointed out our drop zones at the edges of town—nowhere near the sports complex.

| **32**

Mags

It was one thing to come face to face with a zombie. The mutilated bodies merely held together by decaying flesh underneath caked blood and filthy clothes were the stuff of nightmares. Irises hidden behind a white fog gave them a blank stare and allowed you to somewhat detach yourself from remembering that these were once people. It was something entirely different to watch them tear apart the lives that had been like theirs.

The massive blades of the rotors cut through the air overhead, drowning out the sounds below and made it seem as if I was watching a silent movie, although through the open door of the helicopter, I witnessed things that no one would have even imagined making in the early nineteen hundreds. The visual came close to the zombie movies I had seen over the years, and the similarities to what I saw now were uncanny.

I had seen a lot over the course of these fifteen or sixteen months, but this bird's eye view of a city essentially being ravaged by the effects of the

Mortem virus stood on top of a list of things I wished I could erase from my mind.

People were running up and down the streets with no sense of where to flee. Cars slammed into each other, adding to the gridlock that had taken up most of the roads. It seemed bodies lay everywhere, and sometimes I caught sight of a form seemingly dead until it twitched and staggered back to its feet before it hurled itself at an innocent bystander.

As Lieutenant Romero had mentioned, from up here it looked as if the outbreak originated in three separate areas that quickly spread outward. The sports complex along with the football stadium that also contained the refugee camp lay smack in the middle. If I hadn't been able to see it from above, I might never have believed that this could have been a deliberate act. But each point of origin just seemed too carefully chosen to be a coincidence.

Having seen enough, I drew my eyes from the door and searched the faces inside the cabin. Across from me, Angie's gaze was focused as her dark eyes swept over the scenes outside. She had left the helmet behind this time, but like the rest of us, she was dressed in full battle gear. Her black hair was pulled into a tight braid and was sculpted into a Mohawk on the top of her head. Sitting next to me, Mars looked as calm and collected as always. Like the Mars that had rescued me from death by zombie at JFK airport. If I hadn't known him better, I'd say he was fine, but ever so often the muscles in his jaw twitched, and he gripped his weapon so tightly that I feared he might snap it in two.

He might not have said it aloud, but I knew he felt responsible for Dr. David taking Ash, and I would have been lying if I hadn't considered that myself. The fact was that placing blame wouldn't help us get her back, and we needed to get her back. I couldn't bear the thought of losing her. I wanted to reassure Mars that Ash would be okay, but I wasn't sure if I believed that myself. In need of contact, I placed my hand on his arm, but internally winced at my deformed hand. Sometimes, I forgot about the two missing digits. The last time I had seen Mars the hand had sat wrapped in bandages that covered it all. Unwilling to confront him with it now, I tried to pull my hand back, but Mars grabbed it before I could. He squeezed it and then hung on to it tightly.

As promised he had kept us together and even managed to convince Major Franks to deploy us near the refugee camp. We had faced Dr. David before, and we knew what he was capable off. Besides, none of the others had ever met him in person; they'd only seen his pictures.

Leaving Savanna and Toby behind hadn't come easy for me. I still feared some agency would come to collect them and perform whatever tests on them. Luckily, Gibs had offered to stay behind with them, and Preston had agreed. Apparently, he had a bunch of younger siblings and was used to looking after kids. He was happy to do it, although I sensed his reluctance as he watched us depart. Gibs wasn't the kind of guy who enjoyed watching his friends head off in the direction of danger while he sat by and waited for the outcome.

The chopper circled the grounds, and besides a glimpse of other helicopters, I got a clear look at the grounds. The place was some sort of sports complex that held baseball and softball facilities, barns for horses, and a football stadium with the very familiar name Rabobank Stadium.

I couldn't help but think of home at the mention of the Dutch bank that still held most of my funds and savings. The thought was short lived at the sight of the large tents that had been erected across the fields and parking lots and even inside the stadium. From the briefing, we had learned that even the stables had been cleared out to make room for refugees.

Leaning out the door of another chopper, Tom

waved. He pointed at a small field not far from the sports complex. Shortly after, a voice came over the radio and announced our descent.

Several other helicopters hovered over us, veering off to their designated drop-off points. They dropped off inoculated soldiers, airmen, and even sailors, along with ample supplies of the serum. The same thing was happening all around the city, and the sound of rotor blades seemed a constant. The military was determined to stop the virus from reaching the edges of Salinas. The goal was to inoculate as many people as possible, and for that purpose, as many members of the armed forces as were available were supplied with the intradermal vaccination devices. An intricate logistical system had been put into play to collect the devices from all over the country.

Along with the device, I was handed a collection of vials that held the serum and a thick black marker. The idea was that, once you'd given someone an injection, you had to mark them with a big X on the cheek, so they wouldn't get inoculated a second or third time. It seemed a sound enough idea, but I wondered how it would work once zombies came in to play and if people would even let themselves be treated as cattle. Although, I guessed "cure" and "protection against the virus" could become some powerful phrases to use.

I had gotten rid of one of my canteens and filled the now empty pouch with the small vials. As I holstered the device, I glanced up at the rest of the team that, besides the usual suspects in the likes of Angie, Preston, and Tom, was also joined by Mars. Unlike the other men and women who readied themselves at the edge of the small field across from the sports complex area, we hadn't been assigned the task of either defending the grounds or heading up the enormous task of getting a shot of serum into as many people as possible, although it had been made clear to us that if the situation arose, we shouldn't hesitate to use the inoculation devices. The task assigned to us sounded a lot simpler: find Dr. David Warren and bring him in. Implementing that task would probably prove to be a challenge, because we did not have a single clue as to Dr. David's whereabouts. Evidence had been strong that he had been responsible for the outbreak in Carmel-by-the-Sea. He seemed to have followed Ash there.

Initially none of us had any idea what the doctor's intentions might be or what he had to gain by going after Ash, everything from the fact he wasn't finished with his research, to take revenge, to the idea that he might have gone insane. These thoughts remained valid even after he had contacted us and said that it hadn't been Ash he had wanted.

The idea of Dr. David laying his hands on Ash wasn't something I could stomach. The fact that he had taken her because of me was unbearable. It had my heart race and forced me to hold a firm grip on the M4 in my hands, because if I didn't I was afraid, it would show my trembling fingers. The mention of the doctor's name raised the hairs on the back of my neck and thinking about him made my stomach churn, but the idea of stopping him before he could hurt Ash fueled my determination.

"All right," Preston said after we all had loaded up on gear and serum, "slight change of plan."

"Is this a change of interpretation of the plan or have you actually received new orders?" Tom said with a smirk. Preston eyed him with a hard stare before he said,

"You do know that I outrank you or do I have to remind you of that ... Corporal."

Tom raised his eyebrows, clearly not used to Preston's new approach. I shot Preston a curious glance. Maybe he felt he needed to reinstate the proper chain of command again, now that it wasn't just our little team on the line anymore. Not that there hadn't been a chain of command before, but it

354 | Wheels' End

hadn't seemed as if Preston needed to underscore it before. He cleared his throat and I noticed a small tug at the corner of his mouth.

"I always wanted to do that," he said, but kept a smirk in check. It seemed he wanted to lift the mood, but not to the extent that it distracted our focus. "Corporal Harding is correct; this is a change of interpretation."

Mars shot me an impatient look that also kind of screamed, *Who the hell are these guys?* and I could tell he was eager to get inside the camp while Tom threw up his hands.

"You had me scared there for a second," he said in an exaggerated tone. "I was afraid that stick had finally grown up your ass."

"Can we get to the point?" The anger that had edged into Mars's voice was evident. Some intense glances were shared between the men until Preston decided to break the tension.

"I figured you'd wanna go after the kid first, so I suggest you take the main entry and comb through the camp with your focus on her," he said with confidence, but he didn't seem to want to issue an order. "We'll circle round and do the same. That way we can cover more ground."

"What about Warren?" Tom asked.

"If we encounter him, we'll deal with him,"

Preston replied. "If not, he comes later."

Everyone nodded in agreement, and after we synced our radio frequencies, Preston and Tom took off.

Angie had been absently watching the exchange and gave me a worried look.

"How are we going to find her?" she asked. I tried to keep the edge of desperation out of my voice as my eyes swept across the compound, "I don't know."

"That medic, Mike something, told me she was being held in a small building near the softball fields next to the stadium," Mars said. "He also said he had seen them take her inside a truck and hadn't seen her after that. The truck is still there, though, so he assumed they'd taken her back to the small building."

"So that's where we start," Angie added. Both of them readied their weapons and took the first steps toward the entrance to the sports complex. I gripped my weapon with the aim to follow, but hesitated.

"Did he …" I started to say but faltered. Mars and Angie both turned to face me. "Did he say how she was doing?"

"I didn't ask." My eyes grew wide at the bluntness of his inconsiderate reply. They both must have noticed, because Mars opened his mouth to speak, but Angie beat him to it.

"Because she's okay," she said as she took a step to me. Reaching out a hand, she took hold of my upper arm and tugged on it. "That's all we need to know, and now we're going to find her."

I briefly closed my eyes and then let Angie pull me forward. She was right. At this point, that was all I had to focus on, and we set off in a jog.

33

Mags

We had barely passed the gate before we heard the rat-a-tat of automatic gunfire in the distance. The zombie hordes were getting closer, and it became evident on the faces of the people inside the camp.

On what used to be a parking lot stood rows and rows of tents, each of which seemed big enough to hold at least twenty people. To our right stood Rabobank Stadium, and from what I had seen from flying over it inside the helicopter, the field looked much the same as the parking lot. The entire grounds had become a field of green tents. In places, shacks stuck out over the temporary housing, tagged with standard signs for public toilets.

Men, women, and children who had been smart or lucky enough to have fled the East before the Mortem virus could claim them bustled among the tents. Most faces expressed fear as they gathered up their meager belongings or huddled their kids. Some just stared out into oblivion while others flinched at the ongoing gunfire that seemed to be getting closer. Military personnel mingled in their midst as they injected people before marking their faces without too much explanation, and I hoped that wouldn't cause trouble.

The helicopters that had brought us here flew on and off, loading up as many people as possible before hauling them off to safety, although that safety would just be another illusion if we couldn't find Dr. David. He might just as well do this someplace else, for reasons that eluded me.

Weapons pointed at the ground, we hustled between the rows of tents, careful to dodge the frantic masses of people running around. An explosion that sounded way too close had me flinch as I paced after Mars. Angie jogged by my side and pointed at a small building.

"That's where they would have placed her according to that medic," she said. Ahead of us, Mars stopped and addressed a soldier.

I noticed a small ramp that gave a pretty good indication why someone would have chosen this place to keep Ash here. Unable to wait, I walked up the concrete path and entered the small structure.

"Wait up," Angie called as she followed, but I couldn't wait and moved down a short corridor. It opened up to a room that looked like a spot where people might have met up after a sports event. Pictures of kids smiling as they played sports littered the walls and acted as a memory to what this place used to be. Now, bunks sat in rows side by side, some neatly made, others total chaos.

Unfortunately the room sat empty. Except for a piece of clothing here and there, some plastic bags and a cactus, it seemed that everyone had left in a hurry.

"Now who would bring a cactus to a refugee camp," Angie asked in a low voice. Although the sharp-edged plant wasn't something I would have expected to find either, I ignored her question and instead scanned the beds. Ash wasn't here, but for some reason I needed a sign that she had been. Anything that could help me hang on to the hope of finding her.

I walked slowly past the bunks and skipped the ones neatly made. Ash wasn't the type of person who saw the point in making the bed in the morning if you were going to mess it up again at night.

"She's not here," Angie said her voice a mere whisper.

"I know." My eyes fell on an abandoned shoe between two bunks. "It's just—"

The words to finish my sentence eluded me as I caught sight of a door at the other side of the room. I hurried past the rows of beds and barely stopped as I flung the door open. Turning inside another hallway, I found a door on my left that led outside. The door to my right stood open, and I glimpsed a small room. From where I stood, I saw a mattress lying on the floor. With a firm grip on the handle of my weapon, I edged closer. Angie followed closely as I stopped at the entrance to the room.

Except for the mattress and a pillow, the room sat empty. A small pile of bloodied bandages lay discarded in a corner. Blood had also seeped into the mattress and pillow. It wasn't enormous amounts of blood, but enough that it had me worried.

My breath caught as I saw something black sticking out from under the pillow. I entered the room and knelt down by the mattress. My hand was shaking as I pulled the device from under the pillow.

"What is it?" Angie asked stepping closer. I closed my eyes because I had to focus in order to force the words from my throat.

"It's my phone."

Ever since she had gotten her hands on it, Ash had never let the damn thing from her sight. She couldn't have cared less that reception sucked these days. The only thing that mattered was its music library. Music had been Ash's religion ever since she'd been a little kid and had gotten sick.

I swallowed hard as Angie placed a hand on my shoulder and looked down at me. The look on her face told me she was thinking the same thing I was. She knew Ash would never have forgotten it.

"Come on," she said as she gripped the fabric of my shirt and pulled me to my feet. "They can't be far."

At a sprint, we crossed the room with the rows of beds and through the corridor, until I slammed into Mars at the door.

"This way," he said, and without further explanation, he ran down the ramp. My heart hammered inside my chest as I followed, hoping that he might have found her. Maybe that soldier at the door had been able to give him the information we needed.

Loud screams stopped me in my tracks. Gunfire erupted so close to me that I dropped to my knees. In a reflex, I raised the M4 and scanned my surroundings. Not far from me a young woman was holding her child. A man with a wrinkled face and gray hair watched me as he hid behind a crate. Ahead of me Mars had also raised his weapon, but he kept moving.

Angie tapped my shoulder, and as if I were back on that gun range in Alaska, I followed without thinking. Panic started to ensue around us as the weapons fire increased in frequency. People came running toward us, fleeing from the danger; but that was the problem, I couldn't locate any danger.

"Where is it coming from?" I shouted. Angie waved a hand and motioned me to follow. With the side of my face glued to the gun, and my eye locked on the scope, I moved my body from left to right as I tried to prepare myself for the decrepit faces that would surely follow. These days, the sound of gunfire usually meant zombies weren't far off.

A few feet ahead of me Angie, stopped at Mars's side. He seemed to be speaking over the radio.

"Copy that," he said in a loud voice over the people screaming before he started to run for the stadium. We followed him until we had found our way to the main entrance, but I had a feeling this wouldn't be our way in. People rushed out in a panic, while soldiers and airmen admonished them to calm down and keep others from being trampled.

"What the hell is going on?" Preston called over the radio. "I just received an update from the perimeter and they're holding the line around the camp. So what are they shooting at?"

"Just got word from one of the helicopters," Mars said, cutting off Preston. "He said it originated from inside the stadium. Within seconds, all hell had broken out between the tents in the middle of the field—people are tearing each other apart."

"How is that possible?" Tom yelled. "Everyone was screened before they were let in here."

The silence that followed Tom's remark was interrupted by bursts of automatic weapons fire. Still, the air around me seemed to thicken and it became harder to breathe. This couldn't be happening. I shook my head in disbelief, unable to understand how someone could deliberately send people to their death by infecting them with Mortem, but the expressions on both Mars's and Angie's faces said it all. He had done this, but why?

"Goddammit, Warren," Preston cursed over the radio.

"If he did this, then he might still be inside," Mars said. "We're going in."

"We'll be right behind you," Preston replied.

"If this is Warren," Angie said in a hesitant voice, "then he might have …"

"Ash with him," Mars said and shot me a knowing look. "Well then, let's get her back."

Everywhere I looked people were scrambling to leave, but they seemed stuck inside like sardines in a tin. This wasn't the biggest stadium I'd ever seen. Stands ran along the lengths of the fields, and along the width of the field stood a low building on one side and a fence on the other. With the panic rising, it seemed that people were unable to think about finding a safe way out.

We found a side entrance that led us underneath the stands, and then made our way to the steps that would lead us up.

It became increasingly harder to dodge people as they fled the field and tried for safety higher up. A man nearly knocked me over as he pushed past me in the opposite direction. I had to jump up onto the benches, and I struggled to hold my balance as I followed Mars and Angie.

Halfway up the stands, we raced along the benches until we hit the middle of the field. All the while, I kept scanning the area in the hopes of spotting Ash, but who was I kidding? In her wheelchair, I didn't think Ash would be able to keep upright in the middle of the chaos on that field. Three rows of tents lined the field, with pathways carved out between them. Frantic people scrambled down those paths in an attempt to flee the stadium overrun by zombies.

Mars stopped and peered down the scope of his rifle. As Mars took a closer look through the scope, I took that time to make my own observations of the field below. I noticed several tents near the middle of the field hadn't survived the panic that had struck and had been run over by the mob of either fleeing people or the infected. So many zombies already roamed the field, and as I watched them through my scope, a chill ran down my spine.

In these early stages, it was hard to tell the difference between the uninfected and the infected. The bodies of the infected hadn't had the chance to deteriorate, as they would once time progressed, and it made them hard to identify. Especially if you've come in contact with only the decrepit creatures. Except for the white fog that swam in the eyes of an infected person, and maybe the blood that coated their clothes from inflicted wounds, the recently infected looked normal.

Something else struck me as I peered through the scope of my rifle. I wouldn't have noticed it if the magnification through the scope hadn't brought it to light, and once I'd noticed, it wasn't hard to see that these zombies were different. I probably wouldn't have noticed if I hadn't seen them before. In fact, I had created them before by infecting William back at Cheyenne, and it seemed that Dr. David had brought along his 2.0 version of the virus.

The difference lay in the fact that these newer versions seemed aware of what they had become.

This wasn't a proven fact, but I had seen it in their eyes. It wasn't just irises swimming behind a white fog anymore, they seemed to seek you out as if they recognized what they had once been and it looked similar to what I saw in the eyes of the newly turned that crowed the field. Something Dr. David had done had left a form of consciousness behind inside the zombies. Sure, they still craved flesh and would kill and devour any uninfected human they'd encounter, but they would know what they were doing, and they would have to live with that.

"Have you noticed?" I asked Angie, who was standing at my side. She had been there inside Cheyenne and had seen that new version of the zombie up close. Hell, she had even warned me about it after we'd escaped Dr. David's lab in Florida. Angie didn't answer, and I glanced down at her to see what she was doing. She seemed fixated on the low buildings at the far end of the field.

"Oh no," she said in a whisper that I would have missed if I hadn't been paying attention. Instantly, I followed her gaze and used my scope to pull the image closer and gasped.

"What is it?" Mars asked. Angie tapped him on the arm and pointed him in the right direction.

"Son of a bitch," he said.

Across the field, in an outcrop between the small

building and the stands stood Dr. David Warren.

The only thing I could imagine that kept Mars from pulling the trigger was that Ash was sitting next to Dr. David.

34

Ash

"What do you think, Ms. Reed?" Warren asked as he prodded me in the shoulder with his gun. "It's a glorious sight, isn't it?"

I kept my eyes closed. The screams alone made me sick to my stomach, and I had seen enough of what zombies could do. Warren, however, had a different idea. I sensed him kneel beside me, and I felt the cold metal of his handgun pressed against my neck.

"It is not polite to ignore your host," he said and tugged at my hair. My eyes shot open, and I gripped the push rings tightly.

I felt like an extra in a horror movie with an enormous budget. The number of people screaming and running for their lives was horrific. At first, they all scrambled for the exit, but as the infection spread and more and more people turned into zombies, the greater the chaos. One moment a person would be running and a second later someone would latch on and rip their throat out.

Warren laughed as he watched me recoil from

the images that invaded my mind. I wanted to close my eyes again but knew that Warren would force me to watch; he reveled in it.

Strolling through the panicking crowd, Chester took his time getting back to us. Warren's equivalent of the Divus serum established the zombies were repelled by his smell, but that didn't mean they wouldn't attack him in a frenzy. He moved between the carcasses of destroyed tents and fallen bodies and seemed undeterred by what was happening around him.

A while ago, Warren had sent him into the camp that had been set up on the field among the stands of this stadium with the sole purpose to infect a random person. It had been enough. Infecting one person had been enough to first spread hysteria and to then create the perfect playground for spreading the virus.

As a man fell to his knees, holding his entrails in his hands, I shook my head in disbelief.

"Why?" I said in a voice that would never have reached another's ear over the screams of terror, but Warren had his face close to mine as he forced me to watch.

"Why?" he said, sounding incredulous. "This is my insurance of course." I slowly turned my head to look at him. "How else can I make sure that your friend will come alone?" I swallowed and closed my eyes.

"This is just to get Mags," I said as I opened my eyes again.

"Well, of course."

"Assuming the military hasn't developed their own version of Divus," I said. Warren grinned and shook his head.

"My dear girl," he said gleefully, "the development has never been the problem. Testing, however, is something that takes time, especially if it comes to human beings and I doubt even the military has reached that stage yet. They lack both the desperation and the tenacity for it."

Warren stood as Chester neared. "Of course, injecting that Meadow woman with Divus seems to have been the exception, but then Dr. Matley would be the only one bold enough to try an unsanctioned test like that, and don't worry: my men will take care of our friend with the FBI."

I cringed at his mention of Angie. She had been the first test subject to receive Divus and had to endure a hell of a time for the serum to settle into her system. If Warren had spoken the truth and Matley was the only one bold enough to go through with implementing her own research, then Mags and Angie would be on their own. Warren had made sure of that when he'd killed Matley at Cheyenne, and none of the others, Mags, Angie, or even Mars had ever mentioned any progress to the development or testing of the Divus serum. In fact, the reason Mags had been in Alaska for so long was exactly that, because they hadn't been able to make any progress.

"Well done," Warren said as Chester stopped at his side and turned to watch his handiwork.

"It's messy," Chester said, "but it works."

"It'll be well worth when Ms. Vissers shows up and I finally get a chance to look inside that pretty head," Warren replied.

I probably shouldn't have been as shocked as I had felt at that moment, because I knew Warren's intentions were never good, but still. Tears threatened my eyes as I looked up to face Warren, and a single word fell from my mouth.

"Head," I said. Warren barely glanced down at me as a smile spread across his face.

"Ah yes, my dear, it's all in the head," he said. "If there is anything my good friend William has taught me, then it's that, and I'll be sure to enjoy poking around your friend's brains."

I shuddered at Warren's remark as I remembered how Mars had mentioned something about finding William's head in a freezer. Before I could find the words to reply, Warren turned at the sound of a voice calling out to him.

I turned to see who it was, and saw the delivery guy running up to us. I hadn't seen him since we'd left the Marsden house and thought he might have been shot during the shootout, but here he was, alive and kicking.

"Thank God, I found you," he said breathing heavily. He stopped and bent over to catch his breath as Warren eyed him with a raised brow.

"Terrence," he asked questioningly. Still wearing his red cap, Terrence raised himself up to face Warren and Chester. "Please don't tell me you've screwed up setting the charges?"

Terrence shook his head as he said, "No, of course not, sir, but … but …"

"Spit it out, man," Warren said, annoyed.

Terrence swallowed hard. "It's the military," he said. "They're here."

"Well, of course, they're here," Chester said. He sounded as if Terrence had just uttered the most stupid thing he had ever heard. "They run this camp."

"No," Terrence said, shaking his head vehemently. "Troops are coming in by helicopter, and they're inoculated. They're shooting up everyone they come in contact with."

"They're killing everyone," Chester asked.

"No, you dumbass," Terrence said. "They're inoculating everyone with Divus."

Warren stared at him in shock. "It can't be," he said.

I couldn't help the hope swelling in my chest. Maybe there still was a chance to get out of here.

Warren's head turned as his gaze shifted along the stands and past the horrors on the fields as if he were searching for something. I followed his gaze, unsure what to find until my eyes landed on what I was looking for.

I was acutely aware of the danger that hadn't subsided. I still sat among Warren and his goons and felt the nuzzle of his gun pressing into my shoulder now. I assumed he used the weapon as a form of intimidation, because it wasn't as if I were going to run off or something, and I had to admit it worked, but that couldn't compete with the sense of relief that came with seeing Mags maneuvering down a path between a row of tents that crawled with zombies. She moved fast, keeping her body low, but with her height, she still stuck out over most, especially since a lot of the action on the field was now taking place at knee-height with bodies pulling each other to the ground as they tore at flesh with their teeth.

She looked different, held herself different in the way she moved and in the way she held the rifle in front of her. I blinked to check if I was seeing it correctly, but it was her. The way Mags was moving was on the border of being a professional soldier, as if she'd done this all her life. But what was even weirder, and I didn't think Mags seemed to notice, was that the zombies that she passed in her in endeavor to cross the field stopped and followed her with their gazes. It looked just as it had on the security footage that I had seen from inside Cheyenne Mountain. Mags and Angie had told me about it afterward. The zombies had acted strange and had followed Mags around as if she was the Pied Piper.

"Dammit, I knew they'd be trying to evacuate and even stop the spread, but with enough of the infected creating a distraction and blocking the way, they would never have been able to get to us. Are you sure they are immune?" Warren said as a helicopter passed us overhead. We had been hearing them coming and going for a while, but this was the first time Warren looked up at one of them.

He had shown no interest in the helicopters or the troops they carried, because he had probably assumed they wouldn't be able to get to him inside a stadium overrun by zombies. If these choppers had been dropping off inoculated soldiers, then that might change his plans. I shifted my gaze from Mags so I wouldn't be the one to give her away.

Warren pulled my chair backward, but a hand on my shoulder stopped me from rolling off, and as I looked up saw the delivery guy—Terrence?—standing behind me.

"Trust me: they're here," Terrence said. "They arrived not long after I'd set off the first charges, and the infected didn't even look at them. Those solders are definitely on Divus." Warren seemed to take a moment to digest the information.

"Boss, look," Chester said, pointing a finger. For a moment I was afraid he'd spotted Mags, but he pointed at several other figures in military gear pushing through the crowd as they climbed the stands across the field from us. Warren watched the group roam between the benches for a moment before his gaze slit down to me, and he said, "It seems we'll have to postpone our little reunion with Ms. Vissers. Let's get out of here."

He walked around me and toward a narrow alley that led between a part of the stands and a low building. With Warren's back turned to me, I chanced a glance back at the field but couldn't find Mags. My heart sunk as I frantically searched among the raging bodies. Terrence started to push my chair, but I held on to the push rings, keeping him from turning me around.

"Get your hands off the damn wheels," he said, "or I'll cut them off and feed them to the infected."

I didn't listen to him; I couldn't. I was too busy finding Mags. She had to be out there. Fear that she might have been caught in the frenzy and was lying hurt on that field kept me frozen in place, and I didn't care for Terrence's threats.

Not until he grabbed my hair and jerked me back, that is. I let out a small whimper from the pain that ripped through my skull.

"Are you listening to me?" Terrence said in a caustic voice.

"Hey, Terrence," Chester said from where he stood waiting for us, "having a little trouble with the kid in the wheelchair?"

"Shut up, Chester," Terrence replied as he pulled at my chair again.

"Let's get moving," Warren said in an impatient tone from behind me. "We don't hav—" He fell silent, and I was about to turn my head to see what he was doing when I heard a familiar voice.

"Warren," Mags shouted in an angry tone. The other two guys stopped and stared out toward the field. I could only imagine the look on Warren's face. Reflexively, Chester and Terrence grabbed their handguns and pointed them at Mags, who stood with her hands passively at her side in the middle of a path between two tents. She was decked in full assault gear, and an M4 hung across her chest, but she kept her hands angled away from her body as if she didn't want to be perceived as a threat. At the sight of guns in the hands of Chester and Terrence, she called out, "I thought you wanted me alive, Warren."

I had no idea what Mags had planned, and I was torn between voicing my relief to see her and scolding her for standing there like a target. Instead, I kept my mouth shut and searched her face for answers that might lie there. For a brief moment, our eyes met and I could read the concern in them, but as her jaw tightened, a resolve fell over her that told me she was here to set things right. I just hoped that included both of us getting out of here and not some stupid trade off.

"Ms. Vissers," Warren said as he came alongside me, "what a pleasure to see you here, if not a bit early."

"Well, it wasn't because I was eager to see you again," Mags said. They both had to stretch their voices to make themselves heard over the ruckus that was still going on the field and all around us.

Warren turned to look behind him before his gaze swept across the stands and field again. He was looking for Mags's backup, I assumed. Then he turned to Terrence and said in a voice that Mags wouldn't be able to hear, "Fan out and keep an eye out for others."

"Warren," Mags called out in warning as Terrence and Chester moved closer to her. Warren grabbed me by the neck and forced me to move forward. Not sure what else to do, I complied and moved my chair toward the field.

"I'm right here, Warren. You can let Ash go," Mags said as she took a cautious step back. Her gaze shifted from one man to the other.

"Oh, don't worry, Ms. Vissers. The child is of no concern to me," Warren said. He released my neck but kept his weapon pointed at my head. "In fact," he added and then paused. "Except for that pretty head of yours, neither are you." With that he raised his weapon and pointed it at Mags.

35

Mags

I hadn't expected Dr. David to be contented with my dead corpse, but then I wouldn't have put it past him. His plan hadn't turned out that great, and that could have made him desperate. Mars's warning echoed inside my head as Dr. David raised his weapon.

If it had been up to me, we would have taken Dr. David and his men out from a distance. With Angie's and Mars's skills, this wouldn't have been a problem. Even I would have been able to make the shot, but we didn't know the extent of Dr. David's plans. We didn't know how many men he had on his side. All we knew was that he had stolen a decent amount of the Mortem virus from the DC lab and that some branches of the government supported him. We needed to weed those out and find the remainder of the virus before anyone else with bad intentions could get their hands on it. And for that reason, we couldn't kill Dr. David—not just yet. We needed that information from him. But if I didn't shoot him, then what would keep him from shooting me?

It took about a fraction of a second for that information to process, and at the sight of his weapon raising, I dropped to one knee. My hands seemed to move of their own accord as they reached for the M4 hanging from my chest. Ash's scream tore through the air, and from the corner of my eye, I saw her reach for the gun in Dr. David's hand. In that split second, I made my decision and aimed. The weapon in my hands crackled in quick succession as I pulled the trigger.

The man on Dr. David's right went down in an instant. As his body crumpled to the ground, I turned to Dr. David. Fortunately, I had the luxury to count on backup and hadn't immediately worried about the man on Dr. David's other side. The sound of the gunshot hadn't resonated inside my head, but I noticed his body falling to the ground and knew Angie, who had followed me onto the field, had taken care of him.

My focus was on Ash, who struggled with Dr. David for the weapon in his hand. She grunted with the effort when Dr. David managed to tear his hand away from her. He smacked her in the head, but that didn't stop Ash from lashing out. He took a step to create some distance from her as the scene around him registered. His eyes widened at the sight of the two dead bodies at his side.

His face turned red in anger as his eyes shot to me. Still down on one knee, I angled my weapon at his head. Our eyes locked for a long moment, but I couldn't decipher his expression. Except for the anger that radiated from him, he didn't move or flinch. He just watched me like a predator would eye his prey.

As if he knew that I wouldn't or, more accurately, wasn't allowed to shoot him, he stepped forward, wrapping an arm around Ash and pulled her from the chair. The gun, still in his hand, now pointed at her head as he held her around the waist.

He spoke to her in a low voice. I couldn't make out the words he whispered into Ash's ear, but her jaw flexed, and her nostrils flared. It was clear that Ash wasn't happy with what Dr. David voiced, but seemed to be complacent as she stopped thrashing in his arms.

Dr. David straightened his back and shifted Ash higher up his chest so her head was near his and he could use her as a shield.

For some reason, it felt as if we had come full circle, because it had been a similar situation that had led us into the hands of Dr. David in the first place. Back then, it had been the men and women at that church who'd followed Father Deacon. The name of the old man taking orders from Dr. David suddenly came back to me, and I wished it hadn't. The doctor had convinced the father that he could provide them with a cure for the zombie plague. He had twisted the old preacher's head into thinking that he was doing the right thing by handing us over to be tested and experimented on.

This time, it wasn't some oversized woman with curly hair who held Ash and threatened to hurt her. This time, it was Dr. David himself who held her in harm's way. Except this time, I wasn't going to surrender. This time, I wanted nothing more than to put a bullet in the doctor's head. But it wasn't just Ash that kept me from pulling the trigger.

A pattern of colorful flowers shifted between the doctor, Ash, and me. The fabric swayed in the breeze as it blocked my view. Looking up, I gazed into eyes swimming behind that familiar white fog, but they appeared anything but vacant. The old woman had blood pooling down the side of her head from where her ear was missing, and it drenched her flowery dress. She stared down at me as her jaw clenched open and shut in jerky movements, and her head twitched in weird spasms without any control over her own body.

Gunshots rang out from further down the field, and I gathered they came from the side of the stadium where Mars, Angie, and I had entered. As the rapid fire of automatic weapons increased, the zombies surrounding me pushed closer together. It had to be soldiers who had entered the stadium, pushing the zombies back to this side.

I eased myself into a standing position as more and more of the infected surrounded me where I stood. Bodies started to press against each other as they filled the pathways between the tents, and I felt the panic rise inside me as I lost sight of Ash. I had to stay calm so as not to send these newly infected into a frenzy. They seemed agitated enough as it was. There were too many of them, and I felt as if I were back in that distribution center. Dread filled my voice as I reached for my coms and shouted, "I've lost her!"

"I see her," Mars's calm voice replied. "Warren's taking her to the far corner where we first spotted them."

With some idea of where to go, I started to move and shifted my body between the gatherings of newly formed zombies. The crowd seemed to grow by the second and even though my head poked out over most of them, I had trouble locating Dr. David—let alone Ash.

"Get away from me," Dr. David shouted. My blood grew cold as his frantic voice was followed by a gunshot. Deciding calm was overrated, I pushed through the crowd of zombies. This earned me some growls and jaw snapping, but because of the only recent infection, the zombies' reactions weren't as imposing as I had witnessed them at other times.

"You're on the right track," Mars said over the coms. "Keep to your right." He had stayed at a higher position where he could keep a better eye on things, and I felt grateful for his guidance. His calm voice helped keep me keep my nerves in check as I carved myself a path among the infected.

Finally, I spotted Dr. David's head poking out between the mass, and I slammed my shoulder into an unsuspecting elderly man sinking his teeth into a severed arm. He fell to the ground, and I jumped to avoid stumbling over him. Shoving past three other bodies, I saw how Dr. David swung his arm at the zombies pushing into him.

Shifting his body, he again used Ash as a shield, but this time to ward off the zombies. She had her hands pressed against a man's bloodied chest as she tried to keep him from sinking his teeth into her. Ash cried out as the zombie opened its jaw to latch on. The mouth was met with Dr. David's handgun as he shoved it between the zombie's teeth and pulled the trigger. Brain matter splattered from the back of the skull before the body slumped to the ground.

Dr. David stepped backward in the small clearing he had created for him and Ash as he waved his gun in front of him. I had almost reached them and struggled past the remains of a tent as I reached for my own handgun. The space between bodies was limited, and my M4 had become useless. I pushed forward, dodging a lumbering zombie, but as I looked up, I was met with Dr. David's cold stare.

He must have spotted my approach, and he held his weapon raised at my chest. As our gazes held, he seemed to hesitate. Was I still that much worth to him, that he couldn't risk the shot? As his face grew red with anger, and his mouth contorted into a sneer it was easy to see that I wasn't. Out of a newly found instinct forged in the colds of Alaska, I raised my own weapon with the knowledge that I'd never be fast enough, and with Ash in his arms, the risk was too great.

Without warning, Angie burst through the crowd of zombies, slamming her body into Dr. David. He cried out as he fired his weapon, but the impact had thrown off his shot. With Ash still in his arms, Angie tackled him to the ground. Surrounding zombies stumbled over them, and by the time I could reach them, a tangled mountain of arms and legs had formed on the ground.

Among the growls of the infected, I heard the combined curses of the three people still able to voice their thoughts.

"Get off me, you piece of shit," Ash called out while the other two grunted with the effort of their struggle. I shouldered my way between two zombies until I reached the pile, where I grabbed the jacket of a young boy. He nearly felt weightless as I jerked his body from the pile of bodies. Focusing on his foggy eyes, I forced the image of his freckled face from my mind, pointed my weapon at his head, and pulled the trigger. Dropping the boy's body, I reached for the next on the pile as another shot rang out.

For a second it seemed as if everything had gone silent, as if the air had been sucked from the atmosphere and had left us in a vacuum. It was Dr. David's movement that my eyes caught first. On hands and feet he crawled from under the three bodies that still remained of the pile. Without looking back, he staggered to his feet and pushed through the crowd.

My hand gripped the handle of my gun so tightly that I feared I might break it, and I took a step to sidestep the remaining forms on the ground until I heard Ash cry out, "Angie!"

My eyes veered down, Dr. David all but forgotten, and met Angie's face contorted in pain as she tried to push out from under the last zombie that had made it onto the pile of bodies.

I grabbed the old man who had sunken its teeth into Angie's vest and shot him in the same manner as I had the boy. Without further thought, I discarded his lifeless form to the side. Ash pulled her limp legs behind her as she maneuvered closer to Angie.

"Goddammit," I cursed while I dropped to my knees at Angie's side. "What did I tell you about getting shot?" Angie grimaced, but managed a half-smile.

"Ask me later," she croaked and then sucked in a sharp breath between her teeth.

As my hands worked on opening Angie's load carrier vest, I cursed again.

"You're not wearing your armor, you idiot," I said.

Angie jabbed me in the side with a feeble punch and said, "Neither are you, so just shut up." A weak smile followed her words, and I wished I could have returned it with more confidence. I shifted my body and braced myself to shield Angie from the surrounding zombies. Using my back, I nudged at the shuffling forms and managed to create some room on my side. Ash tried the same where she sat at Angie's other side, but she wasn't as successful. Still we managed to keep our little corner on the field from being overrun.

As I worked on Angie's vest, my eyes kept going to Ash. A blood-soaked bandage sat plastered on her forehead while her face and neck were covered with bruises. I had to force myself to focus on Angie or else I couldn't have stopped myself from wrapping my arms around the fragile kid and pulling her into a tight embrace.

I registered Mars's voice, but my pounding heart seemed to drown out his words. Even the weapons fire that had sounded so close before had found a way into the background, and for a moment, I wondered if the soldiers had seized their advance.

"I'm kind of busy, Mars," I shouted back at him.

Angie lifted her head as I tugged on her shirt to reveal the wound. I held my breath in a silent prayer that it wouldn't be too bad.

"Well," she said as I inspected the small hole and instantly spotted the exit wound. I sighed in relief as I determined that the bullet had hit her on the side and should've missed any vital parts. The realization didn't stop my hands from shaking as I reached for the bandages stashed in my side pocket.

"I think you'll live," I said in a shaky voice.

"I'd hope so," Angie replied with a nervous smile. She closed her eyes for a moment as I pressed the white cloth to her side. Then her gaze shifted to Ash who had watched our exchange in silence with a distant look on her face.

"Hey, kiddo," Angie said as she took Ash's hand in hers. "You okay?" As if it took a moment for the words to sink in, Ash's eyes turned to Angie. A faint smile crept onto her face as she nodded her head.

"Hi," she replied in a small voice. Angie smiled, but then moaned as I finished dressing her wound.

For some reason, I suddenly felt nervous facing Ash. I couldn't help feeling responsible for what had happened to her and feared she might hold it against me.

A zombie bumped into Ash, and she grunted her disapproval. The infected man shuffling around on bare feet looked down at her and opened his jaw. At the same time, he seemed to take in Ash's smell and shuttered in distaste. I raised myself up on a knee, leaning over Angie, and shoved at the man until he straggled on.

As I sat back down, I reluctantly shifted my gaze to meet those big blue eyes. Relief washed over me at the smile on Ash's face that, even though small, had reached her eyes.

"Hey, Mags," she said in that same small voice

she had used before.

"Hey, Ash," I replied and couldn't deny that urge to hug her anymore. I wiped Angie's blood from my hands on my pant leg before I wrapped an arm around her shoulders. She replied by throwing both arms around me and pulled me in tight. "God, I missed you."

"Back at ya," she said with a chuckle as she buried her head in my shoulder. I tightened my grip around her for a moment, but then released her and pushed her at arm's length.

"Are you okay?" I asked as I touched her head with a tentative finger.

"I'll be fine," she said at a whisper that didn't have me convinced. I was about to ask for details when I heard Mars's voice over the coms.

"I just saw Warren running over the field, and I'm trying to cut him off. Where the hell are you?"

Feeling calmer than before, I managed to reply. "We're still on the field," I said as I looked up. I could barely see beyond legs and bodies as they surrounded us. The infected had enclosed us and it wasn't hard to understand why Mars wouldn't be able to spot us from his position. "We've got Ash. She's okay, but Angie's hurt; we need to get her out of here."

"How bad?" Mars had gone into soldier mode,

and his voice sounded all businesslike, which angered me, but I swallowed it down as I replied, "I think she'll be okay."

The sentence had barely left my mouth as he said, "Ash will have to stay with her. I've radioed Preston. He and Tom are inside the stadium," he said in a harsh tone. "We need to find Warren." The anger that I had managed to suppress before reappeared.

"No," I said in a raised voice, "I'm not leaving them."

"Goddammit, Mags, I'm on the wrong side of the field," he said, sounding about as pissed as I felt. "We can't let him get away."

I opened my mouth to speak, but before I could utter another word, Angie's hand reached out to grip my hand.

"He's right, you know," she said through gritted teeth, "We'll be fine." She shot Ash that look she used to get people to comply, and at that point, I couldn't appreciate it like I used to. Ash visibly swallowed and nodded before her gaze lifted to face me. Her eyes held fear, but her jaw flexed in determination before she spoke.

"Go," she said. She cleared her throat and then added in a firm voice, "you have a chance to stop this from happenin' again. Go!"

"Are you sure?" I asked and looked around. All I could see were the remains of wrecked tents and the shuffling forms of the infected surrounding us, although they weren't pressing in on us anymore and we had some space to move. Ash took my hand and squeezed it.

"Go!" she repeated. My gaze shot to Angie and nodded at her commanding eyes. I shoved my handgun into Ash's hand and leaned in to kiss the top of her head.

"I'll be right back," I said as I readied my M4 and stood. I didn't look back as I pressed through the wall of bodies that blocked my way.

36

Ash

I watched as Mags walked away, but it wasn't long before she'd disappeared from view. Pulling my gaze away from the ass of a very large man, I turned to Angie. She grunted as she tried to push herself up into a sitting position. I threw my arm around her shoulder and helped her up as best I could.

"Ow," she said and clutched a hand at her side. She sighed as she shifted her butt before her eyes fell on me. Her brows furrowed as she inspected my face. For a moment, I thought she was going to fuss or pity me, but instead she said, "Well, I won't be carrying you very far. Where's your ride?"

For some reason, those words brought a smile to my face, where a moment ago I felt more like crying. I glanced around and spotted my chair. A handful of zombies stood between it and me. I sighed at the daunting task, but at least it gave me something to focus on.

"Do you think you'll be able to walk if you can lean on me?" I asked.

"I guess we'll find out," Angie replied.

"Okay," I said and hoped I sounded more confident than I felt. I checked the weapon Mags had handed me and confirming the safety was on, I tucked it into one of the pockets of my cargo pants. Just as I was about to maneuver into the chair's direction, Angie grabbed my shoulder.

"Hey," she said as she pulled me into a hug. "I'm glad you're all right, kid." The hug felt too good to voice any discontent about her calling me a kid, but I did scowl at her as she released me. With a grin, she waved me off.

"Go already," she said.

With that, I shifted my butt along the ground in an attempt to go get my chair. It wasn't easy getting past the zombies as they roamed around me, but by nudging their legs, I managed to get them moving and created the room I needed to pass.

After glancing up a few times and witnessing the blank stares on the faces of the newly infected, I kept my eyes down. Their noses were raised into the air, and their jaws snapped open and closed just as with every other zombie, but their normal-human-looking faces were an unwelcome distraction. The ones that noticed me kept following me with those foggy eyes, and something in those eyes made it appear as if they screamed for help. Help with being put out of their misery.

I felt exhausted as I reached my chair and turned it into its upright position. Shots rang out as I slid into my seat, and I flinched in reaction. I had removed the gun from my pocket and slid it between my thighs so I would have easy access.

The automatic gunfire sounded close, and my eyes immediately searched for Angie. I could only make out parts of her uniform as zombies crossed my line of sight. In a combination of shoving zombies from my path and pushing the wheels of my chair forward, I made my way back to her. Fortunately, the grass didn't offer that much resistance.

As I approached, I heard her talking, but I couldn't make out the words, until she called out, "Ash, I've called those idiots and told them to stop firing while we're still in here, but keep your head down just in case."

I didn't know whom she had meant by "those idiots," but I figured it meant she and Mags hadn't come alone, and we could use the help getting out of here. Angie was tough, and although it seemed her injury wasn't life threatening, it must have hurt like hell, and I doubted whether I'd be able to help her get out of here.

Easing the final zombie aside, I rolled at a stop by her side. She looked up at me with a silly grin, but it didn't hide the pain along with the exhaustion of her face.

"You ready," I said as I stuck out a hand to help her get to her feet. Nearby voices distracted me. I glanced up, just as the bodies of two zombies were forcefully pulled aside, and I was faced with the barrel of a rifle pointed at my head. The tall soldier holding the weapon raised his head and frowned. My eyes widened as another zombie was jerked from the circle surrounding us and made way for another, stockier soldier.

"Hey, babe," he said as the stocky soldier knelt at Angie's side, "you all right?"

"Shut up, Tom," she replied. If her face hadn't already been flushed by the pain, I think it might have at Tom's words. I raised an eyebrow, and she rolled her eyes at me as the tall soldier, who by then had lowered his weapon, spoke.

"You must be Ash," he said.

I nodded and took the hand he offered.

"I'm Preston, and this is Tom," he added. "We've been traveling a bit with your friend over here." My eyes shifted to Angie for confirmation, and she nodded in reply. Tom had taken it upon himself to check Mags's handiwork and inspected Angie's dressing. He spoke to her in a soft voice as he promised that she'd be okay, but the look on

Tom's face had me worried. That and the color that seemed to drain from Angie's face all of a sudden.

"We've heard Mars on the radio and came here as fast as we could. Where did they go?" Preston asked. The urgent tone of his voice drew my eyes from Angie, and I met Preston's eager gaze.

"Mags ran off that way," I said, pointing a finger. Without hesitation, he tapped Tom on the shoulder and said, "You got this?"

"Right behind you." Tom replied. With that, Preston stepped around us and disappeared into the crowd of zombies. In a reflex, my hands shot to my push rings and turned to follow.

"Wow, there, kid," Tom said as he grabbed my chair.

"Let go," I said and tried to wrench my chair from his grasp. Mags was still out there, and if it hadn't been for Angie, I would have been with her. We would have faced Warren together, just like we'd always done. Now that Tom was here, he could look after Angie.

"There is nothing you can do out there," Tom added.

"The hell there isn't!" I said and lashed out at his arm holding my chair. It shouldn't have surprised me that Tom wasn't at the least impressed by me striking his muscular arm.

"Listen, kid—" Tom started to say, but Angie cut him off.

"Don't call her kid," she said, sounding determined, "Now shut up and help me. We're going with her." She gave Tom a look that made him feel like a five-year-old being reprimanded for stealing candy if his wide-eyed stare had been any indication. Within an instant, Tom released my chair and pulled Angie's arm over his shoulder. I heard her groan as he helped her up, but I didn't wait to see whether they had followed as I pushed my chair past the lingering zombies.

I heard them shouting before I could see them. Mars must have been able to cut Warren off because they didn't seem that far off. I pushed through the remaining zombies standing between me and the edge of the grass, and I stopped where a railing separated the field from the stands. I rolled up next to Preston, who stood unmoving, with his rifle raised and pointed at Warren.

The doctor had found his way up the stands and stood on one of the benches on the ninth or tenth row.

"Give it up, Warren," Mars shouted, standing at my far left in a similar posture to Preston, with his weapon raised and pointed at Warren. Mars had barely climbed the stands, but then there had been no need to go higher. With Mags on my right, they had Warren boxed in. He could go up, but that was it. Angie was breathing heavily as she and Tom came up from behind me. Tom eased her down next to me. We shared a glance that told me she was hanging in there as Preston called out to Warren, "Drop the weapon!"

Just in case, I grabbed the gun Mags had given me and added another weapon pointing in the direction of Warren. Tom did the same.

The doctor didn't seem impressed as he flexed the muscles in his shoulders. He stretched his head from left to right and then said with a shrug, "All right." He released the gun he was holding, and it fell to the ground with a thud. "As long as you don't think that this will do you any good."

"Shut up and put your hands up," Mars said as he took a step in the doctor's direction.

"Why even bother?" Warren said, sounding cocky. "You'll have orders to release me within the hour."

"I wouldn't count on it," Preston said.

Warren grinned as he narrowed his eyes at Preston. "Are you sure about that?" he said.

"What is he talking about?" I asked to no one in particular.

"Politics," Angie said through clenched teeth. I glanced down at her as understanding dawned. Warren had been getting support in high places through all this, and they would get him free to do whatever they needed him to do. I couldn't let that happen and tightened the grip on my weapon.

"No!" I said adamantly, "We can't let that happen." I felt the anger starting to build inside me as my eyes locked on Warren. It seemed as if everything around us ceased to exist except for him, me, and the memories that kept me awake at night —images of box-shaped rooms with glass walls, examination tables, medical equipment, and most of all, those blank, fogged-over eyes of the infected that haunted me in my dreams. As I sat there in the midst of the infected on this field with the man responsible facing the other end of my gun, I couldn't just let him leave so that he might do this to someone else. My index finger slid over the trigger.

Mars and the two soldiers didn't even flinch at my exclamation, but Mags shifted her gaze to me.

"Ash," she said in a low voice. I caught her watching me from the corner of my eye, and I could read the concern on her face, but that wouldn't stop me from pulling the trigger. She lowered her weapon and came down the steps until she met solid ground.

Preston cursed as Mags crossed his field of vision, and he had to adjust the aim of his weapon around her.

"We need him alive," she said.

"No," I shot back at her as I kept my eyes on Warren's cocky grin. I could nearly taste the venom in my voice, and I hadn't meant to spew it at Mags. God knows she had never deserved that, but I couldn't help myself as everything that had happened because of this man stirred inside my head. "He deserves to die for what he has done."

Even Warren shifted uncomfortably at the sound of my voice and the words that fell from my mouth. The smirk on his face disappeared, and his complexion turned into a shade of ghostly white.

"I know," Mags said and I knew she felt the same as me. We had lived through this together, and she hated the man as much as I did, but still she stepped closer and placed a hand on top of mine holding the gun. Tears fell from my eyes and rolled down my cheeks as I looked up to face her.

"That is not your burden to bear," she said. I felt the trust we shared resonate between us, but her green eyes held an iciness that I had rarely witnessed as I let her take the gun from my grasp. "It's mine."

I blinked the tears from my eyes, as the way she had said those words resonated inside my head, and realization dawned. Within the same second Mags swung the weapon around and fired. She kept firing until the weapon clicked, empty and all that was left of Warren was a bloody corpse drilled with holes, and for some reason Dutch cheese came to mind.

Epilogue

Mags

My feet dug into the warm sand as they poked out over the towel that I lay on. A warm breeze caressed my scarcely clothed body, and I couldn't care less that the bikini I wore didn't cover the scars that marked my body. There wasn't a cloud in the sky as the sun started to make its descent toward the horizon, and the weather had been perfect for a day's lounging at the beach.

Children's laughter caused me to raise myself up onto my elbows, and a smile tugged at my lips as I watched Mars lift Rowdy up over his head. The little man was all giggles as he spread his arms and pretended to fly like a bird. A few feet away, Toby chased the waves as they rolled up and down the beach. It hadn't taken long for the kid to warm up to me again, and the smile on his face as he played in the surf was contagious.

A couple of towels over to my right Ash had a look of focus on her face as she mimicked Savanna's hand signing. The two of them had become friends over the past few weeks, and it was good to see Ash hang out with someone closer to her age. Savanna was a few years older than her, but I think Ash's experiences in life more than made up for the age difference. She had become eager to learn sign language, and ever since, the two of them managed to hold up quite a conversation between themselves.

Pushing my sunglasses up, I drew in a deep breath, faintly tasting the salt of the North Sea and felt content. This wasn't where I'd pictured ending up. In fact, I'd thought never to see my home again, but here we were, on the west coast about sixteen miles outside of Rotterdam, sitting at the beach at Scheveningen. Fortunately, the seaside resort had become a safe zone, similar to what we had come to know in the US, and with the help of Divus, the Dutch government had managed to push the zombie plague back as far as below the Waal. The river basically cut the country in half and served as a border much as the Mississippi did. The threat wasn't over, but at least some things had turned back to normal, and I had found my way back home, although it hadn't come easy.

I had pissed off some very high-ranking people by pulling the trigger on Dr. David. The act itself had come as a shock to me as much as anyone. I knew we needed him alive, but seeing Ash nearly torn apart by the emotions of fear and anger that had been left behind by the things that this man had done caused something to snap inside me. The moment I took the gun from Ash's grasp, I'd felt this calm fall over me. I knew what I had to do, and it was easy. That was kind of what had scared me most about what I had done. That it had come so easy.

The shock came afterward as I met the eyes of the people around me. The ones that had looked at me wide-eyed and in disbelief. At least Preston and Tom had. The anger on Preston's face had been evident, but the words he spewed hadn't registered, as if they'd bounced off my ears before their meaning could reach my mind. Nothing had registered except the relief on Ash's face, and anything else did not matter.

As I stood frozen in place, it had been Mars who had taken the empty gun from my shaking hand. The calm I had felt before seemed to dissipate, and the effects of coming down from an adrenaline rush had replaced it. My legs had buckled, and Mars had wrapped an arm around my waist to help lower me to the ground while he'd knelt beside me.

"It's okay," he had said in that calm and soothing voice of his. "It's gonna be okay." I had stared into those pale jade eyes as he'd tucked a strand of hair behind my ear. In those eyes, I had seen something that I'd never wanted to live without, and I'd believed him as he repeated his words. "It's gonna be okay."

"It's over now, right?" Ash had asked, and her voice had pulled my gaze from Mars. She was probably the only one that could ever do that, and I hadn't thought he'd mind.

Hopeful blue eyes had stared back at me, and for once I'd allowed myself to feel it too: hope that everything was going to be okay. I had wrapped my arms around Ash to pull her close, and I'd felt Mars' strong arms wrap around both of us.

"Don't forget about me," Angie had groaned as she sat with her back leaning against Ash's chair. She'd stuck her hand in the air, and I had grabbed it, holding it tight.

Not even getting arrested for what I had done had taken away that newly regained hope. It hadn't taken the soldiers that had followed us inside the stadium long to find their way across the field to us. Injected with Divus, the combined military forces had reclaimed the camp in no time and had kind of caught us by surprise as we'd stood around Dr. David Warren's corpse.

Despite the anger he had displayed moments before, Preston had tried to spin a tale, but that hadn't felt right. Anyone could have seen what had happened, especially with helicopters flying overhead, and I hadn't wanted Preston to jeopardize his career. So under the scrutinizing glares of the others, I had come forward and told the truth.

As I'd sat in some jail cell, I had held on to the memories of those final moments on that field. I had everyone I needed in one place. Mars and his son were okay, Angie was going to be fine, and we had found Ash. She'd been a little banged up, but she was a tough kid. She'd be fine.

Stuck in that cell, lying awake at night, I hadn't been able to stop the fear that I might have forfeited my family with that act of revenge, but I'd never given up hope. Fortunately, those had only been a couple of nights.

For the first time in my life, I'd come to appreciate the perks of being the child of a rich and influential man. If something needed to be negotiated, then my father was the man for the job. Over the years, he had turned his company into a highly acclaimed multinational that sold computer parts all over the world, and he had done it all on his own. His ties with the Dutch government had given him an edge in negotiating overseas, and I guessed he'd approached getting his daughter out of jail with even more tenacity than any deal he had ever brokered.

Of course, there had been extenuating circumstances. They'd had our full cooperation during the development of the Divus serum. The government would not have had this weapon against Mortem virus if it hadn't been for us, and it seemed we had gained some appreciation for that.

It had been one of my dad's main bargaining chips, and with everything that had come to play these past two years, I wouldn't have been surprised if my dad had even threatened to sue the US government, but that would have meant all of Dr. David Warren's little secrets would have become public.

Instead, deals had been made and in the end I think they were just glad to get rid of us. Personally, I'd made a point not to know the details of the arrangements that had been concocted. All I knew was that they'd basically kicked me out of the country and was told never to return. Fortunately, they had left Ash the choice to come with me, and she had chosen just that.

"I'd bet your mom and dad never expected you to bring back four grandkids?" Angie said as she poked her head up. She lay stretched out beside me on her own towel, dressed in a bikini and soaking up the remaining sun.

"If I'm not mistaken, you showed up with the kids," I said, but I couldn't stop the grin from forming on my face. Instead of staying behind,

Angie had decided to tag along after she had visited her family. Together with Savanna and Toby, she had arrived a few days after Ash and I had settled into my parents' home. Expecting our visitors, Mom and Dad, who had welcomed us with open arms, had offered to stay at my place for a while, and with Mars and Rowdy arriving that same week, it had seemed like a sound idea.

"You can wipe that smirk off your face now," I said without looking at her.

"Hey, I blame you for me not having a job at the FBI anymore," she said. Raising my eyebrows, I glared at her.

"You quit," I said, appalled.

"Well, they sort of kicked me out before for being infected," she said, "and I only got infected because you proved Divus worked."

"But they offered you your job back," I replied.

"That's not the point," she said. "It's the idea that counts."

"I ... what?" I said and shook my head in confusion. "I think you're spending too much time with Tom." Angie shot me a mischievous look over her sunglasses and grinned before she changed the subject.

"I have to hand it to your dad, though," she said, "when he's doing business, he's doing business.

How did he manage all those open visas to get us all over here—including a certain tall, dark FBI agent."

"I have no idea," I said, "but remind me to thank my dad again when we get home." As if he sensed we'd been talking about him, Mars turned. I sighed while appreciating the view of Mars in nothing but a pair of boxers as he made his way to me.

"At least your parents live in a castle or else it would have been cramped as hell, us living under one roof and all," Tom said. The sound of Tom's voice surprised me.

The soldier had arrived that morning and had been dozing on his towel for most of the day after a long trip. The war on zombies still raged throughout the world, and even with the vaccination to prevent infection, it would be a while before the world could rid itself of the infected, if it ever could. Tom along with Preston still fought in that war to secure cities, making sure the distribution of the Divus serum went according to plan, but Tom had managed to get himself some well-deserved R&R, which he decided to spend with Angie. Unfortunately for him, she came with quite an extended family, but I didn't think he minded.

I was about to answer, but at that point, Mars decided to make his presence known. He placed his feet on either side of my legs and lowered himself. Holding himself up with his arms, he hovered over me as he flashed that brilliant smile of his. Though he still mourned the loss of his parents—I could tell by the look in his eyes when he thought I wasn't looking—he always managed to throw me a smile that melted my heart.

"Are you planning on doing some pushups?" I asked and noticed my voice came out a little bit huskier than normal. I blamed the toned abs that hover over me and reached up to touch them.

"I might," he said and lowered himself to brush his lips with mine. One of my hands automatically trailed a path from his abs to the back of his neck so I could pull him in closer, but a familiar voice made us both freeze.

"Would you two get a room already!" Ash called out. Mars groaned and I smiled against his mouth as he shifted sideways and onto his towel.

"Kid, I was about to ask you the same thing over there," Tom called back at her. Ash's eyes widened as her face flushed bright red. Savanna gave her a questioning look, and I didn't think she had caught Tom's remark.

"Hey," Angie shot at Tom and chugged an elbow into his side, "you're an ass and don't call her kid."

I cast a cautious gaze in Ash's direction and wondered if the color in her face was an aftereffect of being embarrassed or anger. Unfortunately, Rowdy assured we didn't have to find out. He slammed his tiny body into Ash and wrapped his chubby arms around her.

"Ash," he said, "Toby wants to go round in the chair too. Can he? Please." The little guy's begging brought her full attention on him, and the grin of affection on her face was unmistakable as she answered him,

"Yeah, he can, but he has to wait until we get home, because I can't do it here in the sand." She tickled him and Rowdy's giggles dominated the silence for a while.

Mars had left to get some drinks while Angie and Tom sat engaged in conversation. The two kids had found their way to Ash's and Savanna's towels and played with the toys we'd brought for them.

As the sun descended, most of the people enjoying the day at the beach had started to gather their stuff and made their leave, but there were still plenty of them to go around, although nowhere near the numbers of what it would have been before the outbreak.

I stretched my legs and got to my feet. As he

noticed my approach, Rowdy's head perked up, and he showed me the miniature version of a Porsche he was playing with.

"Look," he said with pride, "it's the same as yours." The toy looked close enough to the car that hadn't left my garage since I'd left for New York two years ago. I had showed it to him once when we had gone out to visit my parents.

"Yes, it is," I said and rubbed a hand over his frizzy head, "and one day you and me are going to take a ride in it." He beamed at my answer and gave Toby a look that could only mean, *See! I told you so.*

I turned my gaze to Ash, who had followed our exchange with amusement.

"You got a minute," I asked. Her brows furrowed as she replied, "Sure."

I tapped Savanna's shoulder to grab her attention away from the boys.

"I'm going to borrow her for a while," I said, pointing to Ash. Savanna smiled and nodded.

On automatic pilot, Ash reached for her phone that had never stopped being the thing she carried around everywhere.

"Leave the phone," I said exasperatedly.

"Oh, hell no. Then there won't be anything to keep you from tossing me in the ocean," Ash replied.

I eyed her with a mock grin as I said, "Are you sure about that?"

Ash seemed to mull it over as she eyed me with suspicion.

"Aw, c'mon already," I said as I sank to one knee and grabbed her arm to pull over my shoulder.

"I'm goin' to regret this, aren't I?" Ash muttered. She settled on my back and I groaned as I got to my feet.

"God, you're getting heavy," I said.

"Oh, shut up," she replied. "Just pray I won't ever get as big as you—'cause that'd be a sight."

"I'm not big," I said as I walked us closer to the surf. "I'm tall; there's a difference."

"Not to me, there ain't."

I shifted her higher up my back and Ash rested her head next to mine as she spoke in a soft voice, "So what's up?"

"Nothing really, just wanted to hang out a little," I said. "The house is so crowded lately, and we haven't had a chance to talk."

"Hmm," she voiced, "this isn't goin' to be one of those parental talks is it?"

"When have I ever given you a parental talk?" I said, appalled at the suggestion.

"Well, never, but I wanted to make sure you

wouldn't start." She fell silent after that as if she waited for what I had to say. I found us a spot in the sand that gave us some space from the group and the remaining beach dwellers and lowered her onto the sand. Sitting down next to her, I stretched out my legs and leaned back on my hands as I soaked up the last rays of the sun. It wouldn't be long before the sun would disappear and bathe us in darkness.

Ash looked at me anxiously as if I were about to ask her some life-altering question. The thing was that I had told her the truth I just felt like hanging out. I missed spending time with her. For a while we'd been inseparable and I had gotten used to it.

To ease her mind, I said, "The nightmares are getting less, aren't they?"

Her eyebrows rose as she asked, "How …" Her words faltered, and I decided to fill her in.

"I haven't heard you the last couple of nights."

"Huh," she started, "I didn't think … that with our rooms so far … well and with all your extracurricular activity, but then, I should have known you'd be able to hear." At that, it was my turn for my face to turn beet red.

"You did not hear us," I exclaimed. "Because what I heard was your chair saying bump in the middle of the night when you set off for the kitchen."

"Oh ..." she added with a chuckle, "well then, maybe our bedrooms are far enough apart."

I bumped my shoulder into hers and grinned. After enjoying the view for a moment and letting my red face settle, I asked, "So what is it you want to do with the rest of your life?"

She pursed her lips and shrugged. "I don't know yet, never thought that far ahead," she said and turned to face me. "How about you? What are you goin' to do?"

"I don't know," I said and mimicked Ash's shrug. I paused, mulling over the question a little longer. Before the outbreak, thinking of the future had seemed futile. Back then, I hadn't had a future. As the outbreak unfolded, this had pretty much stayed the same, until I'd found out Divus had stopped my cancer. From that moment on, I had allowed myself to hope, but that had been still a far step from thinking of the future. A smile crept on my face as I slowly exhaled.

In truth, I doubt any of us had thought much about it. I think we were still in a state of relief that we had survived, and for the time being, it didn't matter. We were all together, and we'd figure living arrangements and such stuff out later. Besides, having rich parents did have its perks. We didn't have to worry about money, although I didn't think my siblings were too fond of us taking over our parent's home, and I had a feeling some if not all members of our new family might decide to stay.

"How about we just sit here and do nothing for a while?" I offered.

"Hmm. Might get cold after a while," Ash said.

"Nah, I'll get Mars to fetch us a blanket." Ash grinned and I wrapped an arm around her to pull her close.

"I think we'll be just fine," I said and kissed her on the top of her head. "Whatever it is the world throws at us."

"I don't really care what the world throws at us," she said, "'cause we'll kick its ass anyway."

"Zombie-killing badasses," I added and Ash chuckled at the old description we had once given ourselves.

We sat in companionable silence for a while until I turned my head at a sound coming from my left. Mars had a big smile on his face as he approached. The fading light bathed the sky in orange and it gave his dark skin a beautiful, almost copper, complexion. The sight of him brought a goofy grin to my face that I couldn't have hidden if I'd wanted to.

"Ladies," he said as he knelt by my side, "I've

heard the strangest thing just now." His tone had this playful seduction in it that had me immediately suspicious of his intentions.

Ash didn't seem to sense anything as she looked at him questioningly and asked, "What'd you hear?"

Without answering, he took my hand as he stood and pulled me upright along with him.

"Mars," I said, drawing out his name. The word had barely left my mouth before he threw me over his shoulder in one swift move.

"It seems you two haven't seen the water up close yet all day," he replied.

As he turned to walk in the direction of the water, I playfully hammered my fists against his back and caught an interesting view of his backside clad in boxers, which made me wonder if he'd ever consider wearing speedos.

A yelp from Ash regretfully pulled my eyes from Mars's butt. Tom grabbed Ash under the arms, and Angie carried her legs.

"Hey, not fair," she grumbled. "You're like harassing a disabled person here."

"And here I thought you would never play that card," Angie said.

"Well, desperate times call for desperate ..." she started to say, but her voice faded as she squirmed against Tom's grip. "You know I never really liked you, Tom."

"No one does," Angie replied. Tom shot her an appalled look that quickly turned into one of a hurt little puppy.

"Babe, I know you love me," he said. "There is no point in denying it."

I couldn't see Angie's expression and perked my ears to hear her reply, but by that time Mars's strong legs marched through the water until it reached his hips and then very unceremoniously he dumped me in.

I came up gasping for air, feeling shocked over the coldness of the water even after the hot couple of days we'd had.

Before I knew it, Mars pulled me to my feet and drew me close. Wrapping my arms around him, I gazed into his eyes.

"So," he said in a soft voice, "this is quite a change for you." I narrowed my eyes and cocked my head at him as I wondered about what he was trying to tell me. When I didn't say anything he added, "To allow this many people inside your heart, and I haven't seen you freak out once." The remark reminded me of the stupid argument we'd had while we stayed inside Cheyenne Mountain about my commitment issues. Hidden under water I playfully kicked him in the chins.

"Hey," he muttered, but he couldn't contain a smile forming on his face. "I'm just checking."

I opened my mouth to answer, but I was interrupted by a loud scream.

"I'm gonna kick both your asses for this," Ash called out without any real conviction. And the pleading gaze she shot at Savanna, who stood watching us with a broad smile on her face, was just adorable. But instead of helping, Savanna gathered up Toby and Rowdy by her side and pointed at Ash's impending bath.

As Tom and Angie, holding Ash, took their first steps into the water, I turned to Mars. My lips brushed his temple before I whispered into his ear, "Have I ever told you that I'm a quick learner?"

"No," he said as his hands cupped my face, "but I've noticed a thing or two." Before I could wonder if he meant killing zombies or shooting M4s, or maybe something entirely else, our lips connected.

"Mags," Ash called out behind me, "you're gonna help me here or what?"

It wasn't so much that I didn't hear her, but at that point Mars deepened the kiss, and I think I might have forgotten.

"Maggggsss," Ash called out in a finale attempt before a loud splash literally drowned out the sound.

Wheels' End

Book IV in the
Wheels and Zombies series

by M. Van

Thanks for picking up this book and I hope you've enjoyed it. I would really appreciate it if you left a review.

If you would like to find out more, visit www.42links.net and join the mailing list.

Other books
by M. Van

The Wheels and Zombies series

Ash: A novella in the Wheels and Zombies series

Brooklyn, Wheels and Zombies

Aground: Book III in the Wheels and Zombies series

Wheels' End: Book IV in the Wheels and Zombies series

Stand-alone novel

Behind the Glass